These Promises are Valiant

M. R. Pritchard

This book is a work of fiction. Names, characters, places, and incidents are the product of the author's imagination or are used fictitiously. Any resemblance to actual events, locales, or persons, living or dead, is coincidental.

These Promises are Valiant Copyright © 2026 by M. R. Pritchard
All rights reserved.

No part of this book may be reproduced in any form or by any electronic or mechanical means, including information storage and retrieval systems, without written permission from the author, except for the use of brief quotations in a book review.

Cover Art and Interior Art: Stockphotos from DepositPhotos. Elements, Filters, Fonts and digital manipulations with Canva.

Photographs by M. R. Pritchard.

Edited by: Kristy Ellsworth & Massiel Lago

Midnight Ledger Publishing

14391 Spring Hill Dr. Suite 203

Spring Hill, FL 34609

MidnightLedger.com

First Edition March 2026

ISBNs: 9781957709888(Hardcover), 9781957709895(Paperback)

Printed in the United States of America

About "These Promises are Valiant"

A Hellion forged by forgotten blood.
An Angel Queen burning under secrets she never asked to inherit.
And a prison older than Heaven that refuses to stay sealed.

Chel survived Hell, the Veil, and a war that should have erased him—but blood remembers what history tries to bury. Haunted by dreams of the Black Mansion and a lineage the Fates never meant him to uncover, Chel is drawn back into battle when ancient fires ignite Teari's kingdom and something long imprisoned begins to stir. This time, the threat isn't just monsters crawling out of the dark—it's the truth of who he is, and what his blood can unlock.

A soul tie awakened.
A past clawing its way free.

Teari has finally claimed her crown, but ruling Heaven comes at a terrible cost. While her kingdom burns and her people flee, she is torn from everything she loves and dragged into the Collector's prison—a realm built by Archangels and fed by broken creatures. To survive, Teari must protect the Queen of Hell, and pretend obedience to a being who wants her blood for his freedom.

Captured. Betrayed. Bound by fate.
 And still, she refuses to break.

Perfect for fans of dark fantasy romance, fallen angels, soul-bound lovers, and slow-burn devotion forged in fire, blood, and defiance.

THESE PROMISES ARE
VALIANT

M. R. PRITCHARD

Chapter One

Some prisons are built of blood, and those are the hardest to break.

Teari sifted through the silver racks of the armory, fingers brushing along empty hooks. She was searching for her blade, given to her by the Archangel Gabriel after her time in his Legion. A blade that would only cut when held in her hand. She'd been searching for days. But this was how the past few months as a newly crowned queen had gone. Items went missing, important documents had been moved, and an awkward hush fell over every room she entered.

Teari's wings flexed, agitation rippling through her as she scanned the rows of weapons again. The walls shimmered, reflecting her image back in fragments of tired eyes, hair mussed, energy dimmed from too many sleepless nights worrying about this damned Kingdom she'd inherited. She felt like it was slowly killing her. But she had never stepped away from duty, and she wasn't going to start now.

"Where is it?" she murmured. "It was here. I know it was here. I put it right here." She hissed through clenched teeth, then closed her eyes and thought back to the weeks before, cursing herself for not remembering where it was. Taking over her father's kingdom had been a flurry of activity for months. She'd needed to make this place a home, because it had never been a true home. It had only ever been a place of heartbreak and trauma. She'd reshaped the small castle. Renovated rooms to match her style, anything to make it different from what her father had left behind. She'd built a chamber for the Legion in the space where her father's quarters had been. Tore it down. Buried the memories with new stone and marble flooring. It was a place for high ranking Legion to stay close even though they never seemed to be there when she went looking.

Teari stepped back and glanced across the room. Most were near the barracks, training and tasking. She focused on the leather club chairs, the long table with maps of her kingdom laid out. Wells had run dry, illness had struck, Angels had left in droves because of the chaos she had yet to tamp down.

It was the side effect of a regime change, Gabriel had warned her. Teari didn't believe him. She felt as though a curse on the kingdom were twisting a knife between her shoulder blades. There was too much history and little of it was good.

She sighed and thought of all the tasks she had yet to complete today. Tallys, remodels, meetings in Babylon, she'd never seen her father running around like this. But then, he'd been at it so long he probably had minions to do most of these things. After he'd died – no, after Chel had killed him – there was a certain distrust about the kingdom. Maybe that was the problem, a lack of trust threading itself through this place.

Teari shook her head to clear the negative thoughts. She needed to teach a lesson on closing wounds with the healers in training. She wasn't going to let her Legion go without proper medical care. She glanced at the time, thankful that there was another addition nearby where her healers were training and she could get to them quickly for lessons.

The Legion Commander stepped from the archway, armor glinting like burnished bone. His name was Lassar, loyal, disciplined —careful. He bowed in greeting.

"Are you looking for something, my Queen," he asked smoothly.

Teari turned. "You scared the shit out of me. I have asked you not to sneak up on me like that."

"My apologies." Lassar's features were handsome, scarred, tanned from the sun of the Seven Kingdoms of Heaven. As a member of her father's original legion, he was the first to approach her and swear allegiance and to protect her throne.

"Forgive me." His voice was soft, but something in it throbbed with warning. "You have been under great strain. It is my duty to ensure your safety and the safety of the kingdom. Are you looking for something?" His brow rose.

The air between them tightened.

"My blade is missing."

"I had it secured," he said smoothly.

Teari's hands dropped to her sides. "That wasn't your decision to make. I want it back."

"You do not require it with my presence. You need rest, not weapons."

"Return it to me now. Do not mistake exhaustion for helplessness," she said. "And do not touch my weapon again."

Lassar's gaze flickered. "Of course." He inclined his head, eyes hooded. "As you command."

He left quietly.

When the door sealed, Teari pressed her palm to the warded wall. The runes pulsed weakly as though something was feeding on her realm's energy, subtle and parasitic.

She wasn't sure how to feel. Lassar had taken her weapon. He had pledged his allegiance but now she wasn't so sure. She had spent so much time running from her father and his kingdom, she was not skilled in the deceptive ways of the Angels here. These were a different breed. So different than the kingdom she'd grown up in. She had an uneasy feeling. A worry that her father's sins might just have infiltrated the entire kingdom.

Did the sins of her father still linger in this place? She'd done her best to cleanse the small castle and give leave to those who did not see her as their Queen. But Teari was sure there wasn't enough sage between the realms to cleanse those sins. Some nights she lay awake wondering if she should have used the sage as kindling and burned it all down.

Maybe Lassar was being overprotective, he knew the risks, or maybe the rot had reached her inner circle.

Chapter Two

The ocean tide whispered against the sand like something half-alive and half-asleep. Chel stood where the surf met the ruins of a pier, boots sinking into cold grit. The night smelled of salt and smoke and decaying fish.

He checked the wards, drew a rune of protection in the sand with a walking stick he'd carved out of boredom weeks ago. He ignored the fact that he leaned on it quite heavily when his knee ached before evening thunderstorms.

The Earthen plane wasn't home to Chel but he was starting to feel comfortable here. Sometimes it was lonely but he'd started fitting in with the locals. They recognized him now, and even if they were human, he was starting to enjoy their presence. The brief encounters on beach walks, the casual conversation at the grocery store, the smiles of recognition at the local restaurants, it was all very different from his experience living in Hell. Although he could see the difference Meg had made in Hell over the years. Hell was a dark reflection of the Earthen Plane, but she'd brought hope to the creatures of Hell and he had noticed it as the markets and trades returned. Lost souls were guided and there was a lot less death occurring.

A voice broke the quiet. "Evenin'. Haven't seen you out this late before."

Chel turned. A man with a fisherman's tan and a beer can balanced in his palm nodded toward him. Tom Danner, if Chel remembered right.

"Where's the wife tonight?" Tom asked, sipping from the can.

Chel managed a small, practiced smile. "Out of town."

Tom squinted. "Seen you alone a lot lately."

"She travels for work."

"What kinda work keeps a woman gone half the year?"

"The kind that saves people," Chel said. It wasn't exactly a lie. She was a healer, and an Angel. His Angel. They weren't married in the normal sense, but they'd made a promise to each other. And in just a few short weeks she'd visit him here on this beach, just like they'd promised. But the locals wouldn't see much of her then because Chel planned to keep her busy and naked and in bed for as long as he could.

Tom studied him, the lines around his eyes deepening. "Huh. Guess that makes you the patient sort." He lifted his chin. "And what do you do for work? Or are you the stay at home wife?" he chuckled.

"Not a wife." Chel's brow rose. "The work I do required clearance."

"Aren't you supposed to say something like, If I told you I'd have to kill you?"

Chel shrugged. "Close enough. Did you want me to kill you?"

Tom's eyes widened for a split second. He looked into the can and shook it. "Either I drank too many of these or not enough."

They fell into a strange, easy rhythm. Tom introduced a few friends who joined them on the sand—locals who smelled of gasoline, salt, and cheap aftershave. They joked about storms, about the tourists who never came back after the dead walked the Earthen plane nearly fifteen years before. For a few minutes, Chel forgot to be on guard. These weren't Hellions, but they were the humans he was protecting. The White Horse had assigned him the Guardian of the gulf portal. He'd made sure nothing from the other realms had slithered out. They were good people, even if they had no idea what he really was.

When Tom suggested card night at the dockside bar, Chel almost declined. But the humans seemed genuine, curious in a harmless way. He was still working on gaining their trust. So he followed them. It would be days before Teari would be back for her monthly visit, as promised. This would be a good way to pass the time.

The bar lights were dim, old Christmas bulbs strung over warped wood. Cigarette smoke curled through the air. Chel sat with them, trying to mimic how mortals laughed—shoulders shaking, mouth curved but eyes watchful.

Cards were played differently in the Hellion barracks. There was much more drinking, growling, and fighting.

Halfway through the game, the conversation turned.

"So where's your family from?" one man asked. "You don't look local."

"Not Florida," Chel said.

"You got that accent, though. Can't place it."

"And those eyes," Tom added. "Not many people got eyes like that. Nearly all black."

Chel stacked his cards carefully. "An old family trait. My father had the same." It was easy to hide some of his features, his wings were invisible when the Veil between worlds was normal. His fangs were set further back in his jaw so he only had to be cognizant of his smiles and laughter so none would see them. He was very much a demon walking the Earthen plane, they just couldn't quite tell. But his size... that was hard to make excuses for, he was giant, muscled and tall, he looked like a body-builder. But the more he interacted with the locals, the more they became accustomed to his size.

The laughter faded. For a heartbeat the room tilted and every shadow stretched toward him. Glasses rattled on the table; the jukebox stuttered and went silent.

Unease passed through the bar and a weather alert blasted from the television mounted in the corner.

The news anchor looked uneasy as he tapped his stack of notes and said, "We're cutting in with a special weather alert for residents along the Gulf Coast tonight. Let's go to our meteorologist for the latest on this developing system."

The meteorologist spoke in a calm, clear voice, "Thank you. Good evening, everyone — I'm Jennifer Hale with your coastal weather update. We are tracking an unusual January tropical system forming rapidly in the eastern Gulf of Mexico. The National Weather Service has issued a Tropical Storm Warning for Perdido Key, Pensacola Beach, and the surrounding areas.

This weather is highly unusual for this time of year. We typically don't see tropical development during the winter months. But warm sea surface temperatures and a stalled frontal boundary have allowed this system to strengthen quickly over the past twelve hours.

At this hour, sustained winds near the center are around 60 miles per hour, with higher gusts possible. The storm is moving northeast at about 18 miles per hour and is expected to make landfall late tomorrow evening near Perdido Key.

Residents should prepare for heavy rainfall exceeding six inches in isolated spots, Coastal flooding and dangerous surf, and gusty winds strong enough to down small trees and power lines.

Storm surge watches are also in effect for Perdido Bay and the lower Escambia River. Low-lying areas should be ready for evacuation orders if conditions worsen overnight.

Again, this is *not* your typical January cold front. This is a tropical system, and it's developing fast.

We'll continue to monitor updates from the National Hurricane Center and local emergency management throughout the evening. Please, secure outdoor items, charge your devices, and have your weather radios ready.

I'll be back at the top of the hour with the latest tracking models. For now, stay safe and stay indoors, if possible. The Gulf is restless tonight. Prepare. Sandbag filling stations are opening now. Residents along the coastline should evacuate to your nearest emergency shelter."

"Storm's coming," Chel said quietly, standing. "We should head home."

No one moved. For a heartbeat, their faces looked too pale, too still, as if someone else were wearing their skin. Chel rubbed his eyes. He must be tired. He downed the glass of beer. Maybe he'd drank too much. Maybe he hadn't drank enough. He swallowed, throat feeling dry. Maybe he needed blood.

Tom was watching him before sliding the cards in his hand into a neat stack. "It's late. New guy's right. We gotta get ready for this storm."

Chel walked the shoreline back to the beach house until the waves steadied his thoughts. Behind him came the crunch of footsteps.

"You do this every night?" Tom asked. He and two others had followed, flashlights bobbing. "Patrol the beach like some kinda guard dog?"

"Keeps me out of trouble," Chel said.

"Thing is," Tom went on, voice low, "we've been feeling something off. The tides are off. A shrimper saw strange lights under the water. Hell, even the sand feels different. Perdido Key ain't right. And now this tropical storm in the middle of winter. Something strange is happening here. And we were glad that man stopped walking out of the ocean to steal our women, but something strange has taken his place."

Chel faced the dark horizon. He could feel the slow, steady hum beneath the island. It echoed through the beach as though the space under was being hollowed out.

"If you know something, you should tell us," Tom said. "Not much will surprise us after the season of the dead walking. I read a newspaper article about some guy in California during that time. The dead followed him. He was darkness. He walked into a bar and when he left everyone inside was drained of blood. It was a big guy. I saw a picture. Do you know anything about that?"

Chel turned back to him, calm and unreadable. "You wouldn't believe me."

He kept walking, boots leaving deep prints in the wet sand. The surf erased them within moments, as if he'd never been there at all.

Behind him, Tom whispered, "He knows."

And in the distance, the gulls began to squawk.

Chel picked up his pace and made it back to the beach house in record time. If there was a storm coming, the wards might get destroyed and all hell might break loose on the Earthen Plane.

Chapter Three

In the city of Babylon heat rose from the streets in a shimmering haze and incense burned from the Church windows, thick and sweet. Teari stood on the balcony of the old citadel, the wind tugging at her pale robes. Below, the world pulsed with noise as traders shouted, bells tolled, and prayers murmured.

"I wondered where you'd disappeared to," came the familiar voice of the Raven King. Sparrow had come for a visit. He was once Gabriel's Legion commander, a cursed Angel, and now he was the King of the Archangel Remiel's land, now deceased. Killed by his mate, Meg.

Sparrow arrived like a shadow, with black, wings dragging behind him like heavy curtains. He wore leather, a blade strapped to his thigh, a black button down shirt rolled up to the elbows. Teari glanced behind him, searching for Meg. She wasn't there.

Teari glanced out of the corner of her eye. Sparrow was beside her, hands tucked into the pockets of a long black coat; typical vampire brooding male. His black wings were now tucked so close against his back she barely noticed them. Those had gotten him the title of the Raven King; the only King in the Seven Kingdoms of Heaven with black wings.

He was trouble bottled in scars and beauty and inked skin. He was one of the few beings in this realm she trusted. Him and Meg. Chaos and fire, both of them. But at least they were honest about it.

"Don't jump," he warned.

"If I have to listen to one more Angel complain about some menial problem I might jump. The conversation about the lack of taxation on water was enough to make me want to stab my ears out."

Sparrow smirked.

Teari's expression didn't soften. "I need to ask how you do it."

"Do what?"

"Split yourself between realms," she said quietly. "The Kingdom pulls me one way, Chel another. Every time I travel, something breaks here. My realm is a mess. I feel like my relationship with Chel is suffering."

Sparrow leaned against the railing beside her. "Ah. The cost of being too divine to rest." He looked out over the city. "Do you enjoy it? The crown?"

She shook her head. "No."

"Good," he said, smiling faintly. "The ones who do are the worst of us. Look what it did to our fathers."

For a long moment, they simply watched Babylon

bustle. Then Teari said, "I don't trust my first in command."

"Lassar?"

She nodded. "He took my blade. Said I didn't need it with him present."

Sparrow tilted his head, eyes glinting. "That's not loyalty."

"I'm kinda pissed about it. I kinda want to lock him in a dungeon."

"And yet you haven't, you let him live?"

Teari gave a sharp laugh. "I'm not my father."

"No," Sparrow agreed. "You're something different."

She turned toward him. "What would you do?"

"If I suspected my right hand of deceit?" Sparrow's grin widened. "I'd let him believe he was clever. Then I'd watch what he touched and who he whispered to. Men like Lassar always betray themselves long before you need to lift a blade."

Her wings tightened. "I didn't want this."

"You can't abandon the kingdom."

Teari turned back toward Babylon's center. "Then help me hold what's left of my realm together before there's nothing left to protect."

A slow dark smile spread across Sparrow's face. "Now that is something I might be able to help you with." Sparrow rested his elbows on the balcony railing and leaned forward. "Let's see who your commander is really loyal to."

There was a pause.

"You are not your father, Teari," Sparrow said.

She looked up.

Teari pressed her lips together, emotion burning under her ribs. She wished she believed him. No matter how she tried to distance herself from her bloodline, she was still the pure blooded child of the Archangel Raphael. And Archangel blood never let go.

Chapter Four

The wind had changed by noon.

It carried the smell of rain, heavy with the promise of ruin.

Chel stood in the flooded street beside the grocery store, burlap sandbags piled high in the back of a flatbed truck. The storm sirens had been wailing every hour, their sound thin and distant beneath the roar of the sea.

"Stack 'em tight, sweetheart!" a woman shouted from her porch as she struggled to lift another bag. Chel moved past her silently, taking two in one arm and setting them down in a single motion. The humans tried not to stare, though one man muttered something about him being "built like a horse."

He didn't correct them. They didn't need to know his truth.

All along Perdido Key, the air buzzed with hurried voices — doors slamming, cars idling, children crying as parents packed the last of their things. The tropical storm had twisted itself into something worse overnight, unexpected for January, unpredictable even for the Gulf. The shoreline had shrunk by nearly a mile as the storm sucked water out to sea, gathering it to douse the coast.

Chel spent the day hauling sand, boarding windows, and tightening shutters. Sweat streaked the back of his neck despite the chill. The sky had gone a strange green-gray, swollen with thunder.

"Appreciate the help, big guy," an older man called. "You heading out soon?"

Chel shook his head, adjusting another board across the beach house window. "Not yet."

The man frowned but didn't press. Most people didn't. They weren't going to argue with him.

By late afternoon, the streetlights flickered on as the darker storm clouds rolled in. Chel helped an elderly couple load their cats into a station wagon, then guided a small convoy of cars through the rising water toward the bridge. He'd helped push a truck whose back tires were slipping on sodden sand. Only a handful of houses remained occupied. The wind howled low, bending palm trees to the ground.

When the last headlights disappeared over the causeway, Chel returned to the beach house. The waves had already crept back, splashing past the dunes, licking the base of the porch. He moved fast stacking the sandbags in neat walls, reinforcing the door frames, dragging furniture toward the center of the room. Every nail he drove into the wood sank clean with one hit.

Lightning split the horizon, turning the glare on the windows white.

A truck engine rumbled up behind him. Tom leaned out the window, his cap turned backward, face drawn with exhaustion.

"Chel!" he shouted over the wind. "You're the last one left on the island. I just checked the evac route—no one else's here. You've gotta go, man! Come on!" Tom slapped the side of his truck.

Chel kept stacking sandbags. "I can't."

Tom climbed out of the truck, rain plastering his shirt to his skin. "You *can't* or you *won't*? They don't want to send a rescue team out for you tomorrow. Don't be that guy they have to fish off a roof."

Chel turned then, eyes reflecting the lightning. "I've survived worse."

Tom huffed, frustrated. "You and your mystery war stories. Look, whatever you're guarding in there, it's not worth your life. Let's go."

Chel's gaze drifted to the dark water beyond the dunes. The White Horse had charged him with watching the gulf portal, storm or not. He had to stay.

"It's not the house I'm guarding," he said. "I must stay."

Tom blinked, confused, but before he could respond, thunder rolled so deep it shook the ground beneath them.

Chel hefted another sandbag, his tone steady. "You should go, Tom."

"You're serious about this?"

Chel nodded once. "I'll see you after."

Tom hesitated, then muttered, "This doesn't convince me that you're normal, man."

Chel almost smiled. "You're not wrong."

Tom lingered a heartbeat longer, then jogged back to his truck. The windshield wipers squealed as they whipped back and forth. Chel watched as the taillights vanished into the rain. He frowned; Tom and the others would have questions and he wondered what would be easier, a lie or the truth. He wasn't sure how far he could twist himself to twist reality after he messed up and told the lady at the grocery store that he was a newlywed.

Chel stood alone on the porch as the first band of the storm struck. Wind screamed through the shutters, salt water spraying the boards. He looked out at the black ocean and the pale line of lightning crawling across the horizon.

The storm had a pulse and it was going to destroy every protective ward and rune they'd set here. Soon, the portal would be wide open.

Chapter Five

Four apprentice healers knelt in neat rows across the marble floor, their palms glowing faintly over bundles of carved bone. Teari moved among them.

"Not too much," she warned. "It isn't about power, it's about precision. You coax the bone to remember. Coax it to mend and reknit its original structure."

A murmur of concentration filled the hall as a cracked femur knit together beneath pale fingers. Teari smiled faintly. "Good. Now again. Until you can do it without thinking so hard."

She needed healers who were well practiced and prepared. It had been too long since anyone trained new healers. As it was, multiple kingdoms went without, including the Raven Kings, Gabriel's Kingdom and Hell. Teari needed healers ready for when they called upon her. She could no longer be at the beck and call of the others but she could train healers to go in her place.

When the last pulse of magic dimmed, she stepped

back, rubbing her hands absently. The light from the stained-glass windows had shifted to amber.

She drifted toward the open balcony. The wind carried the scent of a storm and lemon and sage. From here, she thought she saw smoke in the distance but it mixed with the storm clouds. Just a winter storm starting on the edges of the Kingdom. Soon the snow would drift closer, over the mountains to the edges of Babylon. It never snowed there. Chel always complained about the heat of the sun in the Seven Kingdoms of Heaven, maybe he'd visit and see the snow.

He was probably standing on the beach right now. She could almost hear his dry humor, the quiet steadiness in his voice.

She reached for her phone and called him. Static answered. Then nothing. Teari frowned and tried again. Normally, he picked up before the second ring. Even when busy, even when angry, he *always* answered.

Silence.

She tucked the phone in her pocket and turned toward the corridor just as Lassar rounded the corner. His armor gleamed brightly, and he was walking fast.

"Commander," she called.

He hesitated then turned with a practiced bow. "My Queen."

Teari held in a shiver, she didn't like the title. It felt awkward. "Why are you in such a hurry?" she asked.

"Routine patrol," he said curtly. "I was gathering the men."

"At this hour? Patrols are typically mid-morning and before night fall."

His jaw flexed. "The Legion doesn't rest."

Her eyes narrowed. "Are you not telling me something?"

For a heartbeat, his expression cracked and irritation flared beneath his calm exterior. He bowed again, lower this time. "With respect, my queen, there are matters you need not concern yourself with."

He moved past her before she could reply. Anger was rising in her chest, her fingers started tingling as the emotion grew.

Teari stood in the empty hall, fists tightening until her knuckles turned white. He'd never dismissed her so bluntly before. The nerve of it—and the certainty in his tone—set her teeth on edge.

She turned back to the windows and lifted the phone once more. "Chel," she whispered again. "Please answer."

Nothing. Not even static now

Her stomach dropped. He *always* answered.

The thought pressed sharp against her ribs, something was wrong.

Without another word, she strode toward the chamber doors, calling for her attendants. "I'm leaving for the mortal realm."

"But—"

"Now."

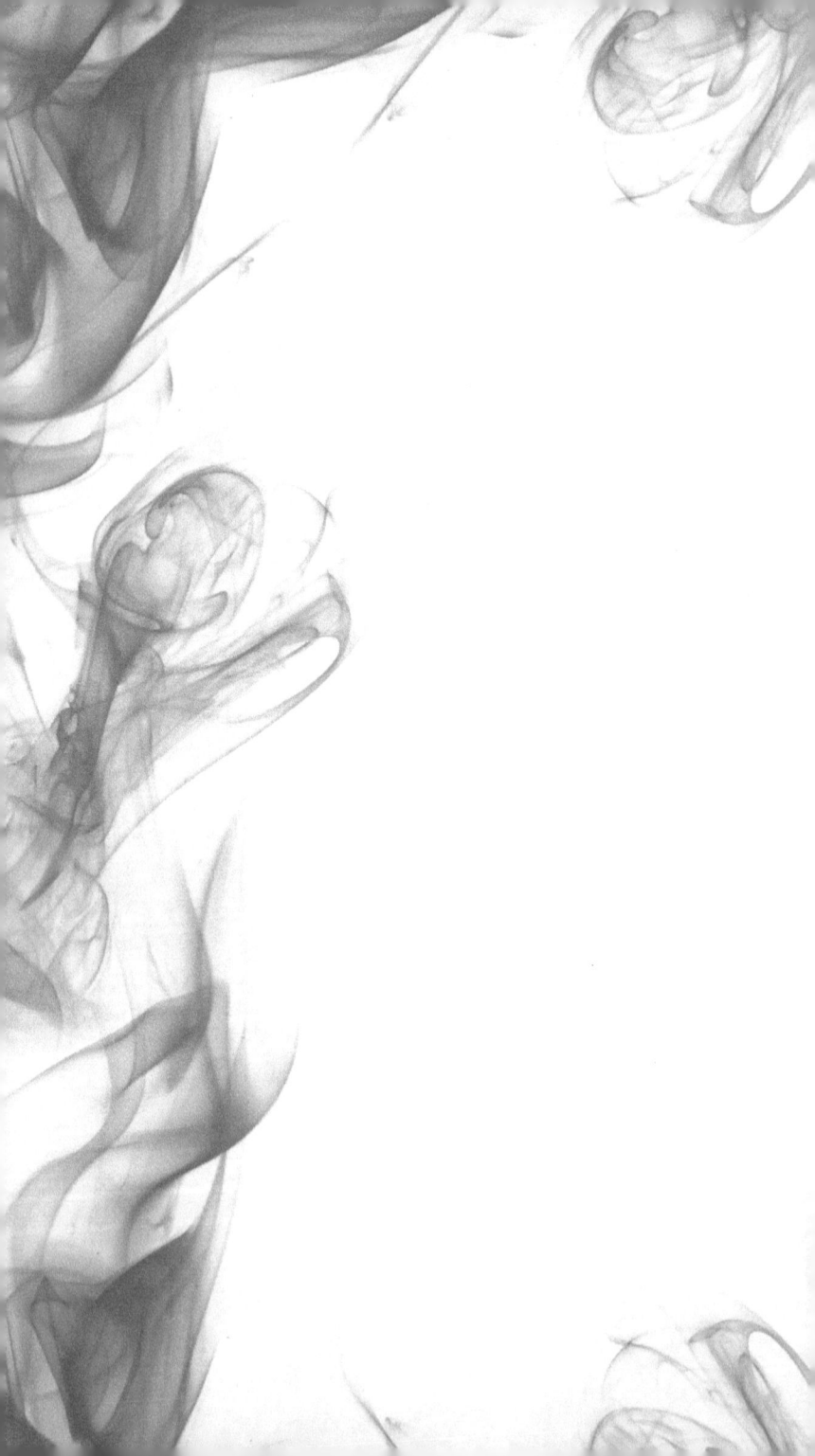

Chapter Six

The storm had turned the world to static.

Wind howled through the shutters, shaking the glass like something alive. The sea had swallowed half the road already, dragging bits of the neighboring houses out into the dark.

Chel stood barefoot in the center of the beach house, water dripping from his hair, the floor slick with salt and sand. Lightning flashed through the windows, white and violent.

He knelt and began to draw along the walks.

The runes were simple—Jed's handwriting burned into memory, every curve and rune carved with purpose. A protection ward meant to stabilize energy through storms both mortal and divine.

"Draw them clockwise," Jed had said. "Never counter. Counter calls the wrong kind of protection."

Chel dipped his finger into a bowl of salt and ash,

marking the first line across the baseboards. The rune flared faintly—white light pulsing through the cracks. The air shifted, a deep hum moving beneath the thunder.

He worked in silence. Outside, the wind screamed harder, and the walls groaned against it.

He had called Jed just before the first squall line hit.

"A tropical storm in January?" Jed had asked. "Storm season's supposed to be months off."

"It's just a storm," Chel replied. "But the locals are antsy. They tried to tell me something is wrong here."

"Yeah," Jed had said after a pause. "I figured. The White Horse has been restless. She keeps pacing the ridge and won't go in the barn."

That had been enough to make Chel's stomach twist. He'd been sent to guard the Gulf, a Hellion on the Earthen Plane. A wolf amongst sheep, he wasn't sure what the White Horse was anticipating or if this storm was part of it.

"You still remember the protection runes?" Jed had asked.

"I do."

"Then draw them. And whatever you do, don't let the water touch your threshold. If it washes away, the beach house is lost to the storm."

Chel had hung up without another word.

. . .

Now, the final rune sealed the circle. The glow deepened, and for a moment the sound of the storm dulled—muted as though the house itself were a steel barrier, something impenetrable.

He pressed his palm to the floor. "Hold," he whispered. He willed the house to stay because he'd made a promise to the White Horse to protect the Gulf portal, and... this house actually belonged to Meg, the Queen of Hell. He was sure she wouldn't take kindly to its destruction. But also, he enjoyed this place. There were memories here. He glanced at the couch and thought of Teari curled up there reading.

The light flickered, then steadied. The wind clawed at the walls but didn't break them. Still, the air felt filled with energy.

He stood, scanning the room. Every shadow stretched too far. The reflection in the window didn't move with him—it lagged a fraction behind, mouth open like it wanted to speak.

Chel blinked then it was gone. He cursed in Hellspeak.

Lightning split the sky again, illuminating the ocean. For an instant, he saw something out there—dark wings folded against the rain, rising and falling with the waves. Watching.

He exhaled slowly, every muscle tight.

"Not tonight," he murmured. He swallowed hard, against the thirst and wished he'd stocked up on blood. He was tired, didn't want to admit it but that was the truth. He'd gone to play cards with the locals and then all hell broke loose. He should have had blood two days ago but now he'd have to wait. He blinked hard and rubbed his eyes.

THE POWER WENT OUT JUST AFTER MIDNIGHT.

The storm had chewed through the light poles, cement and all, the power finally gave its last flicker of life and died, leaving only the sound of wind battering the walls and waves clawing at the dunes.

Chel checked the phone once more out of habit, there was no service, just static. The glowing bars that connected him to the rest of the world had vanished.

He set the phone face down on the counter and opened the refrigerator. The light inside blinked twice before fading completely. Cold air spilled out, carrying the sharp, metallic scent of blood. His blood stock was low.

Two bags left. He'd wait... no. Yes.

He shut the door quietly, the rubber seal sticking in the humidity. Hunger was a dull ache at the back of his throat—manageable, but louder when the world was this still. He flexed his hands, feeling the pulse beneath the skin, the thrum of what he was trying so hard to keep buried. It was easily ignored when he could distract it with pacing the beach or running errands on Main Street or card night.

"Not tonight," he muttered to himself.

Instead, he lit the candles—half-burned stubs in glass jars scattered along the table and windowsill. Their light painted the walls in gold and shadow. Outside, the storm still raged, but the house felt steady inside the wards, the air thick with salt and warmth.

He reached for the book he'd been pretending to read for weeks—a battered copy from the local library, *The Old Man and the Sea*, water-damaged from a storm long past. He read by candlelight, tracing the faded words with a finger, the irony of it not lost on him. A man alone against the sea. A man who refused to surrender to something bigger, older, hungrier than himself.

Lightning flared through the windows, bright enough to bleach the room white. For a heartbeat, he thought he saw movement outside. Shapes flickering along the glass, long wings stretched wide against the rain. He glanced at the fridge. Maybe he shouldn't wait for the blood. He went back to reading.

When the candle light faded, Chel exhaled, lowering the book in his hands. He told himself it was exhaustion, that his mind was playing tricks after too many sleepless nights and too much silence. And he didn't want to admit it but he hadn't been fully himself since the fates ripped his soul from his body. There were still moments when he felt like he was wearing a suit that was a bit too small, a bit too tight in the neck and across the biceps.

He leaned back in the chair, the sound of rain softened, becoming rhythmic, hypnotic. The world outside howled. Inside, everything slowed and he closed his eyes.

And in the half-dream that followed, he thought he

heard a voice—low and familiar, carried through the sound of rain and wind.

Three figures woven of shadow and gold thread, faces hidden behind smooth masks that reflected *him* instead of light. Each step they took pulled the realm tighter, the walls inching closer like a closing fist.

"You returned," the First Fate said.

"You always do," the Second murmured.

"Even when you are told not to," the Third finished.

Chel's jaw clenched. "Why am I here?"

Teari didn't look at him.

The floor shifted. Iron bars rose from the stone between them, slamming down with a sound like a coffin sealing shut. Chel surged forward, slamming his hands against them.

"Angel!"

She finally lifted her gaze. "You should have left when I told you," she said quietly.

The words hit him harder than any blade.

"I didn't—" Chel swallowed. "I couldn't."

Her mouth twitched, almost a smile. Almost pity. "You always say that."

Chains slid from the walls, wrapping around Chel's arms, his chest, his throat. They were cold.

"You think love makes you stronger," the First Fate said.

"But love is just another leash," the Second whispered.

"A thread we can pull," the Third said softly.

The soul tie flared.

Chel gasped as pain tore through his chest, the bond stretching—stretching—until it felt like it might snap. He reached for Teari through it, desperate.

"I did this for you," he rasped. "Every choice. Every bloodstain."

"For me?" Teari interrupted.

Her voice echoed strangely, as though it belonged to someone else.

She stepped closer to the bars, close enough that Chel could see the cracks of light under her skin, the faint glow where she was being *held together* by something not her own.

"You did this because you don't know how to let go," she said. "Because you're afraid of what happens when you're not needed."

The bars trembled.

The Fates leaned in.

"And now," they said together, "you are both trapped."

The floor beneath Chel split open, revealing the Black River far below—inky, endless, whispering his name. The chains tightened, pulling him backward toward the edge.

Teari reached out and stopped.

Her hand hovered in the air between them.

"You should have trusted me," she said.

The chains yanked hard.

Chel screamed, fingers clawing at empty air, heart slamming so violently it hurt.

The room was dark.

He tried to wake, but the darkness pressed harder. The storm outside swelled, the waves slamming against the house like fists. Somewhere, the protective runes flickered and went dark—one by one.

Chel didn't stir.

The last candle went out.

Sleep was like drowning. It felt like the river water of the Fate's realm. The world folded inward. The sound of rain on the roof became footsteps. Thunder became a heartbeat.

Then he was standing in the Black Mansion.

The air reeked of sulfur and burnt wood. The walls pulsed with veins of ink, the floor slick beneath his boots. A map stretched across the wooden table. The lines writhed like serpents.

"You still don't understand it, do you?" a familiar voice made Chel's skin crawl.

Chel turned. His father stood in the doorway—towering, half-shadow, his horns scraping the ceiling. His voice was gravel.

"All this power," the demon said, stepping closer, "and you still cower like a servant. You were bred to serve Hell. A Hellion. Not that White Horse. You do not serve that god."

Chel's throat tightened. "You're not here."

"I'm always here," his father snarled. "Every scar, every nightmare. You were bred in my image."

He moved fast, grabbing Chel by the collar and slamming him against the wall. The stones of the hovel trembled.

"You think you can bury what you are?" His father's breath was Fire whiskey. "You think that Healer can cleanse you of me? You think you can just walk away and forget?"

Chel tried to shove him back, but his strength failed; his limbs felt heavy, sinking into the dream. The ache of having his soul torn from his bones returned ten-fold.

"I'm not you," Chel ground out. His voice sounding much younger.

"You're my son," the demon hissed. "Every drop of blood you spill answers to me. You are more like me every second."

The map on the table began to shift again—corridors spiraling inward, forming the symbol of a cage. Chains rose from the floor, glowing red-hot, coiling around Chel's arms.

"You left this place in ruins," his father said, voice splitting into multiple tones. "But ruins remember their kings."

Chel screamed as the chains sank into his skin, pulling something from him—*not* blood, not flesh, but light. His soul, ripped thread by thread, dragged out of his chest like the Fates had done.

"That's right," the demon whispered. "Give it back. You are weak. You are not worthy of this."

Chel fell forward, gasping and suddenly the world changed again. He stood in another body. Shorter. Broader. Across from him stood Teari in the white dress she'd worn to the celebration in Hell after they'd burned the Black Mansion.

Trembling, and confused. "Have you seen Chel?" she asked softly.

He tried to answer, but the voice that came out wasn't his. It was his father's, low and cruel, echoing through his teeth.

"Chel is dead."

Teari recoiled. "You're not him."

The smile that came wasn't his, either. "Not yet."

The floor split open beneath them. The castle in the burning caves lit with flames.

Chel jerked awake with a choking gasp. The chair tipped over, slamming into the boards. His chest heaved—pain lanced through his arms where the chains had wrapped around him. The scar on his wrist throbbed.

The candles were out. The runes on the floor had gone dark. And outside the storm raged harder, wind howling like laughter. Chel pushed to his feet, unsteady, sweat slicking his back.

A pounding echoed like something broken and flapping in the storm wind.

Chel was blinking into darkness. The house groaned under the pressure of the wind. A beam creaked, grinding like a wounded animal.

Another slam — *thud, thud, thud* — this time against the front door.

Chel froze. "Tom?"

No answer. Only the storm.

"Chel!" A woman's voice, faint but sharp, cutting through the roar of rain.

His pulse stuttered. Teari! He staggered toward the

door, half-tripping over the overturned chair. He shoved aside the sandbags, ripping away the boards he'd nailed in place. The wood cracked under his strength.

When the door finally gave, wind exploded into the room — sheets of rain, sea spray, and lightning all at once.

Teari stood in the doorway.

Soaked to the bone, her clothing plastered against her skin, hair whipping around her face. Her wings hung low and tattered, feathers dripping. One arm was bleeding, crimson streaking down her wrist and dripping onto the porch. Her eyes locked on his.

"Angel?" Chel shouted over the storm. "What the hell are you doing here?"

Lightning flared, painting her in gold for an instant. She looked almost otherworldly, beautiful and furious and utterly out of place in the mortal rain.

"You didn't answer my call," she gasped, stepping forward. "I called you so many times. You didn't answer."

Chel reached for her before he could think, dragging her inside. The door slammed shut behind them, the boards rattling. The storm beat against the walls like it was trying to get in. Water pooled around their feet. She was shaking. Her arm left red smears against his shirt where he held her.

"You shouldn't be here," he said, voice low.

"And you shouldn't ignore me."

He stared at her for a long second, rain running from her hair down his hands.

"You crossed the Veil in this storm?" He asked.

"I saw the storm and your phone isn't working. What if you were hurt. What if something had happened?"

He pulled her closer, checking the wound on her arm. "You're bleeding."

"It's nothing," she whispered. "Debris has filled the ocean. There was a lot to dodge coming through the portal."

Chel's eyes darkened.

"I'm fine." She shook her head, lips pressed tight.

Outside, thunder cracked so violently it shook the floor. For a heartbeat, the candle flames guttered and the air between them trembled.

Chel looked at her, at the rain still dripping from her lashes, the blood staining his palms. "You're freezing."

"Then warm me," she murmured, voice frayed.

Chel's hands found her shoulders, pulling her in until she hit his chest. He didn't mean to hold her so tightly, but the storm outside made everything inside him ache.

"You shouldn't have come," he said against her hair. That burn in the back of his throat threatened to take over.

Lightning flared again, white and furious, flashing across her face. He could see in her eyes the fear she was trying to hide, the same fear he'd felt in his dream.

"You can't stay here," she whispered. "Not with a storm like this. You'll be trapped when the water rises."

"It won't," he said. "The house is warded."

She touched his jaw, rain and blood on her fingertips. "Please. Come with me. Just until it's over."

"The storm could last days," he muttered.

"Then you won't be missed here."

He wanted to refuse. He'd made a promise to the White Horse and Meg. He'd watch the gulf.

"There is nothing out there," Teari said as she pressed a hand over her bloody arm and healed the wound. "Nothing could survive that wind and debris."

The storm roared, pressing against the windows like a living thing.

Chel closed his eyes. "Fine," he breathed. "I'll go."

He re-drew the runes on the floor and around the windows and doors. The runes flared with light. The candles guttered out as the runes burned brighter, the air vibrating with ancient energy.

Chel took Teari's hand.

"The tide's higher than ever," Teari said. "The ocean is at your door."

Outside, the sea raged against the shore, black and infinite. They stepped out into it, wind tearing at their clothes. The rain felt like glass on his skin. The waves clawed at their legs as they walked deeper—knee-deep, waist-deep, chest-deep.

Teari's wings tightened against her back, heavy with water, her grip tightening on him. "Don't let go."

"Never."

The current dragged hard, the weight of the ocean pulling them under. Chel gripped her hands so tightly he knew he'd bruise her skin, but she didn't flinch, only matched his grip.

Lightning split the sky as they sank beneath the

surface. Then her arms were around him and his fingertips spanned her waist as his arms tightened around her.

The sea swallowed them whole. For a heartbeat, everything was darkness—pressure, silence, then light bursting behind his eyes as the portal took them to another realm.

The storm faded. The water calmed.

They broke the surface into a world of white. The Seven Kingdoms of Heaven unfolded in blinding majesty. Even at night this place shined and the threat of heat echoed off the buildings.

Chel fell to one knee, breath shuddering out of him. He didn't like this place. Didn't belong. The last time he stepped foot in this realm, it was to kill Teari's father, the Archangel Raphael. This time, there were no common Angels standing around and gawking. It was the middle of the night.

Teari knelt beside him, soaked and shaking; her arm had begun bleeding again. She placed a hand over the wound and stopped the bleeding.

"We made it," she whispered.

"Barely." He lifted her out of the fountain. He looked up at the endless golden buildings, then back to her. "You owe me a drink for that."

She smiled weakly. "You don't drink holy water."

"I wasn't talking about holy water."

Chapter Seven

They walked in silence through the city streets of Babylon.

The air here smelled faintly of lilies and rain, yet even beauty carried a hum of judgment. The last time he'd been in this realm, he'd killed and he'd made a promise to return Teari. He'd hated the idea of returning her to this place.

Teari led him along a narrow path that wound between terraces of marble and moss. The night air shimmered as they approached a gate grown over with vines and pale blue blossoms.

"This way," she said softly.

Chel paused at the threshold. This Kingdom had changed in the months that Teari had taken over. The gate was just old iron half-hidden beneath flowers. It felt secret.

"Have you always had a thing for secret gardens?" he murmured. "I never knew."

Her mouth curved faintly. "Gabriel said to transform it into something no one expected. So I did. I wanted something alive here. Not polished. Not perfect. Natural and beautiful to cloak the darkness that once ruled here."

He brushed a hand along the vines as he stepped through. They recoiled slightly from his touch, the leaves shivering before settling again. He tried not to take offense.

Beyond the gate, her Kingdom unfurled — a sprawling sanctuary of white stone and green life. The castle rose from the heart of it like a cathedral swallowed by a forest. Balconies overflowed with flowers, and light poured through high glass windows, fracturing into color.

Chel stopped to take it in. "This is so different."

Teari nodded. "I wanted a refuge."

He studied her face, catching the flicker of pain she tried to hide. "I haven't been here since..."

She turned toward him before he could finish. "I know. Do you like it?"

Chel swallowed hard. "It's wonderful."

"Thanks," she said quietly. "Every time I look at these walls, I remind myself that you saved me from what this place once was. I wondered if you'd like this"

He didn't answer. There wasn't anything to say. The storm still clung to his clothes and the nightmare he'd woken from was still fresh in his mind. Plus, he was hungry and didn't think he could trust his mouth at the moment. He liked it very much, but this was not a place for a Hellion.

They continued through the gardens, Teari pointing out the new structures including the rebuilt healing halls, the Legion addition where her father's rooms had once been.

When they reached the castle steps, servants emerged to greet her, winged figures in pale robes, their faces polite but tense... and tired from being woken in the middle of the night. Their eyes darted to Chel and then quickly away, as though his gaze might burn them.

Whispers followed, soft as feathers but sharp as glass.

"That's him..."

"The Hellion..."

"The one who killed the Archangel..."

Chel heard every word.

Teari's jaw tightened. "Enough," she said, her voice cutting through the murmurs. "He is my guest."

The servants bowed low, eyes fixed on the ground.

Chel shifted his weight, the urge to leave already clawing at him. "You don't have to defend me."

"I do," she said. "Or they'll never stop fearing you."

"Maybe they should."

"No." Her tone softened. "They should understand you saved me and them."

She reached for his hand and led him up the stairs toward the castle doors.

As they passed beneath the archway in the hall, Chel looked back once more at the garden, at the vines curling around the gate, the blossoms trembling in the breeze.

It was beautiful.

And for the first time, he wondered if Teari didn't

want to visit him on the Earthen plane each month. Maybe she preferred this to him. She'd nearly broken their promise over the Holidays. December they'd risked not seeing each other. Seeing what she'd transformed this place into, he was starting to understand why it was so hard for her to leave.

Why leave this beauty for him? An old Hellion with scars.

Teari's quarters sat high above the courtyards, the windows looking out over the white terraces and the faint shimmer of the kingdom's gardens. Servants hurried ahead of her, switching on lights, fetching towels, murmuring apologies as they scurried away to find clothing that would fit a Hellion.

Chel stood awkwardly in the doorway, dripping on the polished stone, a black shape in a world made of light. When she turned to him, the smallest smile crossed her lips.

"You look uncomfortable."

"That's an understatement," he said.

She motioned toward the bath chamber. "Come on, before you ruin my floors."

Steam rose, filling the marble room with warmth and the scent of sandalwood. They stepped beneath the water, a gentle fall that hummed against their shoulders. For a few minutes neither spoke. The silence felt fragile.

Chel brushed water from his hair and gave her a crooked look. "Angel, you still owe me that drink."

Teari glanced at him over her shoulder. "You think now's the time?"

"Why wait. You could be pulled away at any moment."

"As could you," she reminded him.

He stepped closer, resting a hand against her arm. "You're bleeding again," he said softly. A thin red line traced down from the wound she'd ignored since the crossing. The sight of it made the air thicken between them.

"The debris in the water," she murmured.

"You have a few cuts and scrapes as well." Fingertips pressed against his skin and Chel watched as she healed him.

"I didn't realize," he grumbled.

"Yes, Hellion, no human could have survived that wind and debris field. And you are not made of stone. I'm glad you listened to me before it got worse."

For a heartbeat they simply stood there, water and light cascading around them. She drew in a sharp breath and stepped back before it consumed them.

"Hellion?" she said quietly.

His gaze lingered on her, the warmth fading. "It was kind of you to save me, Angel."

She reached up, fingers brushing his jaw. "What can I say, there's something about saving a Hellion in distress that just..." she shivered.

His brows rose and his hands moved quickly,

twisting her to face the wall and moving her hands to lay flat against the tiles. He covered her back with his body. Teari moaned and arched her back feeling the length of him against her backside.

"Don't do that, Angel. I won't be able to control myself," Chel whispered in her ear before pressing his lips to her shoulder. One large hand grabbed her thigh and lifted.

"I thought you said I owed you a drink?" she said with a moan, twisting to look over her shoulder at him.

Sharp teeth pressed against the hollow of her neck as he thrust into her. Pressing her against the tile. She tried to move but he had her pinned and she had no choice but to take what he gave. He lifted her leg higher until he hit deep. His free hand roamed over her breasts, massaging, then across her ribs, trailed down her belly, then fingertips pressed against her center in slow motions. Teari gasped and moaned and tried to move but he held her tight. His tongue laved over the bite and then his wrist was in front of her lips.

"Taste," he murmured then groaned.

She pressed her teeth against the soft skin of his inner wrist and bit down.

Chel thrust harder.

This ecstasy was a drug and she felt a twinge of something in her belly, a line snapping taut, snapping into place. Warmth spread throughout her body as she drank his blood. Just a small amount, but a small amount was all it took for the world to explode behind her eyes.

These Promises are Valiant

When they left the bath, the servants had returned with folded linen and dark fabric trimmed in silver. The clothes weren't his style, but they fit well enough. Teari adjusted the collar, her hands steady again.

"You clean up nicely," she said.

"It's not what I'd choose for a dinner date," he replied.

Teari smiled remembering the suit he'd worn to their date on the Earthen plane months ago.

Outside, the bells of the city began to ring—the signal that the Council was gathering. The sound made both of them glance toward the window, where sunlight burned through the mist.

Teari fastened the last clasp of her clothing, smoothing the fabric across her shoulder. "I have to meet with the council," she said, glancing toward him. "You should get some rest. I'll be back for dinner."

Chel leaned against the carved post of her bed, arms folded, eyes still tracing the room like a man studying foreign ground. "Rest sounds dangerous," he muttered. "What if an Angel comes in here to kill me in my sleep."

Teari gave him a patient look. "Are you having nightmares?"

He shrugged, gaze drifting to the massive bed draped in gauze and light. "Still… it looks comfortable enough to die in."

She laughed under her breath. "That's morbid. If I return and you're dead in my bed..." she shook her head.

"I promise I won't die. I'm just tired," he said, softer now. "Didn't think hauling sandbags would do me in in the end."

Her smile faded to something gentler. "I'm sure the people of Perdido Key appreciated it."

He glanced at the floor, uneasy with the praise. "I keep thinking about abandoning my post; if something sneaks through during the storm."

Teari shook her head. "Nothing could have passed through that. Nothing." She stepped closer, reaching out to rest a hand on his arm. "The debris would have shredded anything that tried. We didn't get out of there undamaged."

"Storms end," Chel said quietly. "Things crawl out of the wreckage. Who knows what that churned up."

She studied him for a moment, a flicker of concern tightening her expression. "Then we'll deal with it."

He nodded once, not entirely convinced. She squeezed his arm and turned toward the door.

"I'll send someone with food," she said. "And try to sleep. You look half ghost."

He looked at her over his shoulder, faint smirk tugging at his mouth. "You bring me to Heaven and then complain when I start to fit in."

Teari rolled her eyes but smiled, a flash of warmth before she slipped through the door, white wings trailing light behind her.

The room fell quiet. Chel exhaled, running a hand

through his damp hair, gaze drifting back to the bed. It looked impossibly soft, impossibly clean. Too good for him. But he was tired enough not to care.

He sank onto the edge of it, boots still on, head heavy. Beyond the window, the sky was blinding and endless, but far below he thought he could still hear the faint, distant thunder of the Earthen plane.

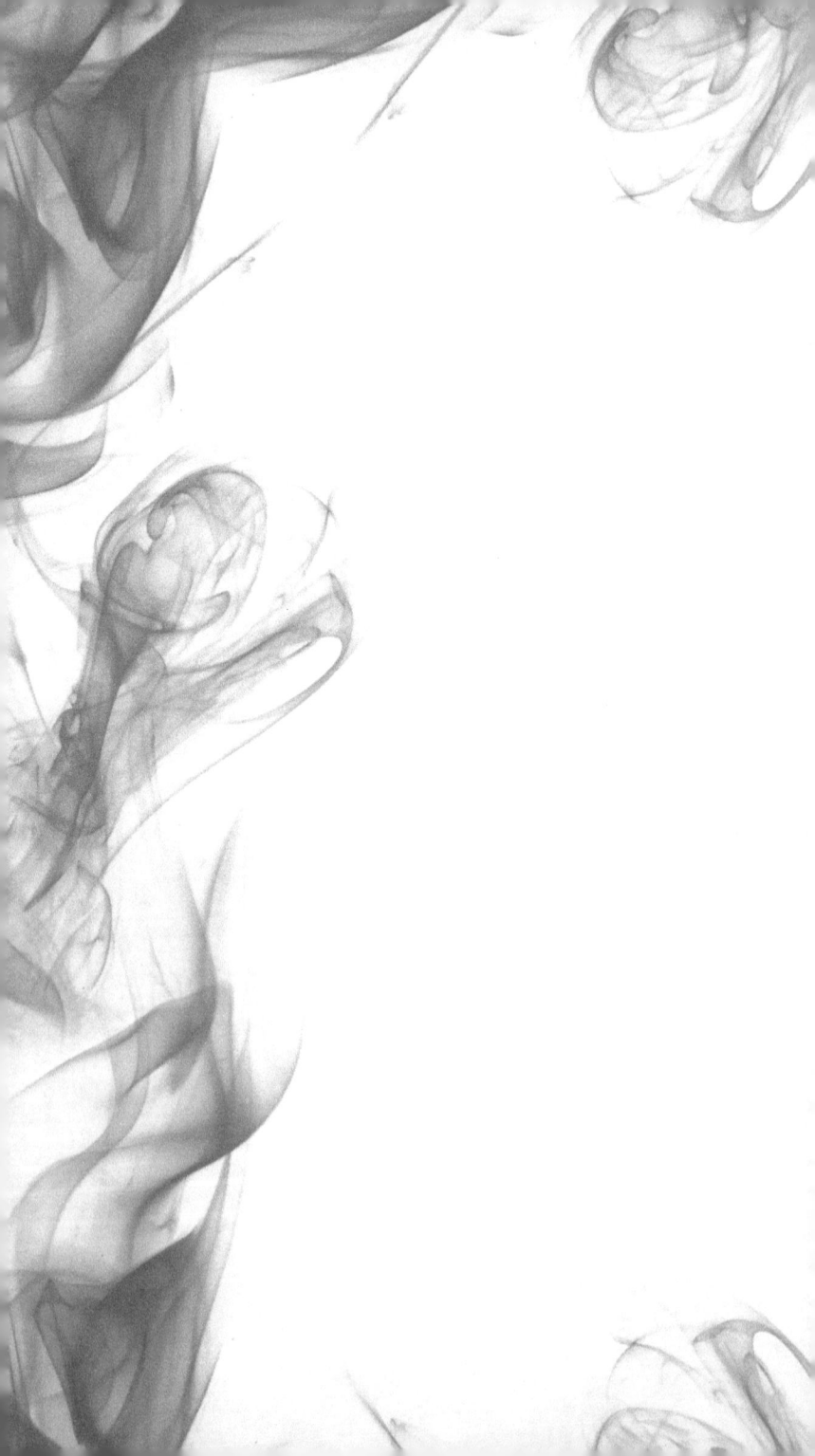

Chapter Eight

Babylon shimmered in the late evening heat, its gold-tipped towers hazy through the dust. Teari landed on the terrace of the old citadel, the air humming with whispers. She'd barely folded her wings when a familiar voice echoed from the archway.

"My queen."

Lassar stepped forward, armored and immaculate, as always. His expression was carved from disdain.

"I heard you went on a little... excursion in the middle of the night."

Teari's jaw tightened. "I had matters in the mortal realm."

"Matters?" he repeated. "That's a generous word for what I heard. Your Kingdom is whispering, my lady. They say you crossed the Veil to fetch a monster. I have heard about your Hellion."

She froze mid-stride. "Watch your mouth."

"I speak only what the others will soon say to your

face," Lassar replied smoothly. "Queens should not dally with Hellions openly or at all. Babylon will not stand for it. Half the Council already frowns upon your reforms, this will undo them."

Teari's wings flexed, feathers rustling. "You watched my father dabble in far greater sins and did nothing. Chel is under my protection. His presence here is sanctioned."

"By whom?"

"By me."

Lassar's face went pallid. "You forget yourself, Majesty. You may rule your Kingdom directly, but Babylon rules all. They will not abide the Hellion who murdered one of their own walking your gardens."

The words struck like a blade to the ribs. Teari's eyes flickered with light. "You think I need to be told that? You think I don't know the whispers in this retched realm? Everyone whispers, you all speak in hushed tones and never confront the truth."

"Apparently, yes." Lassar took a measured step closer. "You forget that he killed your father, my lady. That his hands are soaked in celestial blood. And you," he sneered slightly "invite him into your chambers? Alone? He is there now. Unwatched. Spreading Hellion filth upon your namesake."

Teari's composure cracked, fury flaring beneath her calm surface. "Enough."

"No, not enough." His voice sharpened. "While you sit here in Babylon, that *thing* is wandering your rooms. You've left a predator in your sanctuary. How long before your servants turn up dead? How long before you turn up dead?"

Her wings snapped open. "You are crossing a line, Commander."

"Someone must, when you refuse to see it!"

The air thickened.

Teari stepped into his space, her voice soft but lethal. "I have tolerated your insolence because I believed it came from loyalty. Now I see it comes from fear. And fear is poison in my ranks."

Lassar's mouth opened, but no sound came. Her power brushed against his armor like the edge of a blade.

"You will not speak of him again," she said. "Not to me. Not to the court. Not to anyone."

He bowed stiffly, eyes still bright with barely contained rage. "As you command, my queen."

She watched him turn and vanish into the shimmering halls of Babylon. Only when he was gone did she notice her hands trembled.

GOLDEN VINES CURLED OVER WHITE STONE, AND petals shimmered with dew. The air was warm and clean, heavy with the perfume of lilies and citrus. It was the kind of peace that felt like a dream.

Chel walked alone between the rows of blossoms, his boots leaving faint prints in the soft soil. The storm scent still clung to him, salt and smoke, mortal air that didn't mix well here. He couldn't wash it off, it was stuck in his nose.

A cluster of yellow fruit blooming near the fountain caught his eye. He crouched and reached for one, running his fingers along the edge of its stem. He plucked it gently and lifted it to his nose.

"Lemons don't grow in Hell," he said quietly. The words were half to himself, half to the air. "Too much ash in the soil."

He turned the fruit over in his hand. "But they remind me of Yelena and Teari." His brow furrowed as memories of Yelena wearing a yellow dress flooded his mind.

He almost smiled at the memory, faint and ghostlike. Then his eyes shifted past the fountain, toward the stone archway.

Teari and Lassar were approaching down the path. Her posture was rigid, her expression unreadable. Lassar walked a step behind, his face a mask of calm but he was glaring at Teari's back like he meant to strike or mouth off.

Chel rose slowly, brushing the dirt from his palms. "These grow in this blistering sun?" he asked, still holding the lemon.

Teari gave a strained smile. "They grow best near the fountains. I like the smell of them."

"I remember," Chel said with a hushed voice.

Then he saw the subtle but unmistakable gleam of steel catching light. Lassar's hand was low at his side, fingers wrapped around the hilt of a narrow blade. Not drawn yet, but not sheathed, either.

Chel's gaze sharpened, every muscle in his body tightening with instinct.

The air changed and became thick with threat.

Teari noticed the shift in Chel's gaze. She turned, and her own expression hardened as she saw the weapon. "Lassar," she said warningly.

He didn't answer right away. His knuckles whitened on the hilt. "Forgive me, my queen," he said, voice calm but brittle. "I was simply... ensuring your safety."

Chel's tone dropped, low and cold. "You planning to do that by stabbing me?"

Teari stepped between them. "Enough."

But the light around them flickered, the flowers trembling as the tension built. Lassar's wings twitched, feathers bristling.

"You shouldn't be here, Hellion," he hissed. "Your kind does not belong here. You are poison."

Chel's jaw clenched. "Funny. You talk about poison with your hand on a blade and I am unarmed."

Teari's voice cut sharp as glass. "Lassar, stand down."

The silence that followed was thick and dangerous. Student healers stopped in their tracks in the distance. The fountains seemed to still.

Chel looked from Lassar to Teari then, to Lassar again, his tone turned soft, almost amused. "Careful where you point that thing, Commander. Heaven's full of witnesses. After all, you stood by and watched while I defeated her father."

"Go, Commander," she said. "Put the blade away."

For a moment, Lassar didn't move. Then, with unhurried precision, he lowered the weapon back into its sheath.

Chel turned his attention to the fountain again, but the peace had gone from the garden. The air hummed with the tension.

Only when Lassar was out of earshot did Teari say, "I'm sorry about him. But you didn't need to make it worse."

Chel was watching the Legion Commander and grumbled threats in Hellspeak under his breath.

TEARI'S DINING ROOM WAS SMALL COMPARED TO the grand halls of the castle in the burning caves. A dining room meant for privacy, not ceremony. A single window opened to the gardens below, where the night-blooms were already unfurling their petals. The fountain murmured softly in the distance, echoing through the room.

Chel sat across from Teari, clean and dressed in the borrowed clothing of Heaven. He looked faintly uncomfortable in the soft fabric, a creature built for shadow forced to wear the linens of heaven.

"You look miserable," Teari teased.

He glanced down at his sleeves. "I feel like a wolf that's been doused in bleach."

"No bleach, just soap," she laughed. "You already

know holiness is a shadow in this realm. You're not so different from anyone else here."

He gave a quiet huff of laughter. "That's one way to look at it."

Dinner passed in relative silence with simple dishes of bread, fruit, and amber wine that caught the candlelight like molten gold. Teari ate slowly, her eyes distant.

Chel finally asked, "What are you thinking about?"

"You're going back soon. The storm is beginning to break apart. By tomorrow afternoon it should pass Perdido Key."

He leaned closer, watching her closely, a crooked smile emerged, "You don't want me to leave?"

"No," she murmured. "I want you to stay but we both know you can't."

Chel studied her face in the warm light, how exhaustion and strength intertwined behind her eyes. "You worry too much."

"I'm in charge of this Kingdom now. It's my job."

"You are Queen of this Kingdom," he reminded her.

Teari looked away. "That sounds so pretentious."

"Are you happy here?" he asked.

She shrugged. "You don't like it here."

He smirked faintly. "These people don't like me. And they have good reason."

Her laugh was soft as she nodded. "Something is wrong with this place. I can't put my finger on it."

For a long time they sat there, the conversation drifting between trivial things and shared silences. Outside, the night grew still.

When the last candle burned low, Teari rose and crossed to the window. The moonlight's glow gave her hair a sliver sheen. Chel followed, standing just behind her.

"You've given everything to this place," he said quietly. "But sometimes I wonder if it deserves you."

She looked back at him, eyes luminous in the half-light. "You sound jealous."

"Maybe I am." He touched her waist and pulled her close. "Or maybe I see you giving everything to this place and it gives you nothing in return."

Teari reached out and rested her hand against his chest, feeling the steady rhythm beneath his ribs. "You'll have to return to Perdido Key," she whispered.

He covered her hand with his. "Come with me. Stay with me."

"You know I can't."

"And next month, when this wretched Kingdom tries to keep us apart again?" Chel's brow rose.

She opened her mouth but no words came out.

The moon climbed higher, its light spilling across the floor, painting their shadows against the wall. Outside, the gardens were quiet, the fountain water whispering.

Chapter Nine

Chel dreamed of stone and smoke. He stood in his father's office, in the hovel. The fire in the hearth burned blue, casting long shadows across the walls where dozens of architectural drawings hung like trophies.

Every line of those blueprints was familiar: corridors looping in impossible directions, staircases that led nowhere, doors sealed with runes meant to trap whatever dared to open them. His father's obsession made into form.

Chel reached for one of the pages. The vellum trembled under his touch, bleeding ink that formed words he couldn't quite read.

A voice broke the silence. "You don't belong in here."

Chel turned. His father stood at the door looking massive, cruelly elegant, dressed in black so deep it swallowed the light. His horns glinted in the firelight, his eyes bright and full of scorn.

"You've forgotten where you came from," the demon said. "You think a queen can wash the rot out of your blood?"

Chel's hands curled into fists. This wasn't real, the childhood fear taking over his body wasn't real. It was a memory, a nightmare. "You're not real."

"No?" His father's grin widened. "Then why do you still dream of me?"

He moved closer, the floorboards groaning beneath his weight. The fire flared, throwing monstrous shadows across the drawings.

"You've been pretending to be one of them," his father hissed. "Remember, you'll never be clean, boy. You're my creation. Your bloodline is old as well. Your bloodline means something. You're not meant for filthy Angels."

The words struck like a hammer. Chel looked down at the blueprints again but they'd changed. The Black Mansion had shifted into something new, a city of light, tall spires wrapped in vines, a castle that looked *too much* like something from the Seven Kingdoms of Heaven. Like something from Babylon. His father's claws slammed down on the table beside the image.

"They'll burn you for what you are," the demon said. "And I'll be waiting when they do. We'll find the same ending. Our kind always does."

The fire roared higher and suddenly the world melted.

The smell of smoke became the scent of flowers. The office dissolved into a ballroom bathed in gold.

Teari stood at the center, dressed in white, her laughter echoing as she spun beneath a chandelier. She wasn't alone.

A stranger's hands rested at her waist. They danced together, close, graceful, utterly at ease.

Chel tried to move toward her, but when he looked down, his hands weren't his own. Another body. Another skin. His voice caught in his throat, silent and wrong.

"Teari!" he tried to shout, but the sound came out warped like a whisper in someone else's voice and language.

She didn't look at him. The stranger bent close to her ear, murmuring something that made her smile.

It killed him. The ache was worse than the chains of purgatory, worse than any wound that had ever scarred his body.

The music slowed, fading into static. Teari looked up, finally meeting his eyes and her expression changed. Confusion. Then fear.

"You're not him," she said softly.

The world shattered like glass.

Chel woke with a gasp, drenched in sweat. The room was dark, unfamiliar, and his heart hammered, echoing in his skull. He dragged a hand over his face, breath unsteady.

Teari was still asleep beside him, her wings folded loosely around her like silk sheets. The pale light turned her skin to ivory, her hair dark against the pillows.

Chel lay there for a while, watching the slow rise and fall of her breathing. The lines of exhaustion that had carved themselves into her face were softer here, almost gone.

He reached out, brushing a strand of hair from her temple.

"You're too pretty for a Hellion," he murmured, barely a whisper.

He traced the air just above her cheek, not quite touching.

So much had changed since the war. Since Hell. Since purgatory. Since she promised to pretend to be on honeymoon with him. She was all he'd ever wanted, for ages now. They were so close but living apart from her was killing him slowly. Her absence was a dull ache that never healed, just deepened. She fit here, in this world of gold and light and oppressive sunlight. He did not. He never would.

Chel sighed quietly, easing himself from the bed. The air was cool against his skin, carrying the faint scent of lilies and wet stone.

He dressed in silence, the fabric of the borrowed clothing whispering as he moved. Teari shifted once, murmuring something in her sleep and he froze, every instinct screaming to stay. But he didn't. He needed air.

The corridors were empty, the halls of the castle stretching out like veins of marble and glass. Sunrise had just begun to bleed across the floors, turning the edges of everything gold.

Chel walked aimlessly, letting his fingers trail along the carved walls.

He paused by one of the tall windows, staring out at the city in the distance. Heaven looked peaceful. But peace was a façade and he could feel the tension in the air, a low hum under the stillness.

"Couldn't sleep?" The voice came from behind him and it was cool, familiar and grating.

Chel turned.

Lassar stood in the corridor's far end, armor gleaming even in the dim light. His expression unreadable.

"Shouldn't you be resting," Chel asked.

"I rise before the sun. Some of us still value discipline." Lassar's gaze swept him from head to toe, lingering on the dark smudges beneath Chel's eyes. "You wander the halls before dawn. Strange behavior for a guest."

Chel smiled without warmth. "Old habits from decades of patrols. I'm sure you're familiar with that."

"I'm sure I'm familiar with something completely different. Our realms are not the same."

"True, a Hellion wouldn't be caught dead in this realm before sunrise or sunset. Or at all, really."

"And yet here you are. In her bed. In her home."

Chel's jaw flexed. "Careful, Commander."

"I'm being careful," Lassar replied, voice like silk over steel. "Someone has to be." He stepped closer, his tone softening into mock courtesy. "You're a guest here, but don't mistake that for belonging."

"You sound familiar. Like a Deacon from the old days," Chel said flatly.

Lassar's smile didn't reach his eyes. "A compliment."

Chel's gaze drifted to the commander's hand, resting near the hilt of his weapon. "Do you plan on finishing what you started in the garden?" Chel tipped his head, stretching his neck.

"If I wanted to strike, you'd already be dead."

Chel shrugged one shoulder. "Then maybe you should test that theory."

The air thickened between them.

Before either moved, a bell tolled somewhere deep within the castle.

Chel glanced toward the sound, then back to Lassar, brows raised. "Looks like your Legion needs you."

"The Queen needs me," Lassar corrected, tone sharp. "Don't forget who protects her."

"I have and will continue to protect her. You know not of what you speak."

"Then follow me and I'll show you some of the dangers."

The next toll of the bell echoed louder, cutting through the tension.

Lassar's expression smoothed again, all formal detachment. "We're summoned. Come. Try not to lose your way, Hellion."

He turned and walked toward the stairs, leaving Chel standing in the glow of the stained glass, fists clenched, pulse pounding. He was going to kill the Commander, perhaps within the next five minutes.

Chel started after Lassar, the echo of the commander's boots fading down the corridor. The bell had stopped, but the air still trembled with its vibration.

Something in the silence struck him. There was a pulse of panic.

The faintest scent lingered as Lassar passed. This was earthier and acrid.

Chel frowned. He took another slow breath.

Smoke.

Not incense, not the perfumed kind used in Heaven's chapels. This was pure creosote, like burned wood and ash. Like a building that had charred.

"Lassar," he said sharply.

The commander didn't stop.

Chel's boots scraped against the marble as he caught up. "You smell like fire."

That made Lassar pause, but only for a heartbeat. His head turned just enough for Chel to see the sharp edge of his profile, his jaw tense.

"Mind your business, Hellion."

Chel's voice dropped lower, measured. "Something burn down I should know about. Maybe you set fires? Maybe you're a pyro."

Lassar resumed walking, the sound of his steps clipped and controlled. "You know nothing of this realm's affairs. And you never will."

Chel took a step closer anyway. "If the smoke's

reaching this high, whatever's burning isn't small. You think she won't notice?"

"The Queen," Lassar said evenly, "has enough to concern herself with. And if you care for her as you pretend to, you'll keep her out of this. I can handle it just fine."

Chel saw red. "Pretend to?"

Lassar finally turned fully toward him. His eyes gleamed in the early light but beneath the glow was something darker. Something that didn't belong to Heaven.

"You were made for chaos," he said softly. "Don't drag her into it. I provide safety and calm." Lassar's wings flared once before he disappeared down the corridor, leaving only the faint trail of smoke behind.

Chel stood there for a long time, the taste of hate sharp on his tongue.

He looked toward the window. In the distance, the horizon of Teari's kingdom shimmered but if he squinted, he could see a thin ribbon of gray curling upward from somewhere beyond the outer spires.

Something *was* burning.

He pressed a hand to the glass, the morning's heat faint beneath his palm. "What are you hiding, Commander?" he murmured.

THE REALM CROSSING LEFT SALT IN HIS MOUTH.

Chel stumbled out of the surf, boots sinking into the sand. The wind still clawed at the shoreline, but the storm's fury had dulled.

The Earthen plane was gray and dreary.

He straightened slowly, water dripping from his hair, his borrowed clothing torn and heavy with seawater. The ocean behind him rolled like a restless beast.

Perdido Key was unrecognizable.

The dunes were gone, flattened to wet scars of sand. Boardwalks splintered, roofs peeled open like aluminum cans, palm trees snapped clean in half. The scent of salt and mud and gasoline filled the air. A fishing boat lay capsized across the road, its hull crushed against a telephone pole.

Chel took it all in, quiet and unmoving.

He pushed hair out of his face and started walking up the beach toward the house. His boots sloshed through standing water and he passed scattered debris including an umbrella, a yellow toy truck, a drowned book tangled in seaweed.

When he reached the beach house, it was still standing. Better than anything else. The siding was torn, the porch was missing a railing, windows spiderwebbed. The runes he'd drawn before the storm had done their job.

He pressed his palm to the doorframe. The wood creaked. "You did good," he murmured to the house.

Inside the house, the air was thick and damp. The roof had leaked in three places, and he worked fast to soak up the standing water with towels and place bowls under the leaks.

Chel dropped his coat over a chair and sat by the window. The storm outside had quieted to a whisper, but lightning still flickered far out at sea.

The silence of the house wrapped around him, heavy and familiar.

He leaned back, closing his eyes for a moment, thinking of the people of Perdido Key. He was glad they'd all gotten off the island before the worst of the storm hit. He was thinking of all the work they'd need to do to get the island functioning again.

Outside, lightning flared again.

And Chel's mind went back to Lassar.

The smell of smoke. The smugness in his voice. He rubbed a hand over his face. He wanted to take Teari away from there. But he couldn't, and he couldn't stay.

If Lassar had been near fire, it wasn't some accident. Something had burned, and the commander didn't want anyone to know.

Chel's gaze slid to the runes still carved into the floorboards, faintly glowing with residual light. He'd drawn them to keep the storm out. But storms didn't only come from the sky.

He couldn't help but worry that something strange was going on in Teari's realm, and he didn't want her stuck in the middle of it. There were enough threats to worry about.

Chapter Ten

The Collector's realm was silent but for the sound of turning pages.

Ink glistened on ancient vellum, each line a memory, each word a name carefully stolen and pressed between the leaves of eternity. The air was still, heavy with dust and candle soot. Around him, shelves towered with endless rows of books, maps, bones, relics, and glass jars filled with the things that used to be alive.

He sat at a long table carved from black stone, his hands pale and long-fingered, a quill of raven feather balanced between them. His wings hung motionless, each feather glimmering faintly like oil.

A single candle burned before him, its flame steady.

He wrote in silence. Line after line, a ledger of possession: names, deeds, histories, bloodlines, all recorded in a looping handwriting.

Then he paused.

The quill hovered above the parchment. The air around him quivered faintly.

A tendril of gray mist coiled upward from the floor. It was a vein from the edge of his prison. It reached toward the ceiling like smoke, pulsing faintly with light.

The Magpie tilted his head, listening.

"Ah," he whispered, voice smooth and patient. "There you are."

Through the tendril, he could see the shifting of realms, the brief tear where Heaven's light and Hell's shadow met.

A portal.

He could taste the storm on it. Salt. Blood. Rain. And something else. Teari. The Archangel's daughter.

He smiled and set the quill aside, brushing dust from the open pages of a book older than most worlds. It was bound in pale leather, its cover engraved with runes that pulsed when he touched them.

Inside were family records, written in the language of angels. His old language. One he'd been forbidden to speak again. Teari's line was pristine and tragic. This bloodline was pure gold.

He turned the pages slowly, savoring each entry.

He dragged a clawed fingertip down the page, leaving a faint scorch in the ink.

"You've escaped me for too long, little Angel."

He reached the next section, the genealogy branching into older names, older wars. At the bottom of the column, a symbol appeared it was a bird with its wings outstretched, head tilted skyward.

The Nightjar.

He stared at it for a long time, then began to laugh softly in a low, musical sound that echoed through the empty halls.

"Something tossed away. Oh, but your soul still shimmers."

The candlelight flickered, bending toward him as if drawn by the sound of his voice.

He closed the book carefully, the smile lingering on his lips and an idea forming in his mind. He wanted possession of the Veil, and there were plenty of children to collect to make that happen. He just had to execute his plan just right.

"If the Nightjar flies in the Seven Kingdoms of Heaven again," he murmured, "then a distraction might behoove me."

The tendril of smoke at his feet pulsed brighter, snaking outward across the floor. He knelt beside it, dipping his hand into the fog. The surface rippled like water, showing him flashes of the mortal world. There were waves crashing, the ruins of a coastal town, and a man standing alone in the rain. No, not a man, a Hellion.

Chel.

The Hellion who'd broken a crown and carried its heir to safety.

"I remember you," the Collector said, amused. "Even if you don't know what you are."

He rose, the hem of his dark coat sweeping across the stone. The tendril of mist followed him, branching, stretching, reaching farther toward the mortal plane.

This realm was a prison but he'd figured out how to reach the other realms. He existed between the Veils separating the realms.

"I cannot cross," he said quietly, almost tenderly. "But there are always hands willing to serve."

He reached for another book on the table; this one was thinner, bound in rough cloth. When he opened it, the pages were blank except for a single rune burned into the first one. A summoning mark. He dipped the quill into the ink and began to write names.

Noctara.

Demore.

Nightjar.

He had creatures who would fetch. Each would soon feel the pull. Each one would crave the promise he whispered into the void. Freedom, in exchange for obedience. A swap of sisters would confuse Babylon long enough for him to act. Same blood, same heir. Before they realized it would be too late.

As he wrote, a faint smile curved his lips. "Bring her to me," he murmured. "Bring me my Healer. And then we will collect the next one."

He stopped writing. Looked again at the page with the Nightjar symbol.

"It's been too long since I've added anything divine to my collection."

The candle went out.

And in the darkness, the sound of wings filled the room.

The Collector rose from his desk, the hem of his coat

whispering across the stone. The air in his realm shifted with him, heard in the faint rustle of feathers and the creak of chains.

He moved through the aisles of his library and into the Hall of Cages.

The temperature dropped as he entered. Light came from the lanterns suspended on long silver chains. Their glow spilled across hundreds of cages stacked high to the vaulted ceiling. Each one was perfect. Polished. Maintained. Not a speck of rust.

Inside, creatures from every realm stirred as he passed. Some were too beautiful to look away from, others too terrible to look at. A basilisk coiled beneath a nest of glass. A moth the size of a man shivered its jeweled wings. A river spirit slept in a tank of frozen water, its skin gleaming dusky blue.

The Collector's boots made no sound as he walked.

He stopped before a low cage shrouded in darkness. A faint purr rumbled from within.

"Ah," he said softly, crouching. "My shadow cat."

Two green eyes blinked open, the light of them cutting through the dark like twin lanterns. The creature stretched, its shape shifting slightly as shadows rippled over its fur.

The Collector reached through the bars, checking the tethers that bound the shadow cat, thin silver cords braided through tendrils of shadow. He tugged each one gently, humming in satisfaction when they held.

"Good," he murmured. "You've been restless lately. Best not to test me again, hmm?"

The cat blinked once, slow and unbothered, before curling back into itself.

He stood, brushing a fleck of dust from his sleeve, and moved down the next row. He checked another cage holding a winged serpent with scales like shards of moonlight. It hissed softly, and he smiled.

"Hungry," he said. "Patience. The tides are changing."

He moved on, eyes tracing the shelves that lined the far wall. And then he stopped.

A space was empty.

The faint impression of dust where something *should* have been. He stared for a long moment, head tilting slightly.

"Now that's... curious."

The tag beneath the shelf still hung in place, the elegant handwriting marking its name:

Bell, Winter's Devil.

The Krampus' bell.

He lifted the tag between two fingers, turning it over. "Not misplaced," he said softly. "Taken. What took you." He spun, eyes flicking from cage to cage.

For the first time in an age, a flicker of irritation passed through his expression. His collection was immaculate. Nothing left without his permission. Nothing escaped. He'd been known to trade but never release freely.

He crouched, inspecting the dust closer, fingertips brushing the faint imprint left behind.

The Collector straightened slowly, his voice low and

thoughtful. "So, one of you little ghosts have been playing games again."

He glanced toward the far end of the hall, where the cages disappeared into shadow. "I'll find out which one."

He adjusted his cuffs, composure returning as quickly as it had slipped. "But first," he murmured, "the Healer."

The tendril of mist at his feet pulsed again, whispering the sound of waves and rain — Perdido Key, still trembling on the edge of his reach.

He smiled. "Even gods leave the door cracked, when they think no one is watching."

As he turned to leave, the shadow cat lifted its head and let out a soft, amused chirr.

"Don't laugh," the Collector said without looking back. "You know how he is when he finds a toy."

The cat's tail flicked once, and its purr deepened, sounding like distant thunder.

Somewhere far above the prison realm, a bell rang faintly. The Collector paused mid-step, listening and smiled.

"Ah," he whispered. "So that's where you went."

The tendrils of his realm dug deeper into the Earthen plane and it sounded like the creaking of old wood.

Soon he'd reach the portal in the ocean.

Chapter Eleven

The sky had finally cleared and the rumble of trucks echoed across the ruined beach as the locals returned. Chel leaned against the porch rail, the boards creaking beneath his weight. The air still smelled like salt and damp sand, and though the storm had broken, the wind hadn't quite given up. It hissed through the dunes, tugging at the torn edges of the roof.

He lifted a hammer and began prying the plank from the window frame. The wood groaned, then gave way with a sharp crack. Sunlight spilled through for the first time in days, gold and warm across the floor.

Chel squinted against it. The sudden brightness reminding him of another realm.

He moved methodically, loosening the boards one by one, stacking them neatly against the porch wall. Hell hadn't prepared him for this but it wasn't difficult work. He'd helped the humans of Perdido Key prepare for the storm, read some flyers from the county about how to prepare and how to recover afterwards.

When the last door was free, he stepped back, the house was slightly battered but standing.

"Guess you did your job," he muttered to the wood.

A truck engine rumbled down the flooded street. Chel turned as Tom's old pickup rolled to a stop at the edge of the drive. The man climbed out, sinking into the wet sand, windbreaker flapping.

"You've got to be kidding me," Tom said, staring at the house. "You're tellin' me this thing's still standing?" he motioned to the demolished neighborhood surrounding the beach house.

Chel shrugged, setting the hammer aside. "Appears so."

Tom pushed his cap back, looking around at the wreckage. "Half the islands under water, roofs are gone, the damn pier's missing and you're sittin' here like it's a sunny vacation day."

"This little house has seen worse than a tropical storm," Chel said dryly. It had seen the Queen of Hell on a bender, royal children in hiding, and a Hellion on vacation.

Tom gave him a long, suspicious look. "You reinforce this place with concrete or witchcraft?"

Chel smiled faintly. "Bit of both."

Tom snorted. "You don't even have electrical power yet. How're you livin' out here?"

"Quietly. Serenely. I have some candles if you'd like one." Chel wiped at sweat dripping down his temple. "It would be nice once the AC gets working again but this wind is helping with the heat."

The wind caught the edge of a tarp somewhere behind the house, snapping it like a flag. They both looked out toward the water. It was calmer. Foam and debris clawed at the sand.

"You're lucky," Tom said finally. "Whole east end's a mess. Cops found two boats washed up near the bridge. Folks'll be digging out for weeks."

Chel nodded, his eyes fixed on the horizon. "At least everyone got out in time." Chel was thinking about the old lady who ran the dress shop. She didn't want to leave and cried as Tom and the others loaded up her belongings.

"Sure did. Thanks to you." Tom was watching Chel. "You moved pretty fast helping out everyone in town."

"Just trying to do the right thing."

Tom huffed and shook his head. "You're a weird one, Chel. But hell, I'm glad you made it."

Chel gave a crooked smile. "Yeah. Me too." He shivered, remembering how it had felt when his soul had been ripped from his body by the Fates, he wondered if true death felt the same.

Tom lingered for a moment longer, then climbed back into his truck. "You need anything, generator, food, a ride into town, you holler."

"I'll manage." Chel ran a hand through his hair. "I'm gonna finish fixing things up here then I'll head across the way to help."

The truck rumbled away, tires sloshing through puddles in the road.

Chel was alone again, watching the sunlight creep higher over the water. He was watching the beach. The Gulf portal was wide open. No protection. He needed to get the wards up again before anything noticed.

By morning, generators hummed faintly along the flooded streets, and the sound of hammers replaced the storm's roar and the air was heavy with salt and sawdust.

Chel rolled up his sleeves and joined in the cleanup and rebuild before the sun was fully up.

No one asked why he stayed behind after the evacuation, or why his house still stood when half the island had been gutted. Perdido Key had always been full of secrets, and everyone there understood that you didn't question the ones who helped you rebuild.

He spent the day hauling debris, clearing branches, patching roofs. His strength made him useful; his silence made him trustworthy.

Tom worked alongside him for a while, then left to check the west road. A few kids came by on bikes, handing out water bottles from a relief truck. One of them stopped to watch Chel pull a fallen beam upright like it weighed nothing.

"You some kinda firefighter?" the boy asked.

Chel smirked faintly. "Never fought a fire but I have..." he looked away and thought it better he didn't tell them about training Hellions and fighting Basilisk's and surviving the wars of Hell.

Thankfully the kids rode off, offering water to others.

By late afternoon, the sun broke through the clouds for the first time. The light hit the wet pavement, turning the puddles to sheets of gold.

For a few hours, everything almost felt normal. But when dusk came, the wind shifted. The others packed up, heading inland where the AC and electricity was consistent. Chel walked back to the beach house as the light faded. By the time the moon rose, he was alone again. Good. They didn't need to see him do this.

He pulled the boards he'd salvaged from the wreckage and began sketching symbols across them. Long, looping runes burned into the grain with careful precision.

The new wards would be stronger. He couldn't reinforce with magic like Jed and considered calling the Nephilim to travel down and help, but he'd been there months before and Chel was sure if he returned the locals would ask questions. The wards and runes Jed had taught him would have to be enough.

He worked by moonlight, humming low to steady his mind which kept drifting to Teari.

When the last rune was drawn, Chel carried the planks out to the sand and planted them upright in the dunes. He hammered them with one fist until they sank deep into the sand. The wind tugged at his shirt, throwing his hair into his eyes. The wards pulsed once, then steadied, a faint golden lattice stretching invisible threads across the portion of the beach closest to the house.

"That's better," he murmured. "Now stay closed while I fix the rest."

He knelt and pressed his palm to the wet sand. Something rumbled from below. A pulse that seemed faint thudded through the ground.

Chel's breath caught. He looked toward the dark horizon. The ocean stretched infinite and black, calm on the surface but hiding movement beneath.

Then...

"You'd best decide if you want her free because everything has a price. And I'm always willing to upgrade my treasures."

Jasper stepped forward before Chel could say a word, his wings folding tight against his back. "What's the price?"

The Magpie didn't hesitate. "A trade." His gaze drifted until it landed on Teari.

Now...

He straightened slowly, eyes narrowing. "I know you're there," he said into the wind.

Lightning flickered far out at sea, a thin vein of light tracing the horizon that was too faint to be a storm.

Chel turned toward the house. He needed to make some phone calls and hoped the cell service was working again.

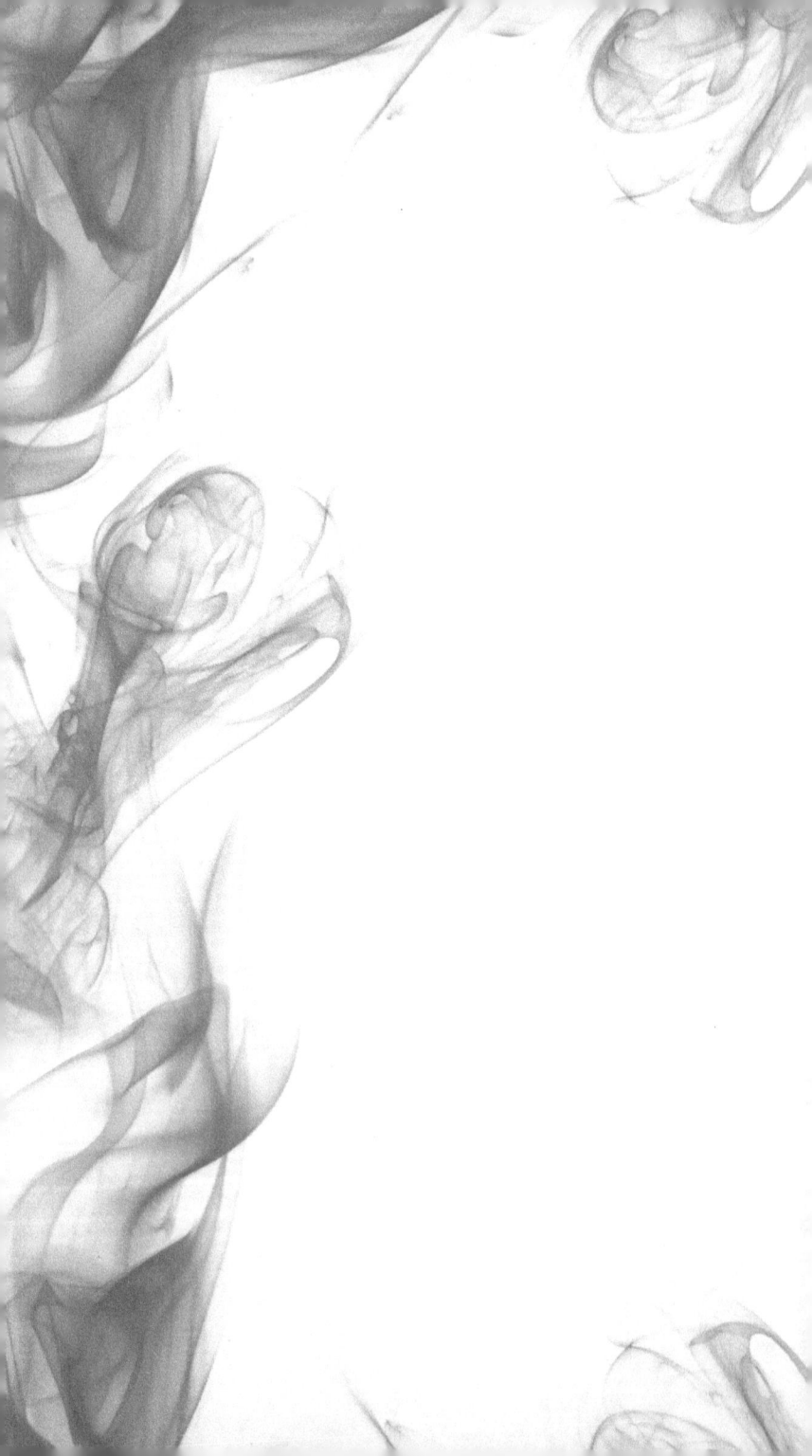

Chapter Twelve

The Nightjar did not arrive quietly.

She was dragged through the threshold in a screaming spiral of wings and smoke by a Wraith that still followed the orders of Gadreel, her cries scraping against the walls of the Collector's realm like broken glass. Shadows snapped at her heels. Chains rattled. The cages sang with agitation as she was hauled past them.

"No—no—no—" Her voice fractured into clicks and hollow croaks, feathers shedding ash with every convulsion of her body.

The Magpie stood at the center of the corridor, hands folded behind his back, watching with polite interest.

"Well," he murmured, head tilting. "That was... dramatic."

The creature that had brought her, slammed Noctara to the stone. She thrashed violently, claws scoring deep gouges into the floor, smoke pouring from her mouth in choking sobs.

"I don't belong here," she keened. "I don't—don't—don't—" It was as though she couldn't catch her breath.

The Magpie crouched in front of her, unhurried. "Oh, my dear," he said gently. "You belong. So many do."

She snapped at him, teeth flashing, but the chains bit down hard and she screamed again, long and raw, a sound that made the lanterns flicker.

Around them, the collection stirred. Mimics pressed against bars. Bone-birds rattled their wings. Soft horrors whimpered, covering too many eyes.

The Nightjar's grief radiated outward, infecting everything it touched.

The Magpie frowned. "That won't do," he muttered.

He rose, pacing slowly around her as she continued to writhe, her shadow stretching unnaturally across the stone.

"She's too unstable," he said to no one in particular. "Too damaged. Too... loud."

She smashed her head against the floor in panic, feathers tearing free, blood smearing.

One of the creatures began screaming in response. Then another.

The Magpie stopped walking.

"No," he said softly. "Absolutely not. This will not do."

He snapped his fingers and silence fell instantly.

The Magpie looked down at Noctara, who trembled violently, smoke leaking from the seams of her form.

"*I could* keep you," he mused. "You are fascinating. A failed heir. A holy mistake."

She croaked, barely coherent now.

"But you would tear yourself apart," he sighed. "And worse, you would cause so much chaos in this form." He glanced at the cages. "You would upset my collection."

The Magpie straightened.

"Which means," he said thoughtfully, "you are better used elsewhere."

Noctara let out a broken sound that might have been a plea.

He knelt once more and reached for her tail.

She screamed.

The Magpie's fingers ignited with cold, deliberate flame.

He set her tail alight.

Noctara shrieked as the flame caught, the fire crawling up her feathers, refusing to consume them— only burn, only spread.

"Run," the Magpie whispered kindly. "Fly."

Her chains dissolved.

She launched herself away with a cry that shook the realm, fire streaking behind her like a comet's wound.

The Magpie watched the doorway ripple as she vanished.

"Let Heaven choke on the consequences," he murmured.

He turned, already disinterested, as the realm settled into uneasy quiet.

Behind him, the cages whispered.

M. R. Pritchard

Fire had been loosed.

Chapter Thirteen

Teari didn't answer her phone.

Chel stared at the cracked screen of his own, thumb hovering over the call button.

Call seventeen went straight to voicemail again.

He exhaled and shoved the phone into his pocket. "What the hell, Angel..."

He tried once more.

Ring.

Click.

Voicemail.

His jaw clenched.

Storm repair could wait. Finishing the wards could wait. Whatever was crawling around under Perdido Key's edges could wait.

Teari couldn't. Chel hadn't forgotten the threats of the Magpie. Nor had he forgotten the glint of disdain in Lassar's eye or the scent of smoke.

He left the beach house and headed straight for the

water, striding into the waves. The runes on his arms warmed, responding to the intent in his voice. The sea swallowed him in a single, breathless pull.

He emerged in Babylon with sand still stuck to his boots, and eyes already scanning the corridors. Angels startled and stepped aside, robes rustling, whispers trailing after him like frightened birds.

He didn't stop. Didn't bow. Didn't care. He nearly ran to Teari's kingdom.

He found her in the outer garden, sunlight filtering through her wings as she sifted through documents with two healers by the fountain.

Her hair was slightly tangled and she looked distracted.

Untouched by the panic that had been chewing at Chel for hours. How could she be bothered? She hadn't answered any of his calls, she didn't know the panic that was rising within him.

She didn't even hear him until he was close enough to cast a shadow over her papers.

"Angel."

She turned, startled. "Chel? Why are you here?"

He held up his phone. "Could you answer your damn calls."

The two healers that were with her sucked in a breath of uncertainty and whispered to each other.

She blinked. "My calls?" She patted her pockets, her belt, her table. "I... I can't find my phone."

He stared at her.

She gave a sheepish shrug. "It's probably somewhere in my rooms. I was looking for it earlier but then I got distracted with this." She motioned to the papers and the healers.

Chel's voice dropped into that low, dangerous rumble he only used when fear curdled into frustration.

"You lost it."

"I didn't *lose* it, I just—"

"You didn't answer seventeen calls," he snapped. "For all I knew, someone had dragged you across realms. Something could have happened to you."

He glanced up as the healers stepped back several paces. One of them, her expression softened as she realized he was simply worried about their Queen.

Teari straightened, wings rising. "Chel, I'm fine."

"That's not the point," he said. "You can't go silent like that. Not with what's moving through the Veil. There were threats..."

Before she could respond, heavy footsteps approached. Lassar emerged from the walkway, his armor gleaming, his expression sharpened.

"My Queen," he said, bowing just enough to be insulting, "all is well. I assured you this morning that your kingdom remains safe under my watch."

Mistrust curdled in Chel's stomach. He hadn't forgotten the scent of fire that Lassar carried on his clothing last time they spoke.

Lassar met his gaze without blinking. "Your presence here is... unnecessary."

Chel took a step closer before Teari raised a hand between them.

"That's enough," she said firmly. "Both of you."

Chel's jaw flexed. "I don't trust him."

Lassar smiled coldly. "Nor I you."

"Good," Chel growled. "Then we understand each other."

The air between them crackled like flint and tinder. Angels along the walkway paused, sensing the tension gathering like a storm about to strike.

Teari stepped between them fully, placing a hand on Chel's chest. Her voice softened, pleading and tired.

"Chel... I'm safe. I promise. I just misplaced my phone. That's all."

He looked down at her hand. Then at her face. Then at Lassar, who watched them with a predator's patience.

Chel exhaled, the anger cooling into something heavier. "Angel... don't do that again. Not now. Not with what's stirring."

She nodded, "Come speak with me in private." She motioned to the small castle.

Chel followed Teari through the gardens, a stone archway, a door manned by a serious looking Angel in armor. Their shoes made hollow sounds on the marble floor. She opened a door and led him into an empty room.

Teari spun before looking at Chel. She motioned to a couch. "Sit. Please."

"I don't need to sit."

"I think you do." Teari was looking him up and down. "I don't think you've slept."

"I have."

She pressed her lips together in disbelief. "What kind of sleep? Good sleep? Restless sleep? The kind of sleep that comes from surviving a tropical storm and then helping everyone around you rebuild."

He didn't reply but memories flashed behind his eyes. The Black Mansion. The Fates. Watching Teari from another body. The maps and plans of the Black Mansion. His father. Yes, he had been having plenty of nightmares.

Teari held her palms over his chest, assessing. "Were you injured crossing the Veil?"

"I'm fine."

"I don't believe you. Show me where you were injured." Light fingertips started tracing over his skin, she found the old scars, a few new ones, but no infection, nothing actively weeping or bleeding. "I'm impressed," she finally said, hands on her hips as she walked around him. "Not even a hint of superglue holding your skin together."

A grumble escaped his throat.

She was behind him and two fingers touched the back of his neck. "Is it blood you desire?"

He sighed. "You just needed to answer your phone." There was a long pause as he considered the blood. "That creature, the Magpie, the Collector, he threatened to take you. Have you forgotten?"

Teari shook her head. "He was trying to scare us."

"I don't think you're safe here." He glanced at the door. "Lassar…"

"Yes I know, my Commander is likely a spy of some kind. Or just a very unhappy Angel. He swore allegiance to my father, now look at him. He probably took my phone just like he took my blade."

"Would you like me to kill him?"

"No," Teari's voice softened. "I've lost so many from these lands, the Angels here trust him. I fear that if he goes, I will lose the entire kingdom. They will all leave."

Chel turned and looked down at her. "Maybe you don't belong here, Angel. Maybe all of this," his hands arced out motioning to the room and the land beyond, "maybe you're just fighting fate."

They both went still at the mentioning of fate.

Teari swallowed hard. "Perhaps," she whispered.

Chapter Fourteen

Lassar

Lassar lingered in the shadowed corridor long after Teari and Chel disappeared into her private rooms. The stone walls carried their conversation.

"I don't think you're safe here." Chel's voice was low and possessive.

Lassar's jaw tightened.

"Lassar..."

"Yes I know, my Commander is likely a spy of some kind. Or just a very unhappy Angel. He swore allegiance to my father. Now look at him. He probably took my phone just like he took my blade."

Teari's words hit like a blade to the ribs.

For a moment, Lassar's vision swam.

Not her. Not her.

Not the one he'd sworn to guard as a fledgling. He

leaned back against the wall, breath sharp, armor plates shifting with the strain. He had sworn allegiance to the Archangel Raphael. He had knelt for him, fought for him, bled for him. Served him without question. And then the Hellion tore his lord apart. He had obeyed. For decades, he had obeyed and looked the other way.

But now?

Now Teari stood at the side of the man who had murdered her father. The universe had twisted itself into a cruel joke. His fingers trembled as he reached into his pocket.

He hadn't meant to take it. Truly.

He had simply... lifted it without thought.

He stared at Teari's phone. It vibrated once, showing Chel's missed calls and more.

Lassar's jaw clenched so hard, pain sparked down his neck.

"So," he whispered to the empty hall, "he came looking for you. And of course you ran to that Hellspawn."

Heat flared down his arm as he crushed the phone in his fist. The metal and glass shattered with a sharp crack, pieces snapping between his fingers like brittle bone. Sparks flickered across his palm as the battery split open.

He stared at the ruined pieces in his hand.

His breath rasped. He swallowed hard and wiped the shards into his other hand. The corridor was lined with ornamental plants with pale fronds and silver-veined leaves. He stepped toward one, parting the foliage, and he buried the broken pieces deep in the soil. Covering them with dirt then smoothed the surface with trembling fingers.

A faint ringing echoed in his ears like a bell far away, muffled and pulling. His vision darkened at the edges. He gripped the pot until his knuckles went white.

"No," he whispered through clenched teeth. "Not now."

He straightened stiffly and forced his breathing to steady.

Voices drifted from the balcony again.

"...probably took my phone just like he took my blade."

Lassar closed his eyes. The weight of those words struck harder than any weapon.

He whispered to himself, voice cracking, "I swore to your father I would protect this Kingdom. Even from yourself."

He turned away from the plant, from the balcony, from the sound of her laughing softly at something the Hellion said.

He walked down the hall, each step heavier than the last. The ringing grew louder. The shadows in the corners seemed to stretch toward him, whispering. And felt something inside him shift. Something that did not belong to Heaven.

Then...

Long before he wore armor, long before he learned the taste of war, Lassar had grown up in the shadow of Heaven's great citadel, Babylon. A child of the Legion, born into discipline, duty, and old expectations.

His earliest memories were not of battle drills but of running through the gardens near the royal grounds, sunlight flickering through the glass towers, his laughter echoing across the courtyards.

His father was stern and immaculate even when off duty and would watch from the barracks steps, arms folded, calling out corrections when Lassar was merely playing tag.

"Feet apart! Balance, boy! Even *fun* is a chance to train."

The other children teased him about it, but Lassar never complained. His world was structured. Predictable. Safe. He knew exactly what his future held.

There were always children on the grounds. Sons and daughters of angels who served the Archangels, all raised within sight of marble halls and healing pools. They hurled practice spears, played at sword-fighting, climbed trees they weren't supposed to climb.

But Lassar rarely approached the white-winged girl at the center of the courtyard. The Archangel Raphael's daughter Teari was never alone, there were always teachers hovering around her. Lessons that lasted from dawn to dusk. Lessons other children never took. He'd seen the healing magic spread from her fingers. It was rare, a gift few had been born with.

And when he asked his father why she wasn't allowed

to play with the other children, he replied with, "It is not our place to question the Archangel Raphael's plans."

So he kept his distance. And, someone else caught his attention. A girl with dark hair, wild curls that escaped every braid, and a smile big enough to warm the entire courtyard. She didn't walk, she darted from place to place. She didn't talk, she babbled endlessly until she was out of breath. And her name was Noctara.

She had a laugh that made his ribs feel lighter. And her dark eyes could look straight into your soul.

While Teari was dragged to endless lessons, Noctara was everywhere. He'd found her at the pond trying to catch silver minnows with her hands, climbing the orchard trees, daring Lassar to climb higher, run faster, break one more rule with her.

And he always did.

They scraped knees. Broke curfew. Shared stolen pastries from the palace kitchens. And got caught, more times than he could count.

When they were ten, they started Legion preparatory school at the same time. He sat beside her every morning, her quill tapping impatiently during lectures, her wingtips brushing his when she leaned over to whisper jokes she shouldn't. She dragged him through the years like a comet pulling a moon.

By fifteen, they sparred together.

By eighteen, they trained together.

By twenty, they spoke the same language of discipline and mischief. Everyone thought they would pledge together someday. Even Lassar. But then, the Archangel Raphael ordered the royal grounds sealed.

Noctara vanished into the inner palace.

And the adults who had once turned blind eyes to their antics refused to speak her name.

After that, he didn't see Noctara.

Instead, he saw Teari more. A girl who grew quieter. Thinner. A girl who trained in shadows he didn't understand. Noctara's absence left a hollow throughout the entire kingdom.

LASSAR WASN'T SUPPOSED TO BE AWAKE. His training began at dawn, and his father demanded discipline in everything, even sleep. But that night, when he padded quietly down the hallway to fetch a book he'd left in the dining room, he heard voices through the half-open door.

His parents were whispering. Which was strange; they didn't whisper unless something was terribly wrong.

He froze in the shadows, heart suddenly loud in his chest.

"...refused," his mother was saying, voice brittle. "He refused. In front of the council."

Lassar's father growled low under his breath. "Raphael has grown arrogant. To deny a baptism? To a child of Heaven?"

A pause. Stiff. Heavy.

His mother's voice cracked. "Not just any child... Noctara. You know Lassar favors her since they were small children."

Every muscle in Lassar's body went rigid. He leaned closer, breath barely stirring the air.

His mother wrung her hands, wings trembling. "Her mother begged. I saw her on the steps. They turned her away."

His father swore a sharp, guttural word Lassar had never heard him speak. "If the mother learns why..." He shook his head. "Grief will kill her. She was never strong after the winter plague."

Lassar's breath hitched. Why would the Archangel refuse a simple blessing? Why would it kill her mother to know?

His father paced once, armor whispering. "Raphael claims it is 'in her nature.' Rubbish. No child chooses what they are."

"What they are?" his mother echoed. "You mean—?"

"Don't say it," he snapped. "Walls have ears."

Lassar pressed closer.

His mother lowered her voice further. "A child born without the baptismal light is a curse. Not blessed. Not marked by the Heavens. A child with shadow in her blood—"

His father cut her off sharply. "Enough."

Silence shook through the room.

Lassar's heart thudded so hard he was afraid his parents would hear it.

Unbaptized? Dishonor? Noctara was simply a child. This didn't seem right.

His mother broke the quiet first. "Raphael protects Teari fiercely, but this? This feels like hiding sin and punishing a child for something they can't control."

Lassar's father drained his cup and set it down with a heavy hand. "I swore allegiance to Raphael. But this..." His voice wavered. "This is cruel. Noctara didn't ask for any of it. She is a child. It was his duty to baptize her."

His mother whispered, "Do you think her mother knows?"

"No," Allon said. "And she must *never* know. It would destroy her."

Lassar's hands curled into fists.

Noctara was being hidden, talked about like a disgrace. Like something *impure*. Like a threat. His stomach twisted. He stepped back from the doorway too fast. The floorboard creaked.

Inside, both parents fell silent. But Lassar was already running back to his room, heart pounding so hard it drowned the distant hum of Heaven's wards.

He slammed the door behind him and pressed his back to it, breathing hard. Noctara. Dark hair. Wide smile. Gone. He didn't believe it. He *refused* to believe it. But the adults' voices followed him into sleep for years afterward.

Unbaptized. Shadow in her blood. Dishonor to the mother. The child must never know. Nightjars are manifestations of the souls of unbaptized children doomed to wander the night sky. She is a child of the Seven Kingdoms of Heaven. She must be baptized in the fountains of Babylon.

But there was no baptism and Noctara never returned to the gardens with him again.

NOCTARA DIDN'T RETURN TO THE GARDENS THE next day. Or the next week. Or the next month. The adults wouldn't say her name anymore.

Children whispered it only when they were certain no angels were listening. The teachers at Legion preparatory never asked after her. Everyone acted as though Noctara had never existed. Except Lassar. He never stopped looking for her. He checked the practice fields. The library windows. The orchard walls. The crystal pools where she liked to skip stones and pretend the ripples were portals.

Nothing.

Until one night, months later, when he returned from evening drills too wired to sleep and wandered near the inner palace gates. He heard a soft, muffled sob. He recognized the sound instantly. Noctara.

Lassar ducked behind a row of carved pillars and crept closer, heart pounding against his ribs.

Two medics stood in the narrow courtyard. Between them sat a small figure wrapped in blankets, knees drawn to her chest.

Dark curls hid her face. But he knew that hair. Knew

that shape. Knew the fierce, stubborn way she held herself.

He opened his mouth, "Nocta—"

A hand clamped onto his shoulder and yanked him back.

His father's grip was iron, his voice a low hiss. "Do not speak her name."

Lassar struggled. "She's hurt."

"Lassar," his father snapped, "this is none of our concern. This is something forbidden."

Those words hit harder than any blade.

Forbidden.

He looked over his father's shoulder. The medics were tending to her. One of them whispered something about containment wards. The other dabbed at the black stain on her wrist that pulsed faintly like a heartbeat.

Lassar froze. She was tainted with shadow. It was true.

His father dragged him back from sight.

"Noctara is unwell," father said quietly, almost pleading. "The decisions of the Archangel are none of our concern. But her affliction must remain secret."

"What affliction?" Lassar demanded. "What's wrong with her?"

His father's jaw tightened. "She will die. Her light was never ignited. Unbaptized children are unstable."

"But she's just a girl!" Lassar's voice cracked.

"That girl," Allon said, "could bring ruin."

Lassar looked up at his father and the world tilted. His friend. His Noctara. Something was happening to her. Something she didn't understand. Something she didn't deserve.

His father's voice softened, "You must stay away, my son. For her sake and ours. Raphael will punish us all."

Lassar stared past him, toward the courtyard where Noctara still trembled under the medics' hands. And something cold settled deep inside him. He didn't want to stay away. He wanted to save her. But his father yanked him by the collar and dragged him away.

The orchard was quiet that evening, the sun bleeding gold through rows of silver-leafed trees. But the moment Lassar stepped between the trees, he felt a coldness creeping through the air. Noctara was sitting at the base of an old pear tree. Her knees were pulled to her chest, her curls tangled, her bare feet dirty. But it wasn't her posture that froze him. It was her arms. Black veins curled up her wrists like spilled ink, flowering under her skin. The marks pulsed faintly, as though something dark and ancient beat within them.

"Noctara?" Lassar whispered.

She didn't look up.

He approached slowly, afraid to startle her. "I've been looking for you for weeks."

Her voice came out sharp and cold. "You shouldn't be here."

He knelt beside her. "Noctara... what happened?"

Finally, she looked at him. Her once-bright eyes were rimmed with darkness, irises dimmed to a bruised violet. She looked hollowed out and tired.

"I'm going to die," she said simply.

Lassar's heart stuttered. "No."

The marks on her arms climbed higher as she clenched her fists.

He reached out, hesitating. "What is happening?"

Her face twisted with fury. "Because I wasn't," She stood abruptly, backing away from him. "Don't touch me."

Lassar rose too, palms out in surrender. "I'm just trying to understand."

"No," she hissed, "you're trying to pretend nothing is wrong."

The orchard darkened around them.

"Noctara—"

"My father chose favorites." Her voice cracked like glass. "He blessed Teari. He taught her. He held her hand. He—" She shook her head violently. "And me? Unwanted. I am nothing to him."

Lassar stepped forward. "That isn't true."

She laughed, a terrible, broken laugh. "Isn't it? Did you see him fight for me? Did you see him hold me when the marks began?" She dragged a hand down her arm, smearing the black veins. "No. He hid me. Like a stain. He didn't do what was required. He doesn't care. He chose one. I am nothing."

Lassar's throat tightened. "Noctara, I care. I always have. Let me take you to the pools. To Babylon. They can baptize you. They can fix this. I'll take you myself. I'll *protect* you."

Her eyes flashed with something wild. "You pathetic child."

The words cut deep.

"You stood by and watched," she shouted. "While they whispered that I'd bring ruin. While they locked me in rooms without windows. You watched."

Lassar flinched. "I didn't know."

"No!" Noctara shoved him hard. "You didn't ask. You didn't look. You believed whatever they told you because it was easy."

He staggered but didn't fall.

"Noctara..." he whispered, reaching for her.

She slapped his hand away. "Don't touch me."

Before he could speak again, a sharp voice split the orchard.

"Lassar!" His father strode toward them, armor glinting, expression thunderous.

Noctara backed against the tree, eyes wide, forehead beaded with sweat. The dark veins spread up her neck.

He seized Lassar's arm. "I told you to stay out of this."

"She's dying!" Lassar yelled. "We can help her."

"Enough!" his father's grip tightened painfully. "You will not interfere."

Noctara let out a sob that sounded strangled, wounded, desperate.

The orchard fell silent. A few attendants appeared at the edges of the grove, staring. Whispering. Watching.

"I will die soon," Noctara sobbed, clutching her arms. "And you will all watch. You'll pretend you didn't see."

Lassar tore against his father's grip, voice raw. "Noctara! I'll find you. I swear it. I'll come back. I'll save you."

But his father dragged him away.

Noctara reached out with trembling fingers, then folded in on herself, crying softly as the attendants slowly closed in like shadows around her.

Lassar's last glimpse of her was a curl of black smoke rising from her arms,

a stain that an Archangel chose not to heal.

Chapter Fifteen

Now...

Teari woke to screaming. Not distant. Not muffled. Not the morning bustle of servants. Real, terrified screaming. Her eyes snapped open. Chel's side of the bed was cold. He had left the previous day after her new phone arrived and they'd spoken.

The screaming grew louder.

She shot to her feet, wings flaring instinctively. The sound of frantic footsteps pounded down the corridor outside her chambers, followed by the slam of doors and someone shouting orders she couldn't make out.

Teari yanked open her door.

Chaos swallowed her.

Angels rushed through the grand hallway, wings half-spread in panic. Some carried children. Some grabbed armfuls of belongings. Others fled with nothing at all.

The air smelled faintly of smoke.

"What is happening?" Teari called, grabbing the arm of a fleeing attendant.

The woman turned, face streaked with soot, eyes wide with terror. "My queen, we must leave. Everyone is leaving. We can no longer survive the fires."

Teari blinked at her. "What fires?"

The woman stared at her as if Teari had spoken in another language.

"The fires across the eastern ridge! They burned through the lower gardens overnight and we thought you had fallen! No one could reach your quarters!"

"That's impossible," Teari said sharply. "Lassar would have..."

A second servant rushed past, overhearing.

"The alarms rang for hours, my queen!"

Teari's wings snapped tight. "No. They didn't."

More attendants surged through the corridor, crying, stumbling, shouting warnings.

Another man, soot covering his robe, paused long enough to bow weakly.

"My queen, the fires have burned for weeks. Has no one told you?"

Teari looked out the nearest window. Black smoke drifted through the sunlit morning sky, rising in long columns.

Her chest tightened.

"Where is Commander Lassar?" she demanded.

The soot-covered attendant swallowed. "He... we don't know, my queen. He was last seen near the southern gate at dawn. Gathering Legion to fight the fires."

"And the remainder of my Legion?"

He lowered his gaze. "Gone, my queen. They left their posts hours ago."

Teari's blood went cold. "My Legion abandoned the kingdom?"

"No." The attendant hesitated. "Not abandoned. Dismissed. Just before the fires reached the inner walls. Commander Lassar said he was acting with your authority."

Teari's vision blurred with white-hot rage.

"I gave no such order."

Angels continued pushing past her, fleeing toward the sky bridges and outer terraces. A vase shattered against the wall behind her as the ground shook again.

Teari stepped forward, forcing her voice to carry over the panic.

"Stop running! Someone tell me exactly where the fires began!"

No one answered.

TEARI FLEW LOWER, HER BOOTS HITTING scorched soil as she landed near the eastern ridge. Ash swirled up around her ankles and heat shimmered off the blackened ground.

The smell of char irritated her nose.

Teari touched the blade at her thigh as she took another step toward the thick plume of smoke curling over the village.

Lassar was there, armor streaked with soot, ordering the Legion to dig a perimeter trench to stop the flames from advancing. They were dragging bodies out of a small house.

The healer trainees were there kneeling beside the wounded, shaking and overwhelmed. They weren't ready for catastrophe healing.

A caravan of Angels drove by, watching. Their vehicle packed to the brim with belongings.

"Better get out before the whole kingdom burns to the ground!" Someone shouted from the passenger seat.

Teari sucked in a breath. He didn't tell her. No one had told her that her Kingdom was burning. How many had died? How many had fled?

Teari ran toward a body on the ground, a man who was barely breathing. She rubbed her palms together and held her hands over the man's chest. There was smoke in his lungs. Internal burns. She pulled the poison out, replaced it with breath, with life and warmth. When his eyes fluttered open, she squeezed his hand once and moved on.

She healed another, then another.

Hours had passed before anyone recognized her. Her magic was drained. She'd healed so many, only for them to get up and leave. They were all heading in the same direction, away from their homes or what was left of them.

"The fires have been spreading for weeks." The old woman Teari was healing said.

A soot stained face looked up at her.

Teari froze mid-heal. "I didn't know," she whispered.

"What are you doing out here?" the old woman asked. "Shouldn't you be up in that castle, doing whatever it is your kind does?"

"Not with this happening." Teari helped the woman sit, a dryness scratching her throat. Teari coughed.

"It's been happening for weeks. Where have you been?" the woman asked.

Teari went rigid. "I didn't know."

"And that is why you do not belong." The old woman moved to her feet and walked away.

Teari looked for the next body, but her gaze landed on one of the Legion.

Lassar.

The commander walked toward Teari with fast strides as he shouted orders to get the fire under control.

His face was streaked with black. His armor glowed red in places, as though it had barely cooled from fire. He strode toward her with fast, angry steps, shouting orders over his shoulder to contain the blaze.

"What are you doing here?" he seethed.

"I will remind you who you're speaking to." Teari wiped soot from her hands onto her pants. "Why didn't you tell me about the fires?"

"It is under control." Lassar leaned in close. "Go back to your castle."

"Stop talking to me like that." Teari lifted her chin,

wings spreading. "You are *my* Legion Commander. You do not tell me what to do."

Lassar sneered before opening his mouth.

Something burned in the back of Teari's throat and when she opened her mouth to shout back at Lassar she felt the scrape of sharp teeth against her lips.

Lassar's eyes widened. "What have you done to yourself?" he looked completely disgusted. "You are tainted." He searched her face, repulsion twisting his features.

Teari slapped a hand over her mouth. Something wasn't right. Her body felt numb, burned out, she'd used a considerable amount of healing magic and now she was losing control.

She turned and ran, feet pounding on scorched soil for a few yards before launching herself into the sky and flying away.

Ash spiraled beneath her. Lassar's shouts turned into distant echoes as her kingdom burned far below.

THE SKY BLURRED AROUND HER.

Teari's wings beat unevenly, each stroke sending a fresh wave of fire rolling up her throat. Her lungs burned. Her veins felt too tight, too hot.

She couldn't keep flying like this. She needed help.

Gabriel's kingdom lay far to the west. Too far for the state she was in. She couldn't go to Babylon; there were few allies there and they would have a field day with her.

Sparrow and Meg were closer. They rotated between Hell and Sparrow's family lands. They'd help her. But she wasn't sure she'd make it without falling from the sky or drawing more attention.

Her vision pulsed, black spots dancing across her sightline.

Wind tore at her wings as she forced the descent, her breath rattling. Her mouth still throbbed where the sharp teeth had grazed her lips.

What had she done to herself?

What was happening to her body?

Was it the exhaustion of healing too many? The rage at Lassar's betrayal?

Her throat burned again and all she could think of was blood. She gasped and the wind caught her wings at the wrong angle.

She spiraled.

Fell.

The ground rushed up in a blur of green grass and black stone.

She crashed hard onto the Raven King's lawn, the impact jolting every bone in her body. Dirt exploded around her in a wide spray. A crack split through the soil beneath her.

Teari groaned, rolling onto her back.

Her wings twitched uncontrollably.

Her throat felt scorched, like claws scraping the inside.

She touched her lips and heat radiated beneath her fingertips.

Footsteps approached.

Teari forced herself to sit up, white breath spilling into the frigid air. The world wavered, vision doubling, then snapping back.

Three silhouettes emerged from the tree line, tall and cloaked in feathered capes. The Raven King's guards.

She tried to stand but her legs buckled. Her wings dragged in the snow like drenched sails.

Her voice came out hoarse, warped.

"I... need aid."

The sentinels stopped a few feet away, tense, assessing her with hard eyes.

One stepped forward, cautious.

"You crossed our borders in distress," he said. "Why?"

Teari swallowed, her throat burning like she'd swallowed embers.

"My kingdom is... burning," she managed.

"My magic..." She pressed a hand to her chest. "It's... something is very wrong. I am ill."

The sentinels exchanged a look.

Then one murmured, "Get her the Raven King."

Teari sagged onto the grass, exhausted, shaking, her breath too loud in her ears. She thought of her people fleeing, wings ash-stained. She thought of the old woman's words, *And that is why you do not belong.*

She thought of Lassar's disgust. And worst of all she felt something shifting beneath her skin, something that wasn't her healing magic.

Something foreign.

Something hungry.

One of the sentinels stepped forward. He crouched and slid an arm beneath her back and another beneath her knees.

Teari stiffened. "I can walk."

"You can't," he said bluntly, lifting her in one smooth motion. His armor was freezing against her skin, but the steadiness of his grip kept her from collapsing again.

As he adjusted his hold, his voice dropped to a low warning, "Just... don't bite me."

Teari blinked, too exhausted to hide her confusion. "Why," she rasped, "would I bite you?"

The sentinel chuckled under his breath, shifting her weight easily. "Last time someone crash-landed here looking feral around the eyes, she nearly took a chunk out of my shoulder. Raven King's wife, you know how she gets."

Teari blinked again. "...Meg?"

"That's the one." He eyed her sideways. "And you've got that same gleam in your eye she had on her worst day."

Teari tried to swallow but her throat burned like fire. "I'm not going to bite you."

"Good," the sentinel said, boots crunching over the gravel path as he started toward the house in the distance. "I'm very attached to all my limbs."

Another sentinel snorted behind them.

"Don't joke. Meg nearly *detached* one."

Teari managed a groan that might have been a laugh. The world tilted in and out of focus as they carried her up the stone steps toward the great doors ahead. They were tall, black, carved with raven wings that stretched from floor to lintel.

Her body throbbed with heat she couldn't control. Her vision pulsed red at the edges.

Her lips still ached where her sharp teeth had scraped.

The sentinel carrying her glanced down again, more serious this time.

"Don't worry," he murmured. "He'll see you. The King always sees the wounded."

Teari swallowed the ache in her throat, her voice a hoarse whisper.

"Am I... wounded?"

"Unless you normally smell like magic rot and wildfire?" he said, giving her a pointed look. "Yes."

She slumped against him, too weak to protest further.

The other sentinel strode ahead, pushing open the massive doors with both hands. A deep, echoing groan rolled through the entry hall as they swung inward, revealing black stone lit by flickering blue torches.

Cold air swept out.

The sentinel carrying her shifted his grip, stepped over the threshold.

Teari's head lolled against his shoulder. They carried her inside.

Somewhere deeper in the home, a low, resonant voice

asked, "Who crosses my border on burning wings?" There was humor in his voice but when he saw her slumped on the bench, ash-streaked and trembling, his expression cracked. "Teari." He swept across the hall in three long strides and dropped to one knee before her.

She managed a weak smile. "Hello, Sparrow. Sorry I didn't call first."

He scowled. His fingers touched the side of her face, thumb brushing the soot from her cheek. "What happened?"

Her throat burned as she tried to speak.

"Lassar. My kingdom burns." Her voice broke. "He kept the fires secret. My people... they ran."

Shadows gathered at the edges of the hall, responding to the pulse of rage that rolled off him.

"Teari," he said softly but dangerously, "look at me."

She lifted her gaze.

He frowned immediately.

"What?" she rasped. "What is it?"

He stared at her pupils, which had dilated unnaturally, then down at her trembling hands. When he inhaled, something in his expression shifted. Tense. Knowing.

"When did you last have blood?"

Teari blinked. "Yesterday. But you know I don't need it regularly. My kind..."

Her voice grew bitter. "Frown upon consuming blood."

"Your kind," he said, "is not your body anymore."

She stiffened. "What does that mean?"

He leaned closer, lowering his voice.

"Have you been drinking from Chel on a regular basis?"

Heat prickled her cheeks. "Yes. For months."

"And you didn't think that might do something to you?"

She frowned. "We were careful."

"Teari," he said, pinching the bridge of his nose, "has your family ever taught you about the birds and the bees?"

She stared at him.

Her wings fluttered with embarrassment.

"I know how... things work," she muttered. "I'm just not... It's not something angels talk about. We're not a... blood for survival kind of species. Blood is frowned upon. You know this. It wasn't so long ago that you were just like me."

His sigh was legendary. He stood abruptly. "Stay here."

Her heart thudded. "Why?"

He didn't answer. He vanished into the shadows, his voice drifting from the corridor.

Teari slumped, shivering. Her body felt aflame, burning from the inside out. The strange sharpness in her mouth pulsed again.

Something was wrong. Something she didn't understand.

Moments later, the Raven King returned, a heavy, black-feathered cloak in his hands. He draped it over her shoulders with tenderness.

"You're freezing," he murmured. "And overheated. And hungry. And poisoned. And—Christ—you're a mess."

She tried to glare. "Thank you."

He scooped her into his arms before she could argue.

"Sparrow!"

"Shh." He adjusted his grip, wings spreading behind him. "You're in no condition to argue with me."

He carried her out of the great hall, down the stone steps, and into the dark forest beyond the fortress. The trees bent toward him as he passed, ravens circling overhead like a protective veil.

"Where are we going?" she whispered.

"To someone who can help," he said.

"Who?"

"Your Hellion."

Her breath caught.

They approached a clearing where ancient stones formed the circle of a portal.

The Raven King tightened his hold on her.

"You're burning from the inside out," he murmured. "Your magic is destabilizing. And the changes in your body... you and Chel will have to stop playing this game of long distance relationship."

She rested her head against his shoulder.

"Why?"

"Because it's not working," he said softly. "Trust me, I know."

He stepped through the portal.

Warm, humid air rushed up around them.

Waves crashed in the distance.

Sparrow emerged onto Perdido Key's beach, holding Teari close as she trembled against him, the black cloak billowing around her like fallen shadows.

"Chel," he called into the wind, voice ringing with authority, "take your angel. She's ill."

Chapter Sixteen

Chel lifted his head at the sound of his name. It was not spoken softly. Not shouted in threat. Simply, called from the beach.

He set the book aside, the cover falling closed with a soft thud, and headed for the front door. His pulse quickened. Sparrow wouldn't be here unless something had gone very, very wrong.

He swung the door open and froze.

Ash drifted from the black cloak wrapped around her. Her hair was tangled, face streaked with soot, wings limp.

Teari.

In Sparrow's arms.

He looked around. Someone could see them. He had to get them inside.

Chel didn't remember moving, but he was suddenly outside, sprinting across the sand. His boots skidded to a stop beside them as he reached out, heart pounding.

"What happened? Give her to me."

Sparrow didn't argue. He shifted his hold, transferring Teari carefully into Chel's arms. Chel cradled her close, jaw clenched as he felt the heat radiating off her skin.

She whimpered softly.

"What did they do to you, Angel?" he rasped, brushing her hair from her forehead.

Sparrow dusted ash from his jacket and crossed his arms. "Congratulations, by the way."

Chel blinked. "For what?"

Sparrow smirked. "On your soul tie."

Chel stared. "...My what."

"Your mate," Sparrow clarified, as though announcing the weather. "You probably shouldn't leave her alone for long. Or a realm away, for that matter. Tends to destabilize things. Makes the females act a certain way."

Chel's mouth dropped open.

He looked down at Teari and her fingers curled weakly into his shirt, seeking him even in unconsciousness.

"A soul tie," he repeated numbly.

"Like you and Meg?"

Sparrow nodded. "The same kind."

Chel swallowed hard. "But... I'm a Hellion." His voice cracked. "I'm not of royal blood. I can't... That's not... That bond is for..."

Sparrow stepped closer. "Are you sure," he whispered and squinted with a critical eye, "about that?"

Chel froze.

The wind cut across the beach, lifting Teari's cloak, scattering ash. The waves thundered behind them, but the only sound he heard was the hammering of his own heart.

"What do you mean?" Chel whispered.

Sparrow smiled, sharp and knowing.

"Oh, Chel. You traumatized disaster. You think your father told you the truth? About anything? Hell, my father didn't tell me the truth about half the shit we've discovered. Are you sure you're just a Hellion?"

Chel's chest tightened painfully.

Sparrow straightened. "Take her inside," he said, voice softening. "She's burning up. And she'll need your blood before the hour is over."

Chel tightened his grip on Teari.

"What's happening to her?"

Sparrow's expression darkened.

"It's the bond. And whether she survives it depends entirely on you."

Chel swallowed, fear curling around his ribs like cold fingers.

He held Teari closer. Her breath hitched, like she was drowning.

"I won't let anything happen to her," he vowed.

Sparrow nodded once. "I know. But we'll have to do something about the fires in her kingdom."

Chel's expression hardened. "Lassar?"

Sparrow shrugged. "Something. I'll investigate. You get her well."

Chel turned toward the house, carrying Teari as though she were made of glass.

Behind him, Sparrow called out, "Oh—and Chel?"

Chel looked back.

Sparrow smiled. "Congratulations, again."

Chel shouldered open the door with Teari in his arms.

The warm, humid air of Perdido Key washed over them. The wards he'd rebuilt hummed faintly beneath the floorboards. The little beach house had become something more with all the work Chel had put into it. Heavily warded with Jed's guidance, nothing could get in there now.

He carried her straight to the couch, lowering her onto the cushions. Her cloak slid off her shoulders, the black feathers falling across the floor.

"Angel," he whispered, brushing soot from her cheek. Her skin was scorching. She smelled like woodfire and her breath came in shallow, shaky pulls.

Chel's jaw tightened, throat thickening. He grabbed a towel, soaked it in cool water, and pressed it gently to her forehead. Steam hissed where it touched her skin.

"What's happening to you," he murmured, "I've never seen this before."

Her fingers twitched.

Chel caught her hand instantly, holding it tight. "Hey. I'm here. Angel, I'm right here."

Her eyelids fluttered. "Chel…" Her voice was barely a whisper, cracked and hoarse.

He leaned closer. "Yes. I'm here."

Teari swallowed hard.

"There was fire on the outskirts. I healed as many as I could," she managed.

Chel pressed his forehead to hers, ignoring the heat radiating off her.

"You should have called me," he whispered. "You shouldn't have done that alone."

Her body jerked and her eyes flew open.

He went still.

Her pupils were blown wide, swallowing up the blue until only a thin ring glowed around the edge. When she gasped again Chel saw sharp teeth emerge from beneath her upper lip.

His heart slammed against his ribs.

"Angel," he whispered, "are you hungry?"

Her fingers dug into his forearm, desperate.

"I—I don't know what's happening. Lassar—Lassar said—he said I was tainted."

Chel's teeth grit. "Don't you listen to him. Not one word."

Teari shook her head weakly. "He might be right. We don't drink blood freely. This is why. It's… it's changing me."

Chel grabbed her face between his hands, forcing her

to look at him. "No. You hear me? *No.* You are exhausted and hungry. Your magic is thinned."

Her eyes glistened, a tear mixing with ash on her cheek.

"But angels don't..."

Chel exhaled, voice breaking. "We don't know what we are when we mix."

She shuddered again, clutching his shirt. "Chel... I'm scared."

Those three words cracked something inside him.

He pressed a kiss to her forehead. "I know. But you're not alone. Not now. Not ever."

She whimpered. Chel felt her magic surging, unstable, like a storm trapped under her skin. He hesitated only a second. Then pulled his wrist to his mouth and bit down hard. Blood welled. Dark. Hot. Hellion blood. He pressed it to her lips.

"Angel," he whispered, "drink."

She hesitated, trembling. Then her lips brushed his skin...and instinct took over. She bit.

Chel sucked in a sharp breath as her teeth broke his skin, sharper than he remembered, sinking deeper, gripping him like she might fall into the abyss if she let go.

Heat rushed through her body. Her heartbeat steadied. Her breathing eased.

Chel held her tightly, fingers tangling in her hair, voice low and steady.

"That's it," he murmured. "Take what you need."

When she finally released him, panting, trembling, her eyes fluttered open.

Teari loosened her grip on his wrist at last, teeth slipping free with a soft, shaking breath. Her lips were stained red, her chin trembling as she fought to stay present. Chel slid his arm around her shoulders, pulling her against him as her breathing steadied.

Chel thumbed a smear of blood from the corner of her mouth and licked it off his finger.

"Now," he said quietly, voice edged like a blade, "tell me about the fires. And Lassar. Before I go and kill him."

Teari blinked up at him, throat working.

"No excuses." He cupped her jaw, not rough, but not gentle either. "I dug you out of the burning edge of Purgatory. You think I won't tear that angel's wings off for simply breathing?"

A shiver rippled through her body and her fingers curled into the fabric of his shirt.

"He lied to me."

Chel's jaw ticked. "About what?"

"Everything." Her voice cracked. "The fires. The evacuations. My people leaving."

Chel went very still and there was murder in his eyes.

Teari winced. Her throat flared with heat again.

"I didn't know. I swear, Chel, I didn't know the kingdom was burning. They said the alarms rang for hours, but I heard nothing."

Chel's eyes darkened. He remembered the Commander smelled like smoke last time he was there.

"And you still think this isn't sabotage?" he asked.

She swallowed painfully, shaking her head.

"No. Lassar... he's been different. He took my blade.

I'm sure he took my phone. I think he's been keeping things from me for a long time."

Chel exhaled slowly through his nose, trying and failing to calm himself.

"Then he must go," he whispered, leaning in, forehead touching hers. "I'll kill him now."

Her eyes closed, her voice soft as she grabbed Chel's arm to stop him. "I didn't want it to be true. He's known my family for ages."

Chel's hand slid to the back of her neck.

She sagged, breath shuddering out of her lungs. Teari's lips parted, panic flickering across her face.

"Chel… I don't know what to do. I am not a leader. I am not a Queen. I'm a healer. I did not ask for this. I cannot save these people. They're better off leaving."

He tightened his arms around her, pulling her into his chest.

"I know, Angel," he murmured into her hair. "There is bad energy there."

"I cannot heal where I was hurt so deeply. That kingdom is cursed."

"Consider not going back without me." A beat. "And if Lassar tries to come near you again, I'll put him in the ground."

Her breath hitched.

"Chel… please don't kill him. There's been enough death. I'll send him away."

He traced a thumb over her cheek.

"I said I would put him in the ground. I didn't

specify how deep. He can live under the soil like the worm he is if you prefer I don't kill him."

Despite everything, a tiny laugh escaped her.

Chel pressed a kiss to her forehead, lingering there.

"Come to bed," he whispered. "You're safe. Do you feel better?"

Teari closed her eyes and leaned into him, letting herself fall against his body.

And Chel held her tightly, like he would never let go.

"I feel better." She sighed.

He led her to the bedroom and peeled off her clothing, layer by layer, slowly. Painfully slow. His eyes lit with fire, like each inch of skin he releveled he'd never seen before. He pressed his lips to her shoulder, the soft space below her ear, the hollow between her clavicle, then lower, and lower still. Teeth nipped her ribcage, then hip, then lower. In a hurried movement, she was on the bed and he was worshiping every lick of skin he could get his hands on.

"Angel?" he asked between slow kisses, "will you stay with me and never leave?"

Teari had never been asked such a question and in her current state of lust and love and torment, she could only say, "Yes."

And when he tore the last scraps of her clothing away and sank into her body, she felt like the world had never been whole before this moment. Every scrape of his teeth, every lick of his blood, every thrust of his hips brought her closer and closer to heaven.

Chapter Seventeen

Teari woke in the middle of the night, breath steady and skin finally cooled from the fever that had raged through her. Chel was sitting in a chair beside the bed, arms folded, watching the door as though daring anything to try and enter.

He didn't look at her at first.

He had felt her breath change.

"Hello," he said quietly.

She pushed herself upright, pulling the blanket to her chest. "Hello to you."

Chel's eyes flicked to her.

"Stay," he said softly. "You're not ready to go anywhere."

Teari hesitated. "I need to return."

Chel's jaw tightened. "To the kingdom that's on fire? Or to the commander who has been sabotaging you?"

"I need to meet with the council in Babylon. I have responsibilities."

"I don't care about your responsibilities," Chel cut in, rising to his feet. "I care about you surviving long enough to deal with them. I care about you being pulled in every direction. I care about you being mistreated by a Commander who is supposed to protect you. I don't want you to go back there."

Teari stood, swaying once before catching herself with a hand against the wall. "I have to face this, Chel. My people fled. My kingdom collapsed. My Legion is scattered. I can't hide on a beach while it all burns. I can't just run off on a pretend honeymoon."

He stepped closer, voice dropping. "You are not hiding. You are healing. And let it all burn. And this is not pretend." His fingers lingered over a fading bitemark on his chest.

"I didn't mean it like that." She touched him, resting her palm over his heart. "I'll only be gone for a day. Just long enough to stabilize things, speak to the remaining healers, and assess the damage and meet with the others in Babylon."

Chel shook his head immediately.

"No."

"Chel."

"No," he repeated. "Not alone."

Teari swallowed, forcing calm into her voice. "I can't bring a raging Hellion; if you come with me, looking like you do right now."

He paused. "How is that?"

She had a point. "Like you're ready to kill everyone."

He hated that she had a point. He would like to extinguish them all.

"Teari," he whispered, lowering his forehead to hers, "I don't feel right about this."

"I'll be fine," she insisted, unable to hide the tremor in her voice. "You said it yourself, our bond is stronger now. I'll call you."

Chel closed his eyes.

Everything in him screamed no. Every instinct. Every pulse of their soul tie.

But she was shaking, raw, and determined. She needed to feel in control after being lied to.

He exhaled through clenched teeth.

"Fine."

Her shoulders relaxed slightly.

"But Teari," he murmured, cupping her jaw, "if you're even a minute late calling me tonight, I will rip open every Veil between here and Heaven to come find you."

She nodded.

He didn't kiss her. He didn't trust himself to let her go if he did. He simply slipped a replacement phone into the palm of her hand.

And when she dressed and left the beach house to cross the portal, Chel watched her vanish, dread coiling deep in his gut.

Chel didn't sleep after her phone call that night. He couldn't.

The house was quiet in the way that made old memories creep out of the corners of the mind. Candlelight flickered across the kitchen table, throwing long shadows over scattered papers, an empty mug stained with red liquid beside him.

He'd had nightmares of his father again.

The Black Mansion rose behind his eyes whenever he closed them. He couldn't escape its impossible corridors, the smell of scorched stone, the echo of voices that were up to no good. The mansion had burned. He'd watched it collapse into itself, watched Hellscape swallow it whole.

And yet. It haunted him. Worse than that, it *called* to him. It was almost as if his dreams were trying to tell him something. Trying to make him remember.

Chel exhaled slowly and glanced down at the sheet of paper in front of him.

He'd been drawing again even though he promised Meg he wouldn't draw while drunk, he'd never promised her he wouldn't draw sober.

His fingers were smudged with graphite. Lines overlapped lines, sharp angles intersecting with curves that didn't make sense at first glance. Doorways and stairwells and strange, oddly shaped rooms.

But this... this was something. His pulse ticked up as he studied it more closely.

It reminded him of the long, rambling tunnels where Lucipurr had once led them, weaving through the dark to find Yelena. That same sense of space bending where it shouldn't.

Chel swallowed.

"I've never been here," he muttered.

And yet... he had.

His jaw tightened as the image of his father crept back in, towering, furious, standing over a desk littered with blueprints that Chel had never been allowed to touch. *Don't touch*, his father had snarled. *One day this will be your burden.*

Maybe the nightmares weren't just nightmares. Maybe they were memories.

Something sharp sliced through his chest.

Chel gasped, hand flying instinctively to his sternum. The ache radiated outward, tightening his ribs, hollowing him out from the inside. The soul tie.

He rubbed at his skin, breath shallow. Every instinct screamed at him that Teari was too far away. Too quiet. Too unreachable.

He closed his eyes.

Where are you, he thought.

That uneasy feeling he'd had when she left returned. That was it. He shouldn't have let her go.

Chel pushed back from the table, the chair legs scraping softly against the floor. Dawn crept in through the windows, pale and pink over the water, as if the world hadn't shifted beneath his feet at all.

But it had. Something was moving. Something was waking.

He folded the paper carefully and tucked it into his jacket.

Then he walked out of the beach house, sand cool beneath his feet, the ocean stretching endless and dark before him.

Chel didn't hesitate, he stepped into the water and vanished.

THE MOMENT HE STEPPED THROUGH THE GATES to Teari's kingdom, he knew something was wrong. It felt empty and cold here. It never felt that way, it was always hot and crowded in the Seven Kingdoms of Heaven.

He ran to her rooms.

"Teari?" Chel called, stepping inside.

The bed was untouched. The blankets neatly folded. Her boots gone.

Chel's pulse spiked as he scanned the room.

"Teari!"

No answer.

He strode into the hall, wings of panic beating against his ribs. He grabbed the nearest attendant by the collar.

"Where is she?"

The angel trembled. "Hellion, she hasn't been seen for hours."

Chel's stomach dropped. "Did anyone think to find her?"

"I don't know," the attendant whispered. "She was arguing with the Commander."

Chel released him slowly, his face hollowing out.

The soul tie pulsed and it was distant, stretched thin, like a thread pulled taut, ready to snap.

Chel's breath shook as he whispered the truth aloud. "She's not here. She's gone."

She wasn't in the Seven Kingdom's of Heaven. He could sense that easily. She was far away. Far from here. He ran for the nearest portal.

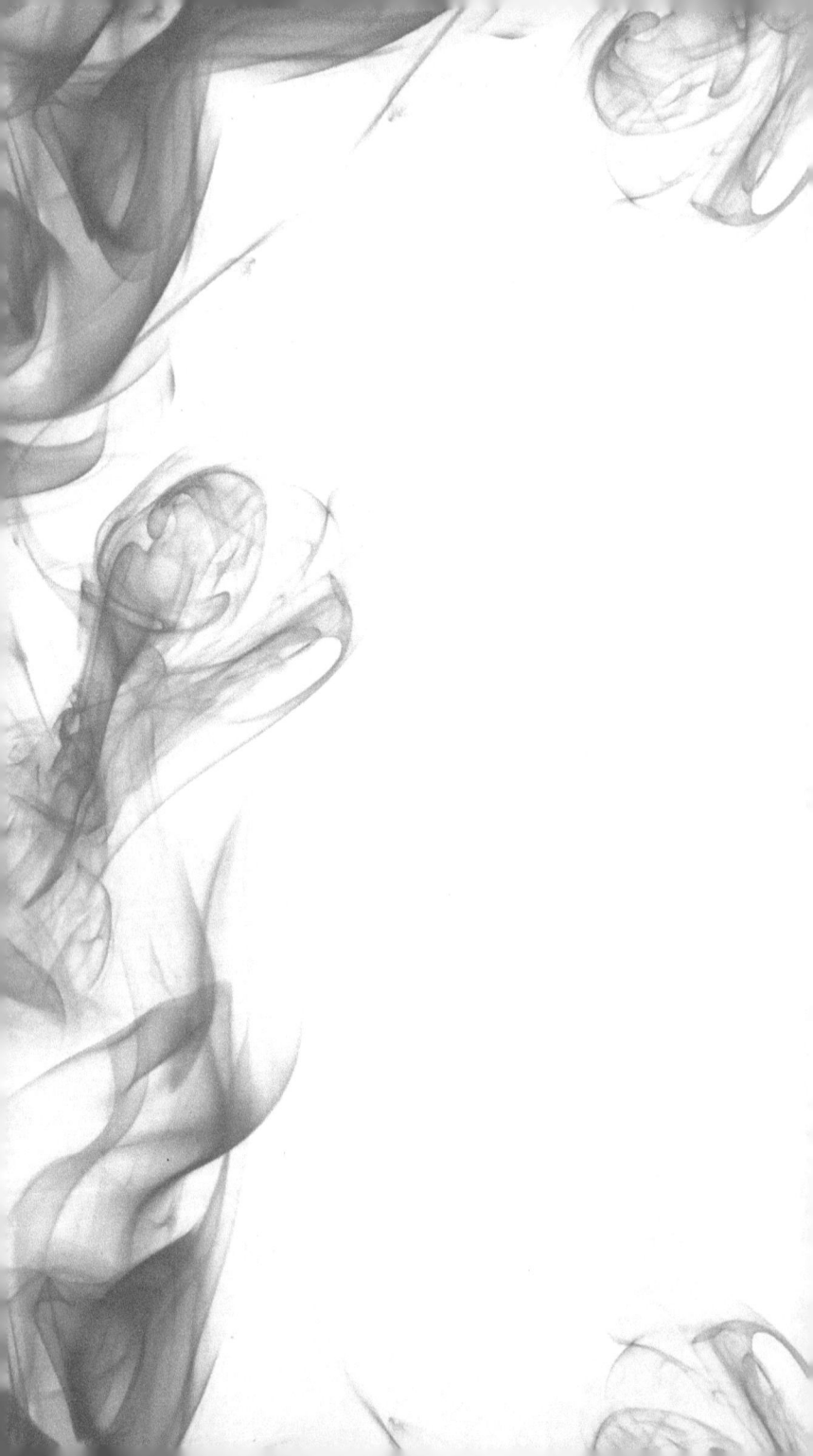

Chapter Eighteen

Meg.
 In Hell.

There is something about midnight in Hell. I glance to my left. Something more about having a creature like Sparrow, the Raven King, standing next to me. I take a deep breath. I'm not ready for this but it must be done.

"Do you hear that?" I ask.

Sparrow tilts his head just so. Birdlike. I will miss that.

"I hear nothing," he says.

Green eyes flash to me and darken for an instant.

"Exactly." I tap my fingertips on the cool stone railing of the balcony. "What has become of our Nightjar? I haven't heard her for days now."

When the Nightjar's song goes cold, a banished Archangel will come into the fold...

Sparrow's face goes slack with shock.

"No." It was more than stern, his voice echoing over the lawn.

A light flicked on at the Hellion barracks in the distance.

"No," Sparrow repeated, a shout now. His eyes going wide and black wings shifting like he's ready to grab me and fly away into the night.

"It's happening," I warn.

"No. It can't. Not now."

He reaches for me, hands desperate to touch, fingers pressing against my skin. "I want more time," he says.

I force a smile but it's crooked, holding in emotion is harder these days. I've known sadness most of my life but this feeling is something else. A black hole waiting to swallow me.

Sparrow drops to his knees, pulling me closer and pressing his face to my stomach. His fingers slide over the thin T-shirt.

"I wanted to see them," he whispers, the heat of his mouth warming my shirt. He whispers words, he does that lately. Soft and soothing and loving. Snowy Owl words. It brings me back to years ago when I first met him and we were nothing but lost souls in Hell. Look at us now. I am still a liar. And his angelic purity has been scorched away by curses, lies and betrayal. He is my monster now. My beautiful dark Raven King. I never knew I'd enjoy having my own monster so much. I never realized I'd enjoy being one with him.

I thread my fingers into his hair and tug at the ends until he's looking up at me. There are wet spots on my shirt, his eyes are red and watery.

"Stay," he begs. "Stay. Please stay. Please don't go."

I'm shaking my head and pressing my lips together so I don't say yes. I finally say, "I can't." My chin shudders and heat floods down my arms.

"Feed before you leave." His hands are drifting over my back, pulling me against him. "Don't go hungry."

Fingers glide under my shirt and across the scars. It's too easy to remember how effortlessly I can be injured these days. I've plenty of scars to show it.

"I won't go in the Bloodlust. I won't risk that." I touch his jaw and run my fingers across his neck. What I wouldn't give for one more taste of him.

He opens his mouth like he's going to say something but he presses his face to my belly again. Whispering. Always whispering these days like he's afraid to use his full voice. Like he's afraid of frightening someone. Maybe he's just holding it all in.

I tug him by the hair again until he's looking up at me.

"Tell Chel to drink the vial of blood. The one he's been saving," I say just before bending and kissing Sparrow over and over and over again until heat swells in my chest and I think I might explode from the thought of being without him. I might turn to stone never touching his mouth again.

"Stay," he begs against my lips. "Please."

"I can't."

"I will come looking for you," Sparrow promises. "I won't stop until I die. I will *never* stop."

I glance away. "I know."

"You are mine and I am yours."

I nod.

"And this is fucked up. We can change it."

"No. Nothing good comes from trying to change fate." That's all I can say. "Don't swear, Raven King." I tease but my voice falters.

My hands roam over his shoulders and I pluck a black feather from his wings. He doesn't move. I tuck the feather in my pocket.

"That's all you will take of me?" His hands are squeezing my hips.

"It's all I can take."

"I won't stop."

"I know."

I step back, out of his grip and the cool night air makes me shiver. I miss his heat already.

And I leave the Raven King kneeling on the balcony looking utterly defeated and wretched. Black wings draped around him like pools of ink; the Midnight sky of Hell as his backdrop. I blink and snapshot the memory. And he watches me go, face set like stone. I know he is angry and miserable because he can't do one thing to stop the predicament we are about to step into. I've seen it from a hundred different angles. This is the only way.

I leave everything behind, my blade, my castle, my

grown children, my hellions, my Basilisk... and the love of my life.

The Hellions manning the door watch me leave, alone. One tries to follow but I hold up my hand and shake my head. An order to stay.

Walking across the courtyard, I wave at the tree where a snowy owl watches me. "Goodbye, Elise," I whisper. She swoops down, gliding beside me until the night swallows me whole.

I didn't know how he'd find me, if he would escape his lair or send one of his minions to collect me when I least expected it. I soon find out, it is neither. The darkness simply swallows me whole like a nightmare.

And through the pitch black I hear the echo of Sparrow as he roars in agony into the night. He'll awaken all of Hell and Heaven and the Earthen Plane screaming like that.

I choke back tears but the emotion gets stuck in my throat.

"Until we meet again, my sparrow man," I murmur.

Some might think this is selfish, walking towards fate with open arms but I know I couldn't have it all for always. My life has been no fairy tale. It has been haunted and dirty and fucked. I want to run back to him. I want to be selfish and take for me. I want to keep him right now.

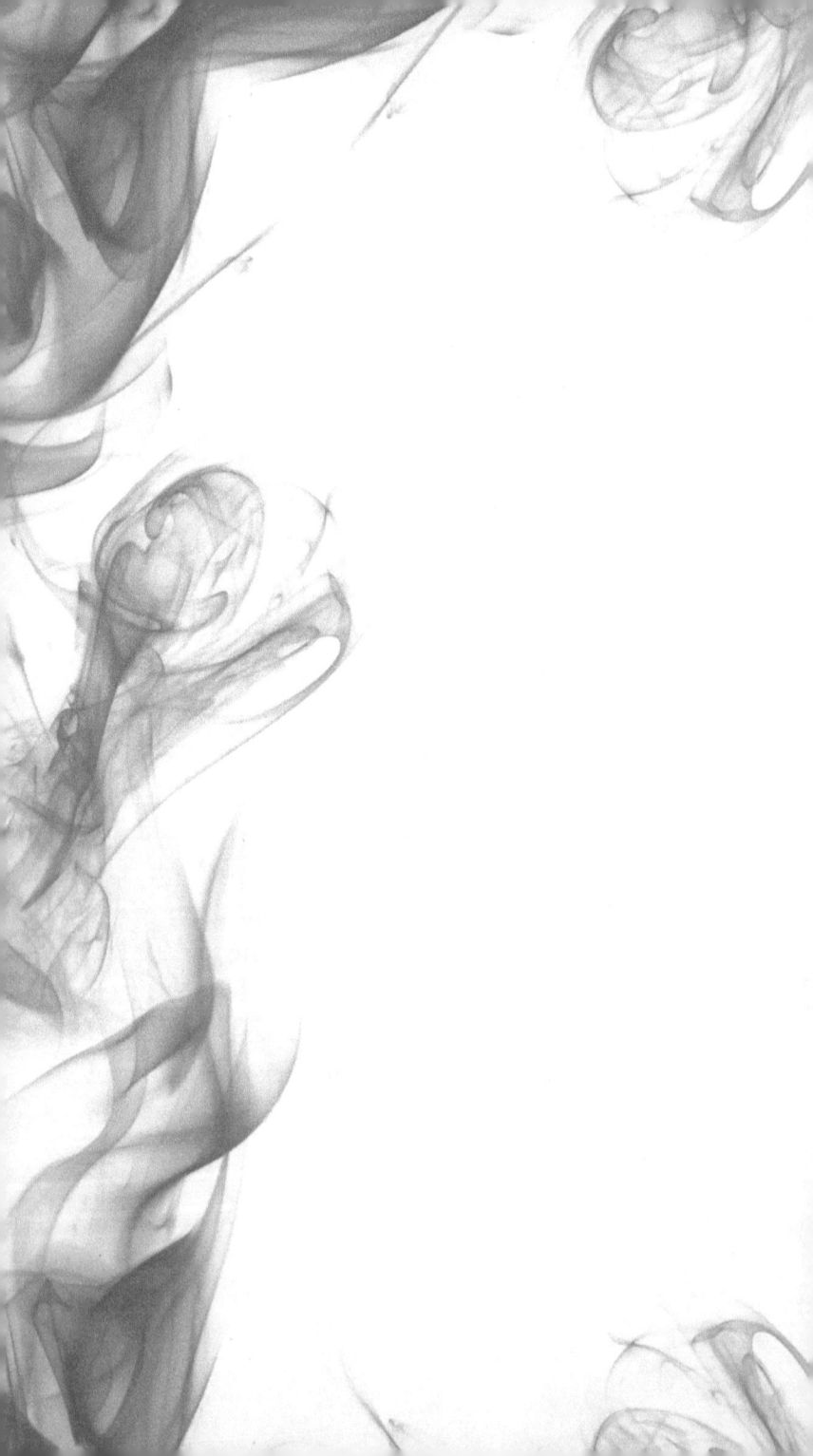

Chapter Nineteen

Sparrow

White, blank swelling rage radiated from the Raven King. Darkness fell around him in pools of ink. But he stayed still, just like she'd told him. Just like she'd warned him. His mind was reeling the entire time. Sparrow had thought his family had the worst of the curses, madness... but hers was worse, to know and see and do nothing and say nothing. He wondered how many times she'd dreamed of this, how many times this had distorted and altered and spiraled.

Rough hands rubbed his face, rubbed away the wetness from his eyes. It took him years to realize that she could *see* like her mother, Clea. Took him years to realize that she'd kept it all to herself and never told a soul. She'd rather let fate play out than try to change its course, interfering with fate never worked out well for Meg.

Chapter Twenty

Chel stormed back into the beach house, dripping water across the floorboards as he crossed the threshold. The walls felt too small. The air too still. Teari's absence hammered against the soul tie like a bruise he couldn't stop pressing.

He grabbed his pack from beneath the table and began shoving in weapons, a change of clothing, a knife made of a Basilisk bone, a vial of blood. He didn't even bother changing clothes.

Teari was gone and he wasn't waiting one more second to find her.

His phone buzzed.

Chel froze at the name flashing across the screen.

Remington.

He answered in a single breath.

"What."

There was a pause, then Remington's voice came

through sounding strained, sharp, colder than Chel had ever heard it.

"My mother is missing."

Chel's fingers tightened around the phone until the plastic creaked.

"What do you mean, missing?"

"No one's seen her since last night," Remington said. "My father won't tell anyone anything."

Chel's stomach dropped.

"Chel," Remington said quietly, "I thought you should know. He's hiding something. Maybe about... something worse. I'm not sure."

"I've got more bad news," Chel growled. "Teari is missing."

Remington exhaled shakily.

"I'll help you."

"No," Chel cut in. "Stay at the Castle in the Burning caves. If your mother is missing, the throne is a target. Don't leave. Protect the throne."

Another pause, thicker this time.

"...Fine. But Chel..."

"It's going to be just fine. Stay where you are." Chel hung up, grateful that he'd been born a Demon, that way he could lie all he wanted.

He tied off his pack, slung it over his shoulder, and reached for the door. A rumble outside stopped him cold. Three trucks. Old, loud, battered Perdido Key beaters. Headlights cutting through the early morning fog.

Chel's breath stilled. Then he heard familiar voices. Tom and the guys from card night.

"Hell of a morning for a visit," Chel muttered under his breath. He stepped onto the porch just as the trucks rolled to a stop in the sand.

Tom climbed out first, slamming his door shut. His face wasn't joking this time.

The other men—Pete, Jonah, and Rick—spread out behind him like some kind of mortal militia, each holding tools, crowbars, or nothing but grim expressions.

"Chel," Tom said, hands on hips. "Mornin'."

Chel stared. "This is not a good time. I need to leave."

"Funny you say that." Tom squinted at him. "'Cause you didn't need to leave in a hurry when that storm was threatening to tear apart this beach."

Jonah spit into the sand. "We came to check on you."

"We heard weird noises from the beach last night," Pete added. "Lights. Flickering. Sounded like... a storm was coming again. But there's nothing left out here to make that kinda noise." Pete swung his crowbar, motioning to the empty lots where houses once stood before the storm that had ripped through nearly a week ago.

Tom squinted at him. "Something's happening, ain't it?"

Chel glanced back toward the house.

"Something *is* happening," Chel admitted, voice low and controlled.

Pete stepped forward. "Are you in trouble?"

Chel stiffened.

Jonah's gaze narrowed. "Your wife hasn't visited in a while. Kinda miss seeing her."

Chel's teeth sharpened against his lips before he could stop the instinct. He turned away slightly, hiding the change.

Rick muttered, "Are you in some type of trouble or not?"

Chel's breath fogged hot. The thirst was burning him from the inside out. These men didn't realize how close they were to danger just standing this near to him while he was like this.

Tom stepped closer, tone gentler than before. "You can go get her, Chel. We can take over whatever mission you're doing here. You helped us. We help you."

Chel turned back sharply. "What makes you think I'm on a mission?"

Tom spread his hands. "What makes us *not* think you're on a mission? You stopped that man from walking out of the ocean and taking our women. But there is something more going on here. We owe you."

Chel's chest tightened and he cursed under his breath. "You need to go."

Tom shook his head. "Tell us what we need to do."

Duty tore at him. Teari needed him.

Sparrow needed to be hunted down. The Veil was thinning. Something beneath Perdido Key was waking. In that moment he caved. The White Horse could kill him, there was no choice that was good.

Chel gripped the doorframe hard enough to crack the wood.

"If anything comes out of the ocean," he said slowly, "kill it."

The men exchanged looks.

"Kill... what exactly?" Jonah muttered.

"Anything," Chel repeated. "Don't take your eyes off the beach."

Tom swallowed but nodded. "Alright. We can do that."

"The White Horse might kill me for this," Chel muttered under his breath, "but I don't care."

He walked into the kitchen, yanked open a drawer, grabbed a pen and scrap of paper. His handwriting scratched hard and fast.

He walked it back outside and handed it to Tom.

"If things get out of hand," Chel said, "call this guy."

Tom read it. "Who is Jed?"

"He'll know what to do," Chel said. "But he's in Montana, so don't wait until you're wading in shit to call him."

Pete raised a brow. "What kinda shit we talkin' about?"

Chel stared him dead in the eye.

"You might see some strange things."

Rick looked Chel up and down slowly.

"Too late. Been looking at some strange things for months now."

Chel huffed a humorless laugh and nodded.

Then he stepped off the porch, wings flickering, old Hellion rage stirring hot and violent.

"I don't know how long I'll be gone," he said. "Keep Perdido Key safe."

Tom adjusted his grip on the crowbar. "You got it. Go get your girl."

Chel took one last look at the ocean and its unnaturally still surface. Then he walked straight into the water and vanished.

Chapter Twenty-One

Then...

Noctara's father, the Archangel Raphael, did not shout when he condemned her. He didn't rage. Didn't argue. Didn't even look angry. He simply looked... disappointed and bored.

"You cannot heal," he said, voice clipped, cold. "You cannot anchor light. You cannot do anything remotely special."

"Father, I can—"

"No," he snapped, hand raised. "You are not ready. Not worthy of this bloodline. I will not baptize you."

Noctara's breath caught. "But Teari—"

"Do not," he hissed, "compare yourself to her."

The words cut deeper than any blade.

"You will not receive the rite," he said. "Not from me. Not from anyone."

A pause. As if he didn't want to say the next part aloud.

"You were a mistake, Noctara. I cannot fix you. You will go with the other mistakes."

Her world collapsed inward.

Before she could speak, before she could beg, he turned his back and walked away. Leaving her standing alone in the hall, trembling.

Night fell fast and heavy. She had been sent out "to pray," the polite way the Legion escort phrased it. She was shoved through a portal without warning and landed in a pile of leaves.

She smelled woodsmoke and pine, could feel the creeping cold under her skin. An ache in her bones. A twisting in her soul. It was too late, she should have been baptized years before. The worst was yet to come. She was in Hell. He'd sent her to Hell.

"No..." She stumbled deeper into the woods, clutching her stomach. "No, not yet... I'm not ready..."

But the Nightjar didn't need her readiness. It needed her lost soul. Her skin split first. A clean tear along her forearms. She screamed, falling to her knees. Feathers that were black and burning at the tips pushed through her flesh.

"No... please... please..."

The pain deepened, spreading through her ribs as her

bones loosened, hollowing. The air around her distorted, shadows stretching from her limbs like smoke. Her fingers curled into the dirt, then elongated, thinning into talons made of darkness.

The dead stirred. They circled her quietly. Watching her become.

Noctara sobbed, the tears turning to salt on her cheeks.

"I don't want this... I don't want this..."

Her voice cracked. Then broke. Then changed.

A feathered plume burst from her shoulder blades, black as void. Her wings weren't angelic, no they were tattered things of soot and shadow, half-formed and trembling.

Her throat seized as she tried to scream but what came out was a harsh croak.

A scraping click. A hollow, echoing sound like something calling from an empty canyon.

She clasped her hands over her mouth in horror.

The Nightjar's song rose from her chest again, unbidden. A call of mourning. A call of loss. A call for help.

But no one came.

Not her father. Not the healers.

Not even someone she loved.

"Lassar..." she whispered, voice breaking around the new sounds swelling beneath it. "My friend. You said you'd... you said..."

Her words dissolved into another croak and the shadows closed around her, feathers falling like black snow. Her limbs dissolved into smoke. Her eyes flickered from soft blue to ink-black pits.

She curled into a trembling heap at the base of a dead tree, surrounded by the silent dead of Hell.

Afraid.

Alone.

Unwanted.

This was how she became the Nightjar.

Not blessed.

Not baptized.

Not guided.

But abandoned. Her soul was lost.

The hollow croak echoed throughout Hellforest.

The moment her voice gave out and the Nightjar's croak replaced it, the forest grew quiet. Every shadow leaned forward.

Every dead thing stilled.

Noctara staggered to her feet, limbs half-smoke, half-feather, every movement crooked and stuttered. Her new wings dragged behind her, too heavy, too sharp, not meant for flight yet. The ground gave beneath her feet. Hell's soil was warm as a heartbeat. She had never set foot here before.

Every angel child knew Hell is where the dead walk. Hell is where the forgotten linger. Hell is where angels do not survive.

A branch snapped. A low groan rolled through the trees.

Noctara spun, breath hitching. Her fingers curled,

but they weren't fingers anymore they were thin tendrils of shadow-talon that trembled and flickered.

Shapes emerged from the darkness. A soldier missing half his skull, eyes burning blue. A woman in a shredded gown dragging her broken legs. A beast that had once been a wolf but now was nothing but ribs, mist, and sharp teeth.

Noctara stumbled back, wings flaring instinctively.

She expected them to attack but they didn't. They watched her. Confused and curious. A few tilted their heads the way animals do when listening to a sound beyond mortal hearing.

Her sound. "Please don't hurt me..." What came out was a shaky croak and a clicking echo that wasn't her voice at all.

The dead things flinched then bowed, backed away.

Noctara froze then she took a trembling step back.

And they parted for her. Not out of fear but out of recognition.

The Nightjar was born and the creatures of Hell mourned outwardly for her. She was so confused.

All she knew was that something monstrous flickered inside her, singing through her bones and skin, whispering for her to run, to hide, to survive to scream and cry and... fly. She'd never flown before but here in Hell the ochre moon called to her. It rippled up her new spine but she was too afraid.

She turned and fled.

Noctara ran until her legs became less smoke and more bone again, stabilizing enough to keep her from collapsing. Twigs scraped her skin, though half of it no longer bled. Her new feathers dragged behind her, snagging on roots and stones.

Every breath hurt. Every movement burned. Finally, she saw a small cabin. Collapsed on one side. Windows broken.

A rotted porch half-swallowed by vines.

It sat beside a pond.

She pushed the door open with shaking hands, hands that sometimes weren't hands at all, and slipped inside.

The air smelled like dust and rotting wood.

Something had died in here once, but long enough ago that only the memory remained.

A table lay overturned. A lantern rested on its side. Blankets half-molded were piled in a corner. Noctara crawled into that corner and curled up small, wings wrapping around her like a cocoon. Her breath hitched. She sobbed until there were no tears left.

She was a Nightjar. A monster.

Demore, was what her father had called her. Demore. Demore. Demore. He took the other name away.

Every time she tried to speak her own name, the sound that came out was a hollow croak, echoing off the walls.

Her father's voice echoed in her mind. *"You were a mistake."*

She dug her talons into the wooden floor to silence it.

Outside, the dead walked by. They didn't enter. They paced around the pond, around the cabin, guarding the perimeter as though she were theirs to protect.

Perhaps she was.

When dawn should have come, the sky changed from black to a deep bruised violet. Noctara forced herself upright, feathers shedding like black petals.

She opened her mouth and croaked a terrible, broken sound. She hated it.

Noctara tucked her wings tighter and whispered into the dark, "I'll never forgive them." The croaking echo repeated her vow. "Demore. I am Demore now."

Chapter Twenty-Two

Now...

"Commander." Teari's voice cracked like dry bone.

He didn't turn.

"Lassar."

This time, he turned slowly as if bored. As if inconvenienced by the Queen of this Kingdom.

"Welcome back, your Majesty," he finally greeted.

Teari took three steps toward him, each one fueled by anger. "Explain why my kingdom is burning."

He didn't blink. "It's being contained."

"It is not contained," she snapped. "People are fleeing and no one told me. Not the Legion. Not the healers. Not *you*."

He folded his arms. "You had other priorities."

Teari's wings flared, ash drifting from her feathers.

There was ash everywhere now, falling from the sky from the fires in the distance.

"You have no right to speak to me like that."

"Oh, don't I?" Lassar's eyes narrowed.

Teari's jaw twitched. "I was spent. My healing magic was depleted. If you had warned me!"

"If you were truly your father's heir," he said sharply, "you wouldn't *need* warning."

Her breath stilled.

"You did this," she whispered. "You let the fires spread. And you hid it from me."

Lassar stepped closer, lowering his voice.

"I did what I thought was best."

"For who?" Teari demanded. "For the kingdom? Or for you?"

"Don't test me," he said quietly. "My family has served this line since before you were born."

"No." Teari shook her head. "You served my father. And now you resent me."

Lassar's expression flickered at the mention of Raphael. Teari seized it.

"You think I don't know?" she whispered. "You think I don't see how you look at me? Like I'm a mistake. Like I stole something that wasn't mine."

"I didn't say that."

"You don't have to," Teari snapped.

"You took my blade. You stole my phone. You kept fires, deaths, destruction from me. Do you have any idea how many injuries I had to heal? How many lives I dragged back from the brink because *you* decided I didn't need to know?"

Lassar looked away.

Teari pressed a hand to her temple, dizzy with exhaustion and fury.

"My magic can only hold me so far," she said. "I am not infinite. I can't heal an entire kingdom overnight. But I would've prepared. I would've called the healers from neighboring kingdoms. I would've rallied the others. If you had told me, if you had even sent a messenger, none of those people would have burned."

Lassar's jaw clenched. "You weren't here."

"I COULD HAVE BEEN!" Teari shouted, voice cracking. "If you had warned me!"

Silence dropped like a stone.

Teari's vision blurred from exhaustion and grief. The soul tie pulsed faintly, like Chel calling to her from across realms. She ignored it and swallowed hard.

Lassar tilted his head, voice low and cold.

"And what would your Hellion have done? Burn the kingdom brighter?"

Teari stared at him, stunned.

Then her voice went soft and lethal.

"You do not speak of him."

Lassar opened his mouth.

"Do. Not." Her wings flared. Light crackled along her skin like lightning. Her teeth sharpened involuntarily, scraping against her lips.

Lassar's eyes widened in disgust. "There," he hissed. "There it is. Proof. You're becoming something else.

Something dangerous. Something unfit. Your father would never."

"My father did plenty while you stood by and watched. He killed. He murdered. He played god and you all stood by and let him."

Teari's hands trembled. Not from fear. From restraint.

"If I lose control," she whispered, stepping closer, "it will be because you pushed me past my limit."

He didn't answer.

So she delivered the final blow.

"You are my Commander. You swore to protect this kingdom. Instead you let it burn. You hid the truth. You failed your duty."

Lassar flinched. Finally. "You want to lecture me on failure?" he spat.

"No," Teari said. "I want to warn you one last time before I kill you."

She stepped inches from his face, wings arching high, magic sparking hot enough to singe the air.

"You will never keep another secret from me again. You will never undermine my authority again. And if you ever take my blade—or anything else of mine—without permission again..." She leaned in, voice dropping to a deadly whisper. "I will remove something of yours. Your soul, your head from your shoulders, anything I want."

Lassar swallowed. He said nothing.

Teari turned away. She fled the courtyard before Lassar could see her hands shaking. Her wings pulled tight against her back, feathers trembling with every step.

The gardens behind the castle were usually quiet at this hour, bathed in soft light and perfumed with jasmine but today the air was humming.

She needed silence. She needed space to breathe. She needed to stop feeling like her skin might split open from the inside.

The soul tie pulsed, quiet but constant, like Chel tapping on the inside of her ribs.

"I'm fine," she whispered into the empty garden, though she knew he couldn't hear her.

She wasn't fine.

She reached the small fountain tucked between two flowering trees. It wasn't a portal. Not officially. Not in any documented warding. But all water was a conduit between the realms.

Teari sat on the stone edge, head falling into her hands as she tried to steady her breath. Everything hurt, her throat, her bones, her magic, her pride.

The water rippled.

Teari froze.

A whisper floated up from the fountain's basin. "Teari..."

Her heart seized and she lifted her head. "...Meg?"

The water, trembling like something beneath it breathed.

"Meg?" Teari whispered again, leaning forward. "Are you here? Are you safe? Tell me where you are. I can help."

The voice returned, sharper, frayed like cloth torn down the middle.

"Teari... help me."

Her pulse spiked.

Meg's voice. Meg's cadence. Meg's... fear.

But something was wrong. Meg was never afraid. Never. The only time Teari had ever heard Meg's voice falter was when she'd found out she was pregnant and then when Remington was born. Meg never showed fear.

The tone shifted, the same voice but a twisted rhythm.

"Teari... stop. Don't listen. Don't..."

Another shift. Lower. Darker.

Like someone wearing Meg's throat as a mask.

"H e l p m e."

Teari's wings flared in instinctive fear.

She glanced around but there was no Legion, no healers, no one to confirm what she was hearing.

"Meg?" Teari breathed. "What's happening? Are you trapped? Tell me where you are."

The water shimmered before blackening, thickening, like ink spreading across glass.

Teari leaned closer, just enough to see her reflection and the whispers grew frantic.

"Teari—no—NO—don't come closer!"

But another voice overlapped, "COME CLOSER."

Her breath caught in her chest.

"M–Meg?" Teari's voice trembled. "Meg, tell me where you are." She couldn't remember if Meg had been with Sparrow the evening she found out about the fires. Sparrow had brought her to Chel but Teari hadn't seen Meg with Sparrow that day.

The water went still. Perfectly still.

Then an arm appeared, dark and twisted with ribbons of shadow that shot up from the surface and latched onto her wrist.

Teari screamed as the cold burned her skin.

The arm yanked.

Hard.

Water erupted upward around her. She clawed at the stone ledge, slipping as her soaked boots scraped uselessly against the marble edge of the fountain. Her wings flailed, feathers scattering like wet petals.

"LET GO!" she cried, healing magic sparking violently in her palms.

The water hissed like it was hungry.

"Teari!" a voice shrieked from the depths. No, not Meg, not human, not anything she recognized. "COME. COME. COME!"

Her fingers lost their grip.

The fountain swallowed her whole.

Water slammed around her, cold and crushing, dragging her down past stone, past root, past realm. Her scream bubbled into nothing as darkness swallowed her.

The last thing she saw was the garden fading above her.

Teari woke choking on cold. She staggered onto her hands and knees, coughing as the world swayed and tilted beneath her palms. The ground wasn't soil. It was slick stone.

Her vision swam. Her lungs burned. The soul tie pulsed faintly like a candle trying not to go out. She forced herself upright and froze.

The air was damp. Smelling faintly of mildew, rust... and something sweet beneath it. Teari's stomach dropped. She knew this place. She'd smelled it when they went to find Yelena.

The Collector's realm. The prison. The Magpie.

THE MAGPIE'S WORDS WERE SHARP IN HER memories, *"She's a rare thread. Beautiful, too. A child of an Archangel... there are whole realms that would burn for the chance to bind her."*

"You heard him. He didn't want Jasper. He didn't want me. He wanted you." Chel's hand slid down her arm, smoothing over the scars below her elbows, until his fingers found her wrist. "You think I'm just going to ignore that?"

"It's not me," she said with a shrug. "Whatever he's after, he's wrong. I'm fine."

Chel's jaw flexed. "Teari—"

"He said those things to get under our skin,"

"No..." Teari whispered, stumbling back until her back hit a wall of damp stone. "No. He didn't want me."

A faint hum echoed through the chamber rising like a chorus of insects trapped in glass jars.

Teari pushed off the wall and forced herself to stand. Her surroundings sharpened through the haze. A long corridor of cages stacked to the ceiling. Gilt bars. Silver locks. Some stood empty. Shadows skittered just out of sight.

On the far end of the corridor, a lantern flickered as though something alive were trapped inside, struggling against the glass.

Teari's breaths came faster.

"I've been here," she whispered. "This is where he kept Yelena. Where he keeps... everything. Everyone."

"Where did you take them from?"

"Everywhere," he purred. "Some from Heaven's shining gates. Some from the bottom-most pits of Hell. A few from those quaint little human cities that think themselves safe from the Veil's reach. I've walked realms your kind has never heard of, plucked the most exquisite pieces, and brought them here."

Teari pressed a hand to her chest, grasping for Chel through the soul tie. It was just a faint spark that answered, weak and distant. She squeezed her eyes shut.

A scrape echoed behind her and Teari spun, wings dusting across the stone floor. But no one stood there.

Only a row of cages, their bars rattling softly. Something inside them was excited she had finally woken.

A whisper curled through the corridor. "Angel…"

Teari's heart slammed against her ribs. "No," she breathed.

"Angel," the voice repeated, closer now.

She backed away. "Stay away from me."

The lantern light flickered—once, twice, then flared—casting a long shadow across the floor. The shadow didn't match anything in the hall. It crawled and then it stood.

A silhouette rose from the far end of the corridor. It was tall, head tilted like a curious bird studying prey. The Magpie stepped forward, face half-lit in the sickly lantern glow.

"Welcome home, Angel. My, have you changed since stepping into the throne."

She froze.

He smiled wide and sharp. "I knew you'd let down your guard for her. Everyone seems to let down their guard for her. There is just something about the Queen of Hell, isn't there?"

Teari's wings pressed tight to her back. "What do you want?" she whispered.

His smile widened, black eyes glittering. "You," he said simply. "And a few more."

The cages behind him rattled violently. The creatures inside were excited, restless, hungry.

Teari swallowed, lifting her chin despite the tremble in her bones. "You won't get either."

The Collector hummed, delighted with her defiance. "We shall see."

Teari didn't wait for the Collector to finish speaking. She moved. Her wings snapped open and she launched herself down the corridor, boots slipping across damp stone.

Behind her, the Collector laughed softly. As if amused watching a bird fly into a window.

Teari reached the first corner and turned hard, forcing her wings tight to her back to squeeze between the narrowing walls. The cages on either side rattled as she passed. She recognized a few of the creatures.

"Almost," she whispered, breath shallow.

She could sense an open space ahead, a chamber, something different was there. But when she burst through the archway the corridor was the same. She skidded to a stop, staring. Heart thumping.

"No," she whispered. "No, I just... This isn't right." She spun, retreating back through the arch. The corridor was the same. Same lantern. Same cages. Same damp stone. Same shadows humming along the walls. Teari's pulse hammered. The realm was shifting.

"You can't trap me," she whispered, but the tremor in her voice betrayed the fear clawing its way up her throat.

She darted to the opposite direction, sprinting until

her muscles screamed. She vaulted over fallen metal, dodged a tangled root of shadow that curled toward her ankle, slipped beneath a low arch and emerged back at the first lantern.

Her stomach twisted. This was a prison after all. Created to contain the Magpie.

He was watching.

Teari pressed a hand against the nearest wall, feeling the pulse beneath it. The vibration was slow, rhythmic, like a heartbeat. She wished she'd had more time to research this place. If the fires and Lassar hadn't distracted her so much she might have prepared. But she was so certain he didn't want her.

"Teari… Little Angel." His voice drifted through the corridor like a breeze. As if he stood inches from her ear. "It took me so long to capture you. Don't run off so quickly. If I can't make it out of here, then you never will," he murmured. "This is a prison. It won't let us out. No one gets out unless I want them too or there's a good trade."

Teari spun. "I don't belong in a prison."

A soft, warm laugh. "Angel, you might not belong here but you are here. You better get used to staying."

The corridor rippled. Light bent. Shadows lengthened. Teari staggered back.

"No," she whispered, pressing her hands over her ears. "No no no. I can't be here. I need to go back."

The Collector's voice deepened, richer, like velvet soaked in ink. "This is a cage, forged by ancient magic. Your forefathers actually helped create it. I'm surprised they never told you about this place. About me. What a surprise. Those Archangels sure enjoyed hiding their darkest secrets." He made a low sound in his throat. "I'm sure you know about some of them."

Her breathing faltered. She forced herself to step back. Then another step. She shut her eyes. Forced her breathing into a slow, steady rhythm.

The air cooled and the walls shuddered.

"Teari?" A familiar voice called from down a dark corridor.

Teari opened her eyes. "Meg?" she whispered.

The Collector's smile curled.

"That's her, isn't it?" Teari faced the Magpie. "You must be royally fucked in the head if you took her. She will slaughter you."

Teari's entire body was humming with disbelief. She staggered toward the sound before she could stop herself, wings dragging across the stone. She knew Meg's cadence. She knew Meg's breath, the rasp when she tried to hide pain, the strain behind her vowels when she lied. But something was wrong. Off by half a heartbeat.

"Meg?" Teari whispered again, voice cracking. "Where are you?"

"Teari." The voice broke. "Don't come closer."

The sound turned inside-out, like someone twisting her friend's voice through a cracked mirror.

"COME CLOSER."

Teari's wings snapped shut. "Stop. Stop it! That's not her."

The Collector tilted his head, delighted. "Isn't it?" he purred.

She backed away, heart pounding so hard she felt it in her teeth. Every instinct screamed that the voice wasn't Meg. But something wasn't right, the echo of it, dug under her ribs and dragged at her breath.

"Teari." Softer now. Closer.

She turned and the lanterns flickered violently, sparks dancing across the dripping walls.

Something moved inside the nearest cage.

Something small and shadow-hinged.

The voice wept. "Teari... please..."

"No," she whispered, breath shaking. "Meg was never here. She wouldn't be in a cage. She wouldn't allow herself to get caught. The Raven King will kill you."

The Magpie stepped closer, footsteps making no sound.

"You're clever. Fearful. Perfect." His shadow stretched toward her, long fingers reaching. "Have you ever heard a mimic? I'm sure they don't have those creatures where you come from. In their own realm, they're little beasts. But here?" His eyes gleamed black as pitch. "Here, they're tools. And the perfect pets."

He snapped his fingers.

All the cages went silent.

Then... every creature inside them spoke at once.

"Teari."

"Teari."

"Teari."

"Teari."

"Angel."

"Angel."

"Angel."

Hundreds of voices. Hundreds of mouths she couldn't see.

Teari slapped her hands over her ears. "STOP!"

Silence fell so suddenly her head rang.

The Magpie leaned in, breath cold against her cheek.

"You hear her because she is here," he whispered. "How else would they learn her voice?"

She flinched.

"Your disbelief," he murmured, "will be the thing that breaks you. Always believe in me. Always believe in the Magpie." He motioned down a dark hallway. "See for yourself."

Teari's pulse stuttered.

Her wings twitched at her back, every feather trembling as she stared down the hallway the Collector indicated. It yawned open like a tunnel carved into the marrow of the realm—breathing, shifting, hungry.

"I don't believe you," she whispered, though her voice cracked, betraying the fear gnawing at her ribs.

The Magpie's smile widened.

His shadow extended down the hall ahead of him, stretching impossibly long, guiding the path like a crooked finger beckoning her forward.

She didn't move.

"You said Meg is here," Teari said, forcing each word past the tightness in her throat. "If you're lying..."

"Lying?" He laughed softly, the sound hollow and

sharp. "Angel, I have no need for lies. I collect truth. I collect rarity. I collect power. I collect the children of the Archangels and they will bring me freedom. I will bind them and escape. I will walk between realms like I am the Veil. I will own the door to every realm that's ever existed."

He stepped closer, his long arm gesturing again toward the dark passage.

"And Meg," he purred, "is the daughter of Gabriel. And you, the daughter of Raphael."

Teari's stomach twisted. "This is wrong. We did nothing to you."

"But your father did," the Collector added, almost conversational. "And now you must pay for his sins."

His black eyes gleamed with mock sympathy.

The Magpie tilted his head, birdlike. "If she means nothing to you, then go. Turn around. Wait for someone stronger to save her and keep trying to escape these shifting hallways. But they built this place to contain me. If I cannot escape, neither will you."

Teari's jaw clenched. Anger flared through her. Meg had been like a sister between the realms.

The Magpie watched all of that flicker across Teari's face and smiled like he'd been waiting centuries for it.

"Go on, little Queen," he whispered.

"See. For. Yourself."

The realm grew still. The cages quieted. The lantern dimmed. The hallway ahead pulsed once like a heartbeat. Teari swallowed hard, lifted her chin, and stepped toward the darkness.

The Magpie drifted behind her, humming softly, the sound echoing through the hall like a lullaby meant for monsters.

With every step Teari took, the mimics began whispering her name once more.

"Teari..."

"Teari..."

"Teari..."

She fought the urge to cover her ears.

Halfway down the hall, the air grew colder and her breath fogged. And a faint, broken whisper echoed from the chamber ahead.

"Teari, I told you not to come."

This time, the voice didn't mimic Meg. This time it *was* her.

Teari stopped breathing. Wings curled tight to her spine. And then she ran toward Meg's voice.

Meg sagged against the bars, chest heaving, sweat beading along her brow. Teari had seen Meg wounded before, bloodied and bruised, but never like this.

Teari swallowed hard and took a cautious step toward her.

"Meg," she whispered. "I'm going to get you out."

Meg's eyes widened in panic.

"No. Get out of here."

Teari ignored the warning.

She shifted her weight, trying to angle her body small enough to approach the cage without touching the shadows curling across the floor.

The air snapped and a high, shrill, metallic scream

cut through the chamber as the runes along the rib-like bars ignited in a violent burst of silver fire. Light slammed up from the floor. Teari staggered back. The ground beneath her feet shifted, groaning, as the floor runes flared to life. A second cage dropped from the ceiling like a guillotine. It slammed around her with a bone-rattling clang.

The bars glowed with the same ancient runes as Meg's, bright enough to sear her retinas. Teari cried out and leapt backward into the bars.

Pain shot through her like lightning. Her skin burned. Her wings spasmed.

"Teari!" Meg screamed, slamming her hands against her own bars. "NO. NO—don't touch it! Don't!"

But Teari was already collapsing to her knees, clutching her chest as the bars pulsed.

The Collector clapped once, delighted, like a child pleased with a well-set trap.

"Oh, Angel," he crooned, drifting toward her cage with the grace of a shadow. "You really should listen to your Night Owl Queen."

Teari forced herself upright, hands shaking violently. Her feathers shed in trembling handfuls, falling around her like snow.

"Let me out," she rasped.

The Collector smiled, pleased by her confusion. "No. You both will stay. I have a plan for you."

Shadow curled around the bars, coiling like a serpent.

"This realm was designed by your forefathers, Teari.

By your divine line. Their blood. Their planning. Their magic. Their punishment."

He tapped the bars lightly.

"And now they respond to you. Stop touching the bars and they'll stop burning you."

Teari's breath hitched.

The soul tie pulsed hard in her chest. Chel's anger surged through her, sharp as a blade. He must have realized she was gone.

Meg's voice broke through the ringing in her ears.

"Teari. Listen to me." Meg's fingers curled around the bars. "I'm going to kill him."

Teari tried to breathe. Tried to stay still.

But the Magpie stepped closer, eyes gleaming with victory. "At last," he whispered, "the plan is coming together."

Teari's wings flared, teeth sharpening, rage boiling.

"I will kill you," she hissed.

"I will kill you," Meg echoed.

The Magpie only smiled when he replied, "I'm counting on it."

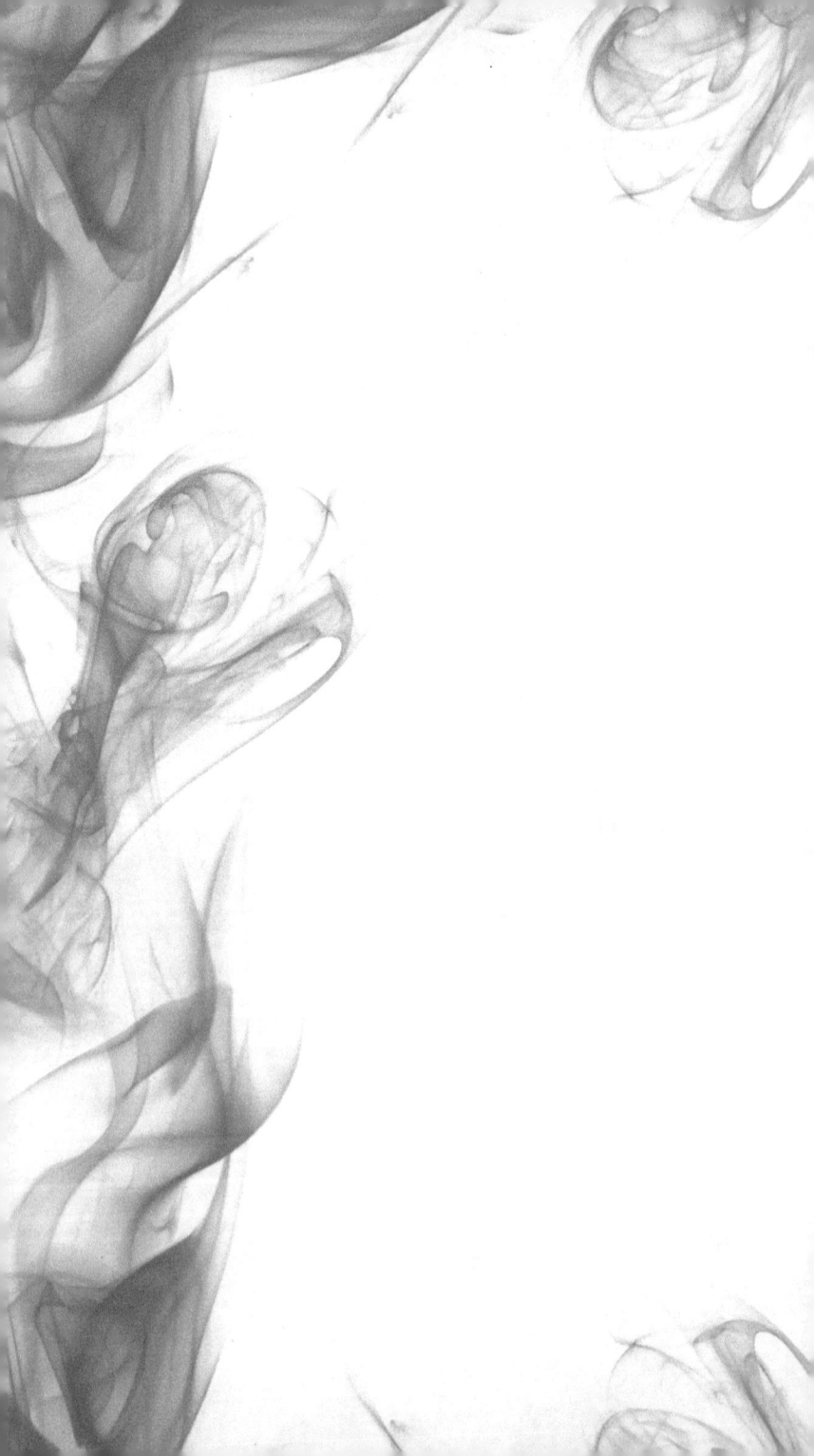

Chapter Twenty-Three

Only a portion of the library within the Castle in the Burning Caves was made of stone. The back half was carved from the fossilized ribs of something that once walked the land of Hell. With each arching bone forming a vaulted ceiling, each hollow spine packed with scrolls, grimoires, and relics.

Lanterns flickered along the walls, their flames blue-white, casting restless shadows over the endless stacks.

Sparrow's voice cut through the quiet, "Where is it... Where is it... Where did that *idiot* archivist shelve it?"

Books slammed as he rifled through another shelf.

Remington leaned over an enormous table strewn with brittle architectural drawings of black ink lines depicting the Black Mansion, its hidden chambers and twisting staircases.

Evelyn hovered near his shoulder, steadying one edge of the parchment whenever a draft fluttered it.

"That door again," Evelyn murmured, tapping one

scribbled symbol with her finger. "It keeps repeating. Every blueprint, every redesign. It's the same. We've seen it in so many books."

Remington's gaze narrowed. "Okay. It must be the access point now that the Black Mansion is gone. It's the same door, the same runes, but different locations."

"It moves," Evelyn said, leaning closer.

Sparrow hissed a curse from across the room and yanked a crumbling tome from a top shelf. Dust exploded into the air.

"Aha!" Sparrow crowed. "Ritual elements of the First Cages. I *knew* this had to be here." He spun on his heel. Just in time for the door to slam open hard enough to rattle the rafters.

Chel stormed into the room like a hurricane given a body.

Remington jerked upright. Evelyn stumbled back. Sparrow froze, blinking once.

Chel was pissed and the bone-blade strapped to his back steamed as though he'd crossed a portal of boiling water. It was the heat coming off him, anger was a flame.

"Hellion," Sparrow said slowly, lowering the book.

"Where is she?" Chel demanded, voice low and dangerous enough to make the lanterns flicker.

Sparrow tilted his head.

Chel crossed the room in three strides and slammed his hands onto the table, rattling the Black Mansion plans.

"Teari!" he snarled. "Where is she?"

Evelyn gasped softly, stepping back.

Remington's hand drifted toward the dagger at his belt.

Chel glanced at Evelyn and then softened. "Sorry. I didn't mean to scare you." He poked a finger in the Raven King's direction. "But I did mean to scare him. Because you've kept important information from me."

A protective darkness whispered off Remington's shoulders and curled around Evelyn.

Sparrow's expression didn't change but his pupils narrowed.

Chel's breathing was ragged, barely controlled. "She's gone."

Sparrow went still he closed the book slowly, the blood draining from his face.

"This is bad," Evelyn whispered, hand covering her mouth.

Chel's voice dropped to a graveled whisper, "Meg and Teari."

Sparrow cursed softly. "Chel," he said carefully, "you need to calm down so we can find them."

Chel shoved a nearby table, sending scrolls sliding. "Don't you dare tell me to calm down. She's gone, Sparrow. And you knew something was wrong. You knew Meg was missing too. Why didn't you SAY something?"

Sparrow's jaw twitched, the first crack in his composure. "Because we need a plan," he snapped back. "Because," His wings bristled, black feathers rising, "I can't say anymore."

Chel slammed his fist down again. "I want her back."

"You think I don't?" Sparrow shot back. "Meg is

trapped too! I vowed to keep her safe, to never allow her to be hurt again and now she's gone. Gone! And I had to watch her—" His mouth snapped shut and he shook his head.

The room fell silent.

Evelyn stared wide-eyed. Remington swore under his breath. Chel blinked. Shaken for half a second. Then the rage returned tenfold.

"Then why are we standing here?" Chel growled. "Why are we reading books? Why aren't we tearing open realms? Killing someone? Ripping the meat off their bones, cracking their femurs over our knees? Why are we here?"

"Because we don't know HOW," Sparrow snapped, shoving the ancient tome toward him. "The Collector's realm is sealed by the first Archangels. It's Gadreel. That is his prison."

"And who the fuck is Gadreel?" Chel hollered.

"One of the original fallen angels who rebelled against God. Infamous for seducing Eve in the Garden of Eden. He brought weapons to humanity and taught them warfare. He brought violence to the world. Gadreel, the Magpie, the Collector. They are one in the same."

"Three names is a bit much, don't you think?" Chel huffed.

Sparrow swallowed. "Access to his prison was destroyed when the Black Mansion burned."

Chel paled.

Remington stepped forward. "We found something on these blueprints."

"We found an entrance on the Earthen Plane when he took my sister months ago," Chel argued.

"It's gone," Remington said. "Sealed up and moved."

THEN.

"Okay," Evelyn was biting her lip. "I don't know where the missing Archangels went. I read about a battle and some of them were cast out."

"That's the Black Mansion blueprints," Chel pointed out as he pressed his hands to the table and leaned closer.

"Watch this." Evelyn moved the blueprints over the drawings on each book. "They line up." She traced a line. "And it appears the Black Mansion wasn't just a building, it was a moving realm of its own."

"So we burned it and did nothing?" Chel said.

"You definitely damaged it." Evelyn pointed to a drawing of a black and white bird.

"Oh, that's a magpie!" Meg said. "I read about those in one of Sparrow's books. I think it was titled, *Birds of Western North America*."

"And here, under the Magpie image, these runes say Collector." Evelyn moved to the other book and ran her *finger under the runes on the page.* "Ah, here it is. Collector."

"Magpies do like to collect things," Meg said, tapping her lip with a finger.

"Uh hm." Evelyn slid the books around and moved the blueprints. "So I found a stone with this marking." Evelyn pointed to the half-page. "One of the sacrifice stones." She swallowed hard.

"They called to Lucifer's bloodline," Meg reminded Chel.

Chel was nodding, following along but still pissed that the Black Mansion wasn't done with completely.

Evelyn pressed her eyes closed and took a deep breath as if she were remembering. She pressed a finger to the paper again. "There are all of these tendrils underneath the Mansion."

"We entered through one," Chel said.

"They seem to be ley lines into each realm." Evelyn cleared her throat.

"There's too many tendrils," Chel leaned closer, counting at least ten. But there was a rip in the page. "There could be dozens more."

"You entered through Hell's tendril." Evelyn licked her lips. She moved the blueprints over the books again, flipping pages until she found the drawings that matched. "Here's one that leads to Heaven. The Astral. The Earthen Plane."

"Where do the rest lead to?" Meg prompted.

"Now we know of the realm of the Fates." Evelyn tapped a finger on the page. "Then the rest is missing. We haven't found the other realms. Yet."

Chel exhaled and rubbed his face with both hands, stepped back and turned in a tight circle. "Let me get this straight. The Black Mansion still exists?"

Meg held up a finger. "Only a small piece of it."

"Sure." *Chel frowned.* "Its lower levels reached into each realm, some we haven't heard of in ages. I've never heard of anything like this."

"Fucking Archangels and their coverups." *Meg was shaking her head.*

"Your father is an Archangel," *Chel reminded her.*

"True. I asked him about this. Seems the Deacons and some bad players were highly involved. Gabriel actually gives a fuck about humanity. Which has gotten him imprisoned multiple times. They locked him in a cage for being my father just after the Fast-Zombie War. But he does know who was cast out and imprisoned below the Black Mansion."

Chel continued. "It sounds like you're telling us, Ev, that we've been halfway right but halfway wrong the entire time."

"Rue actually put all of this together but she ran back to her research lab to grab some notes we needed. And there was a book Layla found for us at Loyola University Library that has another map in it." *Evelyn was gripping the edge of the table.* "I'll present this theory. What if you were banished from heaven, banished to a singular realm, a building of sorts, a private island that thrived on blood and moved from place to place, hard to track... and you spend your time collecting all of the shiny souls you want. Because you have a back door into every realm. And no one *noticed because you were forgotten about and slowly dug into every realm to get what you wanted. So you could collect and collect and collect under the radar. Magpie. Collector."*

"Shay, Rue, Evelyn, Layla..." Meg whispered. "Who else?"

"Binding the child of an Archangel would keep the Veil thin enough for possession. We were wrong, it wasn't a forgotten sect. It wasn't possession of a body. It was a banished Archangel. It is a banished Archangel. Whoever it is possesses the Veil between worlds."

"It wouldn't really be an Angel any longer." Meg was rubbing her teeth with a finger.

"Binding the child of an Archangel..." Chel whispered then stared at Meg. She was the child of an Archangel and the Raven King was clearly on edge these past few days. Meg hadn't let Chel leave her side since he'd returned in this new skin.

"It's not me." Meg finally told Chel.

"How can you be so sure?" he asked.

She shrugged. "I don't think it's me."

"Who else is there?" Chel asked.

There was a beat of silence.

"Jed," Evelyn said. *"There aren't many. Nightingale is in the Astral. Nothing with a spec of survival instinct would touch the Raven King."*

"The Nightjar," Meg said.

Chel looked up. "Teari."

Now.

"This," Sparrow said, "is the prison the Archangels helped build to hold Gadreel. The Magpie, the Collector and Gadreel are one in the same. Thrown out of Heaven with Lucifer. The Archangels didn't build this themselves, no, they used Demons and creation magic." Sparrow flipped open the book he'd been holding. "This is written in Hellspeak. Ritual Elements of the First Cages, *written in Hellspeak*," he emphasized again. "Why would this be written in Hellspeak, Chel?"

Chel's eyes widened. A dream flashed through his mind. His father's office. Papers, shouting, promises... Chel rubbed his face, his entire body trembled in fury and terror.

"No," he whispered. "No, she's not a lock. She's not a key. She's not part of that cage." His voice cracked. "She is mine."

Sparrow exhaled slowly. "And Meg is mine."

"Then we find a way to break the oldest cage in existence," Sparrow said. "And we do it before the Magpie walks free using the blood of the women we love."

Chel lifted his head, fire blazing behind his eyes. "Good," he said. "Because if we don't," He drew the basilisk bone blade and slammed it into the table, "I'll rip his realm apart myself."

A sickening feeling tore through Chel's stomach as he stared at the blueprints.

"Do you know something more about these?" Evelyn asked, tucking a blonde lock of hair behind her ear.

Chel pressed his lips together and nodded. "I've been having dreams about my father and blueprints in his office. I was a child. I can't remember everything. But... I know how to access the memories."

"How?" Sparrow asked.

"The Fates have them."

"Purgatory," Remington whispered with the shake of his head.

Silence fell heavy in the room.

Chel exhaled a long, shaking breath. His bones ached. His soul was already cracked and roughly stitched from his last encounter with the Fates. It throbbed like a bruise under every inch of skin. Teari had been helping the healing but it was a deep injury, a soul injury.

"But that's where we have to go," Chel said finally. "To get them back."

"I'll go with you," Sparrow promised.

And then the two creatures, Hellion and Raven King, were walking swiftly through the castle to gather weapons and blood.

Chapter Twenty-Four

Chel never thought he'd be standing in front of the muddy tunnel that led to Purgatory ever again. He had an uneasy feeling in his gut.

Sparrow slapped him hard on the back. "Now's not the time to turn tail and run."

"Never," Chel growled. "I am not a coward."

"I watched Meg crawl through this hole when she went after you," Sparrow was crouched down, inspecting the passage. "She barely fit."

Chel rolled his shoulders. "I barely fit. Have you ever crawled through a Basilisk's rectum? That's what it feels like."

"And how do you know that feeling, personally?" Sparrow flashed a smile. "Had to ask. If I don't laugh, I'll kill something. Or cry. Or both."

Chel tried to chuckle but the searing pressure behind his eyes stopped him short. He stepped toward the tunnel and got down on all fours. "See you in Purgatory, Raven King."

They got on their hands and knees and started crawling.

The world twisted.

No up, no down, only swirling mist carving shapes from the dark.

Whispers slithered along Chel's ears as he moved to his feet.

"Little Hellion..."

"You left pieces behind..."

"Shall we show you which?"

Chel clenched his jaw until his teeth ached and he stumbled remembering the sharp slicing of his soul being removed.

Sparrow elbowed him. "Keep walking."

They moved deeper.

The mist parted.

And the Fates stood ahead—three figures, faces masked with woven gold thread long as rivers curling at their feet.

Chel had seen a lot of monstrous things in his time: bloodlords, soul devourers, Angels twisted by pride. But nothing had ever unsettled him quite like the sight of these creatures once again.

The one on the left was tall. Her eyes were milky and unmoving. When she spoke, it was with a voice like shattering glass, "You brought us a friend. So handsome. So dark. The Raven King has defied many odds. Welcome, dark thing. It seems you have brought your wrath."

The Fate in the center moved more fluid, her robes flowing like ink in water. Her gaze fixed on him. "You risk much returning."

The third smiled as if she knew every secret he'd ever tried to bury. Her voice was warm, almost kind. He knew better. "You were always going to save her."

The First Fate lifted her head. "Chel of the Blood-Torn Line," she said softly, voice echoing like bells submerged underwater.

"You have returned."

Chel's pulse hammered. It was unsettling how her voice changed. He forced the words out. "I need my memories."

The Second tilted her head. "You ask for much, Hellion. Memories like that cost much."

The Third spoke last, voice ancient enough to vibrate the marrow in their bones. "And you give... what?"

Chel opened his mouth but Sparrow stepped in front of him.

"He offers nothing," Sparrow snapped. "You already owe him. You took too much last time. You took beyond what was needed."

The First Fate smiled. "Perhaps we took what was necessary. Your memories hide the key to the Collector's cage. They will hurt you. They may break you. They may unmake you."

Chel didn't blink. "I don't care."

Silence.

Then the Fates extended their hands, threads drifting off their fingertips like strands of starlight.

"Very well," the First Fate said. "We shall show you."

The world collapsed into white and Chel fell into the memories he never wanted to see again.

Chel hit the ground hard.

He blinked his vision swimming as the world materialized around him.

A desk. Stacks of papers. Ink pots. Piles of ash. Half smoked cigars and burnt leather. Oil lamps flickering low. This was his father's office.

Chel's breath hitched as Sparrow appeared beside him, one wing brushing the desk as he steadied himself. "Hell of a place to raise a demon."

Chel swallowed hard. "I haven't seen this place since..."

"Don't say since you were a child," Sparrow muttered. "I can tell."

Chel moved forward, heart thundering. The papers were more vivid than in his dreams. Detailed sketches, narrow ink strokes, everything preserved exactly as his memory had sealed it. He reached toward the desk.

Sparrow narrowed his eyes at the pages. "Those aren't blueprints for a house."

Chel traced the topmost sheet. Black lines. Corridors. Arched chambers. A central circle with runes he'd never understood as a boy.

"It's not the Black Mansion," Chel whispered.

Sparrow frowned. "Not quite."

The ink shimmered and the structure shifted. Ink shifting. The lines thickened, deepened, reconnected and then the mansion dissolved into something else.

A cage.

A labyrinth.

A prison.

Chel's stomach dropped. "This... is it."

"Yes," Sparrow said quietly. "This is a real map of the Magpie's realm."

Chel staggered back as more papers shifted, reshaping themselves to match the first into corridors turning into tunnels, staircases falling into spirals, windows sealing into solid walls. Each blueprint transformed into a piece of the Collector's cage.

"You are connected somehow," Sparrow whispered. "Your father knew how the prison realm was built."

A cold wind rippled the papers and Chel's blood froze. A deep voice like gravel and hate-filled, rolled through the room. "That's because I helped build it."

Chel's heart slammed into his ribs.

Sparrow pivoted, blade drawn.

The office door stood open and a silhouette filled it. Horns scraped the threshold, shoulders broad enough to blot out the lamplight pushed through. Chel's father.

The demon stepped forward. "Look at you," he growled. "Digging through scraps of our past like a starved dog."

Sparrow raised his blade. "You're not real. This is a memory. You can't touch him."

The demon smirked. "Oh, Raven King. You misunderstand." He stepped further into the room. "The Fates don't just show memories. They open doors. And this door is fate changing."

The lamps flickered violently.

Sparrow grabbed Chel's shoulder. "Don't speak to him."

Chel couldn't breathe. The demon's presence filled the room, thick, choking. Exactly like the dream.

"All this power," the demon said, advancing, "and you still cower like a servant."

Chel's throat constricted. "You're not here."

"I am always here. Right here. Waiting for you to return."

His father blurred and seized Chel by the front of his shirt, slamming him into the wall so hard the wood cracked.

Sparrow surged forward.

Chains erupted from the floor, glowing red-hot and coiled around Sparrow's wings, pinning him in place.

"Stop!" Chel choked.

Sparrow snarled through clenched teeth. "Don't let him pull you in, focus."

But Chel was already losing his footing in the memory. He was just a boy when this happened and his body reacted with fear, just as it had so many years ago.

"You were bred to serve Hell," his father hissed. "Not that White Horse. Not that healer. You do not serve another god."

"I'm not you," Chel ground out.

"You think you can bury what you are?" The demon's breath was fire. "You think the Healer can cleanse me out of you? You think you can just walk away and forget what you were made for?"

The papers behind them fluttered violently, maps reshaping into the cage and corridors spiraling inward like a noose.

"You're my son," the demon growled. "Every drop of blood you spill answers to me."

Chel's limbs felt heavy. His soul pulsed, raw, exposed and ready to tear off his bones again.

"You left this place in ruins," his father said, voice splitting into multiple tones. "But ruins remember their kings. Your sister was nothing, but you… you were something. But you took her away and now everything is warped."

The chains lashed upward, wrapping around Chel's arms.

"No!" Chel gasped as something tugged at him. The same tearing sensation he'd felt in the Fates' hands.

His soul being pulled.

Thread by thread.

"Come back," the demon whispered. "Come back and live out your fate."

Chel screamed, collapsing to his knees and the world shattered into white fire.

Chel hit the ground so hard the air punched out of him. Cold mist surrounded him.

He gasped, chest heaving, clutching at himself as if he could hold his soul together with his bare hands. His vision flickered between white and black spots.

Sparrow knelt beside him instantly, wings flaring, fury rolling off him like heat.

"Chel." His voice cracked. "Hey. Look at me."

Chel tried. His head lolled. His skin felt too tight, his bones too loose.

Sparrow grabbed his face between both hands, forcing his eyes up.

"It's over," Sparrow said. "Focus."

Chel shuddered.

"He wasn't here," Sparrow snarled. "Just a memory the Fates let crawl too close."

Sparrow stood abruptly and wheeled toward the three masked Fates, wings flaring to full span. "That was too close."

The masked women stood still as statues.

The First Fate tilted her head. "We did not expect... the resonance."

"The hell does that mean?" Sparrow barked.

The Second Fate stepped forward, golden mask shimmering. "It means destiny awakened it."

Chel pushed himself unsteadily to his knees.

The Third Fate's voice rolled across Purgatory like a cathedral bell, "You are not simply Hellion."

Chel blinked. "My father was—"

"You do not understand," she interrupted.

All three Fates lifted their hands.

Threads of light poured from their fingertips, weaving into a tapestry of symbols runes and writings older than Heaven or Hell.

Sparrow's breath hitched. "Oh," he whispered. "Oh, shit."

The First Fate approached Chel.

"You are of ancient blood," she said. "A line erased from Hell's records. Forgotten. Buried. Drowned, if you will."

The Second Fate added, "A Duke once appointed to oversee the boundaries between realms."

Chel stared blankly. "No. My father was a violent demon. A Hellion. Nothing more."

"Your father," the Third Fate said, "was not."

Sparrow turned sharply.

"Your *mother*," the Fate continued, "carried the Duke's line."

Chel's heart stopped.

"My mother is…" he didn't want to tell them where she was, he'd spent enough time hiding her away so his father could never find her again. "Somewhere."

"Yes," the Fates said in unison.

"As every child of that line is destined."

Chel staggered back, throat tight. Sparrow caught his shoulder again.

"Chel, do you understand what they're saying?" Sparrow asked gently, "Your existence is older than Hellion. Older than demon. You were bred into Hellion but that wasn't your origin."

The First Fate nodded.

"The Duke's line carried the knowledge of the ancient cages. The original designs of the first cages."

Chel's pulse hammered. Remembering the conversation he'd had with the White Horse.

"You will be a Guardian of the gulf portal. You will keep my realm safe from whatever comes through that portal until the Veil strengthens."

A shiver went through Chel. "It is my honor."

"My father had them," he said slowly. "Blueprints and plans."

Sparrow stepped closer, jaw tight. "He doesn't have them anymore."

Chel blinked.

Sparrow reached into the inner pocket of his jacket and pulled out a rolled bundle of brittle parchment with ink faded, edges frayed, sealed with black wax.

Chel stared. "You stole them," he breathed.

Sparrow exhaled through his nose. "Stole is a strong word. The Raven King does not steal. I borrowed. Forever."

Chel's pulse stuttered.

"These are different from the ones Rue and Evelyn found," Sparrow said quietly, "the originals were in your family's possession. And because the Magpie was one of the fallen Archangels your ancestors were sworn to keep caged."

Chel's vision went hot. His whole life had been a lie. His history twisted. He'd had nothing but honor and duty all this time. It was all he'd ever needed. But now... now things had changed. Now he was truly something more and the idea of it seemed insurmountable.

One of the Fates spoke again. "The Duke's blood can open the cage or seal it."

Chel's heart stopped.

Sparrow's wings snapped open, protective.

But the Fates did not flinch.

"You fear the truth," they said, "because you know it."

Chel shook his head. "No. No, I'm not opening anything. I'm not—"

"You've walked between the realms before," the First Fate reminded him. "I saw it, right here." She pulled a thread of time taut and it sparkled in the dim light of Purgatory. "I watched you walk the line of Purgatory and death and retrieve your sister. No one else has survived that river."

Chel swallowed hard, breath shaking. "I'm trying to wrap my head around all of this."

Sparrow's grip tightened.

"This explains the soul tie," Sparrow said. "If you were just Hellion, it wouldn't have happened."

Chel let out a ragged breath.

Sparrow tucked the blueprints into his coat.

Chel rose to his feet, still shaking, soul aching, but

ready to leave and tear open the Collector's realm, and get Teari back.

"Let's go," Sparrow said, wings flexing. "We don't have time."

They turned, in search of the tunnel that would lead them back to Hell.

But the Fates stepped forward in a single, perfect motion. All three. Moving as one. Blocking their path.

"You will not leave."

Sparrow bristled. Chel stiffened.

"Move," Sparrow snapped.

"No," the Fates said.

Their voices weren't loud.

Mist surged around their feet.

Chel's breath came faster. "We need to get Teari and Meg. Move."

The Fates stared at him with their woven gold masks.

The First Fate raised a hand. "Teari is not your only responsibility."

Chel froze. "What the hell does that mean?"

"The fires," the Second Fate whispered. "The ones burning her kingdom."

Sparrow's wings snapped open. "We know about the fires. Lassar is responsible."

"They are not natural," the First Fate said sharply.

"They are not political," the Second added.

"They are not sabotage," the Third finished. "They are fear."

A shiver crawled down Chel's spine.

Sparrow hissed, "Do not speak in riddles. We do not have time."

The First Fate stepped closer to Chel. "You both know who it is," she whispered. "When Teari was a child her father chose favorites."

Chel's blood ran cold. Teari had a sister.

Sparrow's eyes narrowed. "Say it."

The Fates tilted their heads in eerie unison. "The Nightjar," they whispered.

"Demore..." Sparrow breathed.

The Fates nodded once.

"She has been stolen in the night and deposited where she cannot survive," the First Fate said.

"She is confused," the Second murmured.

"She is burning everything," the Third finished.

Chel took a step back. "We *cannot* go deal with someone else. Teari and Meg need help."

"You are wrong," the Fates said together.

Sparrow snarled openly. "We are not leaving our queens."

The ground underneath their feet pulsed violently.

"You misunderstand," the First Fate said.

"You *cannot* reach Teari without addressing the fire that burns at her doorstep."

Chel shook his head. "What does one thing have to do with the other? The Nightjar is a lost soul, she's not connected to this."

"She is," the Second Fate said.

"She is tied to Teari's line, as Teari is tied to you."

Chel froze.

"The Nightjar is not a monster," the Third Fate whispered. "She is a broken heir. You must seal her. Heal her. Or she will burn the gates of Teari's kingdom to its foundations."

Threads of gold spun around the Fates.

Sparrow clenched his fists. "Not our problem."

"IT IS NOW," the Fates thundered, voices merging into one deafening boom that cracked the floor.

Chel staggered.

Sparrow snarled. "You expect us," Sparrow growled, "to baptize that creature? Do you know what that would do to Teari's Kingdom? Two female heirs. Demore returning would change things."

"Yes," the Fates answered calmly.

"We know exactly what it will do. Worse things if you don't. We do not reveal fate often. You should take this warning and act on it."

Chel's pulse pounded in his ears.

"Tell me," he demanded.

The First Fate lifted her hand toward him. "Her fire will consume Teari's kingdom and kill many. The throne will weaken considerably."

The Second Fate's voice trembled with something like regret. "Her grief will unravel the realm's wards."

The Third Fate stepped forward. "And when Teari returns she will face a kingdom burning under a Nightjar she cannot contain. She will be weak. She will be nothing. She will be at the mercy of Babylon. They will make her pay for the deaths."

Chel swallowed hard. "Then what do we do?"

The First Fate's answer was simple. "You must find her."

The Second Fate's voice deepened. "You must baptize her."

The Third Fate whispered the final command, "You must heal her."

Chel whispered, "I can't leave Teari any longer."

"You cannot reach her," the Fates replied, "until you save what she once loved. She saved your sister. Now you save hers."

Sparrow stepped beside Chel. "Hell," Sparrow muttered. "That means we're doing this."

Chel exhaled, breath shaking.

"I'm going to get her back," he whispered.

"Let's get this show on the road."

The Fates nodded. "But first," they said, "You must save the girl who burns. The one who was tossed away."

Chapter Twenty-Five

Chel clawed his way out of Purgatory like a man dragging himself from a grave. His hands hit wet mud. Then cold earth. He hauled himself upward, gulping a lungful of bitter air as Sparrow scrambled up beside him, wings coated in black muck and dripping from the tunnel they'd used to cross realms.

They collapsed on solid ground.

Chel gagged. "I hate that place."

Sparrow wiped sludge off his face. "I think Purgatory hates you, too. Consider it mutual."

Chel spat mud, shoved himself to his knees, and looked around.

Sparrow was already standing, shaking out his wings like a soaked raven. "Nearest portal will drop us in Babylon. It's over that way." Sparrow pointed. "Let's go before the Fates decide to give us homework again."

Chel grunted. "Too late. They already did."

Sparrow didn't argue. "You were right. It did feel like crawling through a Basilisk's asshole."

THEY SHOT OUT OF THE BABYLON FOUNTAIN like cannon fire. Pedestrians screamed and scattered. Sparrow shoved his dripping hair out of his face and glared at a mortified angel frozen on the steps.

"Go away," Sparrow snapped before the man even spoke.

Chel staggered out of the fountain, soaked, muddy, and shaking. His leathery wings flexed instinctively, flinging droplets everywhere.

A few angels covered their heads.

One fainted.

"Move," Sparrow barked.

He didn't wait. His wings shot open and he launched skyward, black feathers slicing the air.

Chel followed, flames crackling at the edges of his wings as he pushed upward into the sky.

They flew fast, the wind whipping the mud off their clothes, the sun turning Sparrow's wings into black fire. For a moment, neither spoke.

Then Sparrow yelled into the wind, "Meg said to drink the blood."

Chel's stomach dropped. "What?"

"Her last message before she left." Sparrow's voice

was strained, strained in a way Sparrow rarely let anyone hear. "She said, *Tell Chel to drink the blood.*"

Chel's breath hitched.

Drink the blood…

He had a vial of blood but he'd been saving it for Teari. Just in case.

Sparrow turned mid-air, flying backward for a moment as he looked Chel dead in the eyes. "Do you know what she meant?"

Chel hesitated.

His hand went instinctively to his pack. The inner pocket held a small glass vial containing Raphael's blood he'd taken the night Chel killed the Archangel.

Then Chel remembered. The blood. He dug the vial out of his pocket and began scooping up Raphael's blood until the vial was full. He capped it and tucked it away.

Chel's heart hammered. He pulled the vial out and held it up. Sunlight hit the crimson liquid.

Sparrow swore loudly enough to echo through the clouds. "Is that it?"

"You think I throw things away?" Chel muttered.

Sparrow flew in close, expression dark and worried. "Drink it."

Chel stared at the vial. "What if I die from it?"

"The fates already told you," Sparrow yelled over the

wind. "Your mother's line is ancient. You're not just Hellion. Not just demon. You will survive."

Chel swallowed thickly. "What happens if it changes me?" He asked, voice nearly lost in the wind.

Sparrow gave a humorless, vicious grin. "Then you'll be strong enough to break open the Magpie's realm and kill him."

Chel stared at the vial.

His heart hammered.

His wings burned.

The soul tie throbbed like a bruise.

He uncorked the vial.

Sparrow hissed through his teeth. "Wait until we land."

Chel didn't.

He drank it.

THE ARCHANGEL'S BLOOD HIT CHEL'S TONGUE like liquid lightning.

A metallic sting. A warmth down his throat.

A heartbeat skipping. Then the world detonated.

Chel's spine bowed violently mid-flight, wings flaring wide as a ragged snarl ripped from his throat.

"Chel!" Sparrow shouted, diving toward him.

But Chel didn't hear him.

His veins lit up like molten metal. His bones felt too

large. His skin burned as if something inside him was clawing to get out.

Archangel blood.

Raphael's blood.

Divine. Ancient. Unforgiving. It tore through him with no mercy.

Chel's scream was a sound so raw and brutal it split the sky. His wings spasmed, nearly folding. He plummeted several feet before he managed to jerk upward again.

His vision blurred. Power surged through him and it was too much, too fast, too violent.

Sparrow caught up, flying dangerously close. "You need to breathe!"

Chel's breath came out as a roar.

"Chel!" Sparrow barked again. "Stay in the air!"

"I can't." Chel growled, voice warped as if two voices spoke through him at once.

His back arched in agony.

Something shifted under his skin. Bones cracked. Muscles reformed. Wings expanded, the leathery edges humming with power.

Sparrow's eyes widened. "Oh, you've got to be kidding me."

Chel's wings doubled in span, membranes stretching, runes etching his bat-like wings in black fire tipped with gold light. The air around him warped, heat bending it like glass.

His skin split in thin glowing lines, as though the

Archangel blood was carving runes into him from the inside.

Chel screamed again and the clouds above them parted in a circle, blasted away by the force of it. Lightning cracked across the sky.

Sparrow flinched. "Chel! Stay conscious!"

Chel's face twisted, teeth sharpening into something not entirely Hellion or demon but something not seen in ages.

Flashes of memory stabbed through him. Raphael's hand raised in judgment. His father's voice whispering, *You were bred to serve me.* Teari's hand on his cheek whispering, *Come back to me.*

Chel seized onto the last one. Her voice. Her touch. Her soul tie. It anchored him and he clung to it like a lifeline. But the transformation wasn't done. Another surge of power slammed into him. His wings snapped wide again. He lurched upward, then downward, then sideways.

Sparrow swore loudly. "You're going to fall!"

It was truth. Chel dropped like a sack of shit. Wind tearing past him. Clouds streaking by.

Sparrow dove after him, wings slicing the air.

"Focus!" Sparrow bellowed. "Remember you must find Teari!"

He reached through the soul tie and felt Teari's terror, he felt the cold edge of something, felt her whispering his name in her sleep. The power inside him responded.

A snap echoed.

Chel's wings thrust open again, catching the air just before he hit the cloud bank. A shockwave burst outward, rattling Sparrow as he pulled up beside him.

Chel's eyes lifted. They burned. Two lineages locked in war inside his body. But he was still standing. Still flying. Still himself.

Barely.

Sparrow hovered nearby, chest heaving. "Well," he rasped. "You look terrible, but at least you're not dead."

Chel's voice was gravel and thunder.

"I can feel her," he growled. "Every heartbeat." A beat. A pulse. A thread of fear down the bond. "Is this what you feel with Meg?"

Sparrow's expression hardened. "Let's move."

The two of them shot across the sky like twin comets. Headed for the smoke in the distance.

Teari's kingdom came into view like a slow-forming nightmare.

Smoke rose in thick black columns across the horizon, darkening the skies until daylight resembled dusk.

Angels fled in droves, wings singed, belongings stuffed into carts and crates.

The fires were so hot they burned blue at the edges.

Sparrow cursed under his breath. "Well. That's... worse than she described."

Chel's wings beat powerful and unsteady as he took

in the devastation. His jaw flexed. His teeth ached with the urge to rip something apart.

"Teari was hiding all this," he growled.

"She didn't know," Sparrow said. "She was lied to."

Chel's blood ran hot.

They descended lower.

Heat blasted upward as they reached the lower valley where the fires had eaten through entire rows of homes. Chel could smell the burning wood.

Sparrow veered right, scanning the landscape.

"Nightjar," he muttered. "What have you done?"

Chel's wings twitched. "How do we find her?"

Sparrow banked hard and pointed toward the forest.

They landed on a charred ridge overlooking the forest line. The fires hadn't reached here yet.

Sparrow paced a few steps, then turned sharply.

"All right," he said, clapping once. "How does one catch a Nightjar?"

Chel stared at him. "You're asking me?"

Sparrow rolled his eyes.

Chel folded his arms. "Do *you* know how to catch one?"

Sparrow hesitated.

Chel narrowed his eyes. "Oh Christ. What."

Sparrow cleared his throat. "I read... something."

Chel waited.

Sparrow looked away. "...in a book."

"What book."

Sparrow's expression was deeply, tragically serious "Birds of the Northeast."

Chel blinked. "Meg had that book."

"She stole it from me."

Chel stared.

Sparrow held up a finger. "Don't mock it. It was extremely informative."

Chel rubbed his jaw. "Fine. What did it say."

"That if you want to attract a male Nightjar," Sparrow said matter-of-factly, "you stand in a clearing, wait until dusk, and wave a white handkerchief until it swoops down."

Silence.

Chel blinked slowly. "...Sparrow."

"Yes."

"Demore," Chel's voice darkened, "is not a male."

Sparrow shrugged. "Then we cast a net."

Chel cracked his knuckles, wings flaring with black-and-gold markings. "I don't have a net."

Sparrow shrugged again. "I know."

Chel exhaled, frustrated. "So what now."

Sparrow gave a helpless little shrug toward the burning horizon.

"Well," he said, "we could always try another idea."

Chel arched a brow. "Which idea."

"You grab her around the throat."

Chel smiled slightly. "I like that plan."

Sparrow pointed at him sternly. "It is a *terrible* plan."

Chel nodded thoughtfully. "You're probably right."

They both stared into the dark, twisting forest where the Nightjar lurked.

Sparrow sighed. "We're doing it, anyway, aren't we?"

Chel's eyes glowed when he replied, "Yes."

Dusk slid over Teari's kingdom like a bruise.

The fires had slowed. Their blue edges curled upward, flickering against the tree line. Shadows stretched long and sharp, merging into the deeper darkness of the forest.

Chel and Sparrow stepped beneath the first boughs, the air thick with smoke.

Sparrow whispered, "Stay quiet."

Chel could feel a tremble in the earth, a vibration in the air, a pulse of grief so deep it scraped the inside of his skull.

The Nightjar was close.

The woods darkened. Trees bowed inward, branches warped by heat, leaves withering into ash.

Low, hollow and mournful sounds echoed. A long tremolo call that rose and fell like a dirge echoing across the scorched forest.

Chel stiffened. Sparrow held up a hand.

Another call drifted through the trees.

Closer. Lingering. Sad enough to make them shudder.

Chel whispered, "She's crying."

Sparrow nodded grimly. "That's worse than ever. She must hate it here."

Chel flexed his wings. "I know the feeling."

The woods shifted again.

The call grew sharper, shrill at the edges, slicing through the underbrush.

Sparrow whispered, "There. Left."

Chel saw a shape darting between the trees, too fast, too fluid, trailing sparks of blue flame.

Her wings were shadows. She perched on a charred branch, body contorted, shadows molting into drifting embers.

Sparrow breathed, "She's hurt."

Chel took a half-step forward, voice low. "Demore."

Her head snapped toward him, jerking at an unnatural angle. She hissed, the sound split into two tones of a girl and a monster trying to speak at once. Demore leapt from the branch, wings unfurling into a wide, smokey spread as she attacked.

Chel lunged first. His newly empowered wings giving him a burst of speed Sparrow could barely track. He dodged her first strike, her claws carving a glowing streak in the air where his chest had been a moment before.

Sparrow darted to the side. "I'll flank!"

"No!" Chel snapped. "She's too fast."

Too late.

Demore spun mid-air and slammed Sparrow into a tree. Black feathers exploded around him as he grunted and rolled aside just before her talons punched into the bark where his skull had been. The fire was closer now.

Chel snarled, "Demore!"

The creature slowed just enough for Chel to dive. He

hit her from the side, grappling her wings, heat searing his arms as he forced her down into the underbrush. She screeched a sound that vibrated his bones and thrashed violently.

"Home!" Demore shrieked, her voice splitting into two different tones. "Take me home home home!"

Chel flinched but didn't loosen his grip.

Sparrow staggered to his feet, holding his side. "She's lost it."

"Demore," Chel growled, muscles straining as her claws scraped the earth inches from his face, "you need to stop."

She snapped her beak-like jaw toward him, fangs grazing his cheek. Blue fire curled around her feathers.

Chel forced her down harder. "Enough!"

She writhed, struggled, screamed and then suddenly collapsed beneath him.

Her wings folded like torn paper.

Her body shook with weak, broken sobs.

Smoke leaked from her mouth with each breath.

Sparrow approached cautiously. "We are here to help you."

Chel swallowed, then did exactly what he threatened earlier.

He wrapped a hand around her throat, not to hurt her, but to anchor her, to keep her from thrashing as he shifted his wings and pulled her upright.

The Nightjar didn't fight. She sagged in his grip. "I remember you," she whispered with a guttural voice.

Her voice cracked in a girl's pitch, fragile and painful,

"Don't... hurt me. Father hurt me. Father hated me. Father killed me. Father threw me to the dead."

Chel's breath wavered. "I'm not here to hurt you," he murmured. "I'm here to fix this."

She trembled.

Sparrow assessed her, wiping blood from his lip. "We have her. Now what?"

Chel met his eyes, grip steady on the broken creature in his arms.

"Now," Chel said, "we baptize her."

Demore whimpered the sound echoing with decades of abandonment.

Chel tightened his hold. "You're safe," he whispered. "We're not sending you back... you're safe."

They dragged the Nightjar across Babylon. She clawed and hissed the entire way, wings snapping open in broken bursts of shadow. Sparrow held her legs. Chel held her torso and throat, muscles strained, the creature twisting like a burning storm in his grip.

By the time they reached the Babylon courtyard, angels had gathered in clusters to watch. Whispers rippled through the crowd.

"Move," Sparrow barked.

The angels backed up instantly.

Chel marched straight to the base of the fountain. Water sprayed over the stone lip.

The Nightjar thrashed violently.

"No—NO—NO—" she shrieked. "You'll throw me over the edge like him." She howled.

Chel gritted his teeth, breath ragged. "Hold her."

Sparrow tightened his grip.

Chel stepped into the fountain and the water churned. Lights flickered. The last royal to have been baptized in the fountain was Thrush, Sparrow's nephew.

Chel flipped the Nightjar so her back hit the water first. She screamed, the sound splitting the air as steam erupted around them.

Angels gasped. One fainted. Another crossed themselves repeatedly.

Chel snarled, pinning her under as the water boiled around his arms.

Sparrow began chanting old words, sharp and rhythmic. The water turned blindingly bright.

The Nightjar shrieked underwater, her voice rising in the bubbles. Her wings convulsed. Her shadowy feathers disintegrated.

Chel pushed harder, holding her submerged as the baptism continued. Her eyes went wide as she struggled under the water, her mouth opened and bubbles of air came to the surface. He faltered, not wanting to hurt the woman she was transforming into.

Sparrow snapped. "Don't let go she will drown if you do, but she can't change if you don't!"

"I know!" Chel roared.

The water exploded upward in a column of blinding light.

And then... A sound like glass shattering echoed. The courtyard went silent.

The Nightjar went limp.

Chel caught her before she slid to the bottom of the fountain.

Her body changed in his arms, bones rearranging, feathers dissolving, shadows drawn back like ink retreating from the edges of parchment.

When it was over, the Nightjar floated in his hands but she was no longer the Nightjar, no longer Demore.

A young woman. Broken but breathing. Her hair long and dark. Her eyes closed. Her limbs thin and trembling.

The kingdom inhaled collectively.

"That's her."

"That's her."

"The lost one."

"The un-baptized."

"She was unwell."

"No one has ever reversed a curse like that before."

"It was a Nightjar."

"Her name was taken."

"Her name was taken."

"Her name was taken."

"That was Noctara."

"Noctara, Noctara, Noctara, Noctara," the name echoed across Babylon as the Angels watched, waiting for the next move.

An apprehensive voice broke the silence. "What have you done?"

Chel turned sharply.

Lassar stood at the edge of the fountain, blade half-drawn. "You," Lassar snarled, "have no authority here, demon. This is not your kingdom."

Chel's new wings spread wide.

"Oh?" Chel growled. "You sure about that?"

The ground trembled beneath them.

"Are you sure I don't belong?" Chel took a step forward, the air heating. "Sure my blood is not pure enough?" Another step, wings blazing. "Sure I have no claim?"

Lassar paled.

"Stand down, Lassar," Sparrow warned.

He stepped back. Then further. His blade dropped from his hand. Then... He bowed. Head down. "I apologize," Lassar whispered, voice breaking. "My king."

Chel's wings faltered. Rage twisted in his chest.

"I am king of nothing!" Chel bellowed, the courtyard shaking. "I have NOTHING."

His voice cracked. "Without the Queen you betrayed, I have nothing until I find her again."

Silence fell heavy and the air turned choking.

Sparrow was watching closely.

Noctara stirred in Chel's arms. Blinking and dazed, confused as water dripped from her dark hair.

Lassar lifted his head slightly, eyes widening as he truly looked at her. Recognition slammed into him so hard he swayed.

"Wait..." Lassar whispered. His skin turned ghostly white. "I... I know you."

Noctara blinked up at him.

Her voice was hoarse, fragile as she tried to make a sound. It had been ages since she could speak normally and not as a Nightjar.

"Noctara?" Lassar choked. "You... you were dead. They told me you died from the curse."

But the girl shook her head slowly.

"I was alone," she whispered, voice cracking. "All alone."

Lassar stepped closer.

Sparrow muttered under his breath, "Oh, this is going to be a problem."

Chel looked down at the silent girl in his arms. The nightjar was gone and in her place was a broken heir.

Chapter Twenty-Six

Teari lay on the cold floor for a long moment, letting the dizziness ebb. Her shoulders ached. Her throat burned. Her entire body felt scraped raw. There was something wrong with the energy here. She felt dulled and cold.

A soft voice cut through the silence, "I told you not to come."

Teari looked up and found Meg was sitting cross-legged in her cage, dark hair tangled, skin pale as steam, blue eyes dim but sharp. The runes carved into her bars flickered with restrained violence whenever she shifted as though the cage she was kept in was anticipating her violence.

"I didn't come here on purpose," Teari muttered, rubbing her wrists. "I was dragged through a fountain."

Meg snorted. "Figures. Water portals are rude like that, they'll allow anything through. Always dumping people into places you don't want to be."

Teari sat upright, blinking away the last of the realm-sickness. "Meg... you look like shit."

Meg smiled weakly. "Aw, thanks. And you look like you haven't slept in a week."

"I haven't," Teari said flatly. "Probably been longer than a week. You've lost weight. Are you eating?"

Meg tilted her head lazily. "The Magpie feeds me, you know. Not enough, though. I'm used to... more. I miss pizza and soda." Her smile twisted.

Teari's chest tightened. "How long have you been here?"

Meg looked away. "Long enough to memorize every rune on these damned bars."

Across the corridor, one of the cages rattled, its invisible occupant slithering along the shadows. Another cage whispered curses. A third hummed like a mother singing a lullaby.

Teari shivered, her gaze stayed fixed on the shifting hallway, the cages, the flickering ward-light. "We need to escape."

Meg exhaled through her nose. "Yeah, and I'd like a vacation on a Florida beach with a fruity drink, but here we are."

"I'm serious," Teari hissed. "We can't sit here and wait for someone to rescue us."

Meg hesitated. Her eyes softened for a moment. "Sometimes we simply have to wait for the right time," she whispered.

Teari looked down. "Okay. Fine. I don't think I want to wait."

A clattering echoed from down the hall and a cart jerked into view. It was wheeled by a hunched creature made of stitched-together shadow and bone. It slid bowls through the bars of each cage. Thick, reddish liquid in Meg's bowl. A faint glowing nectar in Teari's.

Teari recoiled. "What is this?"

Meg sniffed her bowl. "Definitely not waffles and mostly caloric disappointment."

The creature pushed the cart onward, leaving them alone again.

Teari picked up her bowl with suspicion. "He gave us actual beds."

"Yes," Meg said dryly, leaning back against her cell's feather-soft mattress. "This is the nicest cell I've ever had. Usually my captors give me something paper-thin on stone floors. Honestly, my back is a little insulted. I was hoping for aches and pains when I woke up."

Teari blinked. "You're joking."

Meg gave her a crooked grin. "Keeps the tears away." The smile slipped.

She stared past Teari, toward the flickering lanterns and the shifting shadows.

"He wants us rested," Meg murmured. "He wants us alive. That's worse than if he wanted us dead. He wants to keep us here and use us."

Teari swallowed hard.

Meg turned back to her, eyes dim but fierce.

"We'll figure something out," she said softly. "But you can't panic. And you can't lose hope."

Teari hugged her knees. "Chel is coming."

Meg's breath caught. "Of course he is."

Teari looked at her. "You don't sound relieved. Sparrow is coming too. I know it. Neither of them will leave you."

Meg's smile cracked. "Yes."

Silence settled between them.

Distant cages rattled and shadows slithered along the floors.

Meg looked away first.

"My whole life someone has always trapped me up in prisons and dungeons," she whispered. "I'm used to it now. I imagine soon I'll have lived more of my life locked up than freed." Her voice was thick. "So yeah," Meg said, wiping her cheek, "the mattress is nice. I could use a carpet in here though. Maybe if I'm good enough he'll gift one to me. I'm thinking shag."

Teari reached through the bars, fingers brushing Meg's hand.

"We're getting out," Teari said.

"We're both getting out."

Meg grabbed her hand and squeezed back.

"You know something, don't you," Teari asked.

Meg looked away as she pulled her hand back.

Before Teari could press her, a sharp creak echoed down the corridor. Then footsteps echoed, soft, measured, predatory.

Teari stiffened as the Magpie's shadow appeared, stretching long across the stone like an omen. The corridor lanterns flickered to life in sequence as he walked.

A servant with gray skin and eyes downcast, followed behind him carrying two trays. More food.

The creature placed the trays in small alcoves of the cages and scurried away.

The Magpie smiled. "Perhaps a snack, my rare birds."

Meg lifted her chin defiantly, silent.

Teari glared.

The Magpie didn't enter either cage. Instead, he stood between them like a man admiring artwork.

"You've been upgraded," he said. "Pillows. Mattresses. Blankets. Comfort eases distress."

Teari sensed Meg go rigid.

Meg joked loudly, voice shaky only at the edges, "Luxury. Thank you."

The Magpie looked between them. Then his eyes settled on Meg. "You're weakening," he said softly.

Meg smiled razor-thin. "Still strong enough to break your jaw."

The Magpie didn't laugh. "What's wrong with you? The lying Queen is always eager to bite." He tapped the bars of Teari's cage, making the runes light up. "Tell me what you need and I'll get it," he whispered. "I won't have a trophy like you ill."

Teari snarled, "You should have left us alone."

"I cannot do that. You are both the key to my escape," he replied. He drifted away, humming, his shadow trailing across the cages like a living thing.

The silence that followed felt suffocating.

Teari waited until his footsteps faded, then turned back to Meg.

"Meg," she whispered, gripping the bars, "please tell me what you know."

Meg stared at her tray. At the food she wouldn't touch. At the wall she wouldn't look past. When she finally spoke, her voice was low and cracked.

"Teari," she said. "I'm not meant to leave this place."

Teari had drifted in and out of sleep, never fully unconscious, listening to Meg shift and breathe in the adjoining cage. Every hour, Meg jolted awake with a sharp inhale, sometimes cursing under her breath, sometimes trembling, sometimes whispering Sparrow's name like a prayer. She would lick her lips, gnash her teeth, grinding the molars until it made Teari cringe. She whispered, *"Not now. No no no. Them, they're too small..."*

By morning, Meg looked half alive.

Her skin was even paler than yesterday, stretched tight over high cheekbones. Her hair stuck to her face, damp with cold sweat. She moved slowly, strain in every motion.

The breakfast trays appeared via a quiet creature that resembled a small mountain troll from children's books. It placed metal bowls set on the small tables the Collector had gifted them. Eggs. Fruit. Some kind of nutrient-heavy porridge. Too much for Teari. Too little for Meg.

As soon as Meg saw the bowls, her eyes flashed.

She devoured hers in seconds. Barely chewing or taking a breath between bites, like she'd been starved for days. Maybe weeks. When she finished, her gaze slid to Teari's untouched meal.

Teari's stomach tightened. "Meg... are you okay?"

Meg wiped her mouth with the back of her hand. "I'm fine."

She was definitely not fine.

Teari hesitated. "Is it the blood bond with Sparrow? Is it pulling on you? Draining you?"

Meg snorted. "No. I've survived the blood bond away from him before. This is... this is fine."

Teari didn't look away. "You're lying."

Meg's jaw ticked.

Teari pushed her own bowl toward the bars between them. "Here."

Meg froze.

"Take it."

Meg's eyes flicked from the food to Teari's face. She reached through the bars, hands shaking, pale fingertips gripped the lip of the bowl and dragged it toward herself.

Teari pretended not to watch. Meg pretended not to care that she was being watched.

When the bowl was empty, Meg sat back against the bars, breathing hard.

Silence stretched between them.

Finally Teari said softly, "Meg... tell me why you're like this."

Meg stared at the empty bowl in her lap.

"That's not the blood bond," she murmured. "It's not Sparrow."

Teari frowned. "Then what?"

Meg's hands tightened on the metal rim, knuckles white.

"I told you last night," she said quietly, not looking up. "I told you not to come."

Teari moved closer to the bars. "Because you knew you were starving. You wanted to starve alone?"

Meg's laugh was a brittle thing.

"I'm used to eating six full meals a day. Sparrow feeds me like we are preparing for war on the daily. The Magpie," Her expression flattened, "feeds me enough to keep me moving. Not enough to keep me strong."

Teari swallowed. "Why? Why starve you?"

Meg finally met her eyes.

In them, Teari saw despair. And fury.

And something very close to fear.

"Because he doesn't know any better," Meg said.

Teari's throat closed.

Meg leaned her head back against the bars, eyes half-lidded.

"We're getting out," Teari whispered, reaching through to grip Meg's hand again. "We're both getting out."

Chapter Twenty-Seven

Noctara had collapsed, twitching in Chel's arms as the holy water finished burning through her curse. She looked small and frail, trembling in the Hellion's arms in the middle of the fountain.

Chel dragged her up and out of the water. Lassar passed them his cloak and Chel wrapped her in it.

Now she lay wrapped in a cloak, unconscious, hair matted to her forehead, smoke still curling from the cracks in her skin.

Chel stood beside her, chest rising and falling heavily. His wings flickered gold at the edges before burning away to black again, still unstable, still changing from Raphael's blood.

Sparrow watched him carefully.

"Don't pass out," Sparrow muttered. "I'm not carrying you."

Chel ignored him, staring at the girl in the cloak.

"She's... really just a kid," Chel murmured.

Sparrow nodded. "Most monsters start as children someone forgot to save."

Lassar swallowed hard. "What do you need from me?"

Chel turned toward Noctara's fragile, unconscious body. "You're going to help her."

Lassar blinked. "Me?"

"Yes," Sparrow said sharply. "You'll take her to the castle. To the healers. You will make sure she eats. You will not leave her alone. And if she is harmed..."

Chel took a step forward. "I'll make sure you never walk again," he finished Sparrow's sentence.

Lassar's wings shuddered.

"Fix yourself," Chel said.

Lassar bowed deeply, voice trembling. "I understand."

"No," Sparrow corrected. "You *don't*. But you will."

Chel lifted Noctara gently. She was feather-light and barely breathing, he held her out.

Lassar hesitated. Then took her. Carefully.

His face went white as bone.

"I know you," he whispered, staring at the small woman in his arms. "I know you."

His voice cracked.

And he carried her away.

These Promises are Valiant

The infirmary was quiet. Just the low hum of healing wards and the soft rustle of linen echoed from the hallway.

Noctara stirred.

Her fingers twitched. Her breath hitched.

Her wings were no longer shattered shadow but not fully feathered either. They trembled against the blanket. She groaned, curling in on herself. Then, she jolted upright. Her scream ripped through the infirmary, sharp and instinctive, shaking the crystal jars on the shelves. She was panicked, disoriented. She flew from the bed onto the floor.

The nearby healers flinched. One angel dropped a bowl of salve.

Lassar stepped through the doorway.

Noctara backed against the wall, panting, eyes wild and darting in every direction as if seeking a way out.

Her hands shook violently. Her pupils were blown wide. Her breath came in short, broken gasps.

"Noctara," Lassar said softly. "You're safe."

She froze.

Her gaze snapped to him, her expression twisting, recognition flickering behind the terror. Then, like the collapse of a dam, she launched herself at him.

Lassar barely caught her as she slammed into his chest, clawing at his tunic, burying her face against him. Her breathing was frantic, her whole body shaking. He stiffened, hands half-raised in shock.

"Easy, easy," he muttered.

But she didn't let go.

Her fingers curled painfully into his shoulders.

The Healers in the room whispered, "She knows him."

"They were children here."

"He was never the same after she was banished."

Lassar turned and glared at the healers until they hushed and backed away.

Noctara hissed over her shoulder, baring her teeth at the healers, prepared to defend the one familiar thing in the room.

Lassar swallowed hard. "Noctara," he tried again, softer this time. "Do you remember me?"

Her breathing slowed just enough to sound like a sob.

"You," her voice cracked, raw and hoarse, "you left."

Lassar closed his eyes as guilt punched him square in the ribs.

"I was a child," he said quietly. "I didn't understand what they were doing to you. I couldn't…"

"You didn't come," she whispered. "I thought you would come find me."

Her words stung sharper than any blade.

She finally pulled back enough to look at him. Her face was pale, her eyes rimmed with red, but stripped of the monstrous shadow-form she'd carried as the Nightjar.

She looked young. Broken. A girl abandoned. Her eyes searched his. "I hoped and prayed you'd find me. But then… I changed. Father took my name. I became ugly and rotten. I did awful, terrible, horrible things. I lived with the dead. I stole..." Her eyes went wide as memories tore through her.

One of the healers stepped forward.

"Commander," she said nervously, "we need to assess her vitals."

Noctara bared her teeth again, pressing into Lassar.

Lassar's spine straightened. "No one touches her," he said coldly. "Do it another time."

"But sir," the healer protested.

"*No one*," Lassar repeated, hand firm on Noctara's back as she trembled under his touch.

As the healers backed away, Noctara clung tighter.

When she spoke again, her voice cracked. "He tossed me into the shadows," she whispered. "Left me there to turn. Left me alone with the dead. I was just a child. Alone."

Lassar's jaw clenched. He didn't have answers. Not ones she deserved. Not ones he deserved to say.

"You're not alone now," he managed.

She looked up at him with wide, broken eyes. "You won't leave me this time?"

He hesitated, just for a second.

Her breath hitched and she began to pull back.

He grabbed her shoulder. "No," he said.

"I won't leave. And you won't leave. No one will touch you."

Her lip trembled as she gripped his shoulders and pulled him closer.

The healers watched, silent, unsure.

Noctara pressed her forehead against Lassar's chest again. He stood stiff and helpless, not knowing where to put his hands, not understanding why his throat felt tight. He let his hands stretch across her back and hold her close.

Chapter Twenty-Eight

Teari jerked awake.

Her heart hammered, breath sharp as the cold stone beneath her cheek. For a moment she didn't remember where she was. Then she heard a sound like claws scraping inside bone. A guttural growl. A suppressed, desperate whine.

Meg.

Teari sat upright instantly, she pressed her hands to the bars, ignoring the sting.

"Meg?"

A ragged breath answered.

Meg sat hunched on the opposite side of her own cage, arms wrapped around her stomach, hair matted against her pale cheeks. Her eyes dark, shadows darkening beneath the skin. Her shoulders trembled with hunger.

"Meg," Teari whispered.

Meg shook her head violently. "Just," She swallowed, throat bobbing. "I'm hungry."

The words were soft. Ashamed. Painfully human sounding. But the hunger in her eyes was not human.

Teari's chest tightened. "He's not feeding you enough."

Meg huffed a humorless laugh. Her voice dropped into a low growl. "I could eat a horse."

Teari recalled last night as Meg thrashed in her sleep, teeth snapping at the air, fingers digging into the mattress as hunger ravaged her from the inside. Teari had considered reaching for her, holding her, but one look at Meg's fangs in the lantern light had stopped her.

Meg would never forgive herself if she lost control on Teari.

Teari took a steadying breath. "Here." She pushed her untouched bowl toward the bars. "Take mine."

Meg stiffened. "No."

"Yes."

Meg's lip curled. "I won't take from you."

"You need it more," Teari insisted. "Don't argue. Just eat."

Meg stared at her for a long moment, eyes hollow, body shaking. Then she reached her hand through the bars and pulled the bowl toward her.

She ate quickly.

Teari watched, heart breaking.

When Meg finished, she wiped her mouth with the back of her hand and pressed her forehead to the bars.

"Sorry," Meg whispered. Her voice cracked and her eyes closed. "I don't like you seeing me like this."

Teari scooted closer, pressing her palm to the bars even though they burned her skin. "I've seen you in worse situations." Teari's forehead wrinkled. "I remember when Sparrow brought you back after Alastor had cut off your wings. That was bad back then, Meg. I think worse than this."

Meg let out a soft, strained laugh. "Maybe."

"You know something," Teari said quietly. "The other night you were muttering in your sleep. You know something, Meg. Tell me."

Silence draped over them like another cage.

Meg's jaw flexed. Her eyes filled with something sharp and pained. "I told you not to come," she whispered. "Because I knew he wanted you. He's going to do terrible things."

Teari's blood went cold. "Why?"

Meg looked away. "When you get out, I need you to find Rue and tell her about this place. It's important to her research."

Footsteps echoed down the corridor, patient and unhurried. The Magpie was coming.

He appeared from the shifting shadows as if peeled from them, lantern light glinting along the bars of their cages. A silver tray floated after him, delicately balanced, carrying food covered in ornate lids.

Meg stiffened immediately.

The Magpie smiled faintly. "Good morning, my queens."

Teari's wings tightened behind her. "Don't call us that."

He ignored her, eyes focused on Meg. "You had a rough night. Sweet, Meg. Dear, Meg. I would like you to tell me what you need so I can keep you healthy." Dark eyes were looking her up and down. "I don't like this."

Meg glared, lips peeling back over sharp teeth. "Let me out. Let me go home."

He tapped a rune on her cage. The metal unwove just enough for the door to slide open, still barred at the threshold, but open enough for Meg to stumble out into the corridor.

Teari gasped. "Meg don't!"

"It's fine," Meg muttered. She leaned her shoulder into the wall to steady herself as the Collector approached. He made sure to stand three careful paces away.

"Do not bite me," he warned gently. "I won't enjoy it, and you'll regret it."

Meg gave a humorless snort. "Trust me, you don't taste good. You taste like rotten shit."

The Magpie frowned before he offered a dish. "Eat."

It was a whole roast chicken. Meg grabbed it like she might throw it at him, but hunger won. She tore into the meat with clumsy desperation. Teari watched her, stomach twisting at the sight.

Meg had devoured the entire chicken in seconds. Her hands shook. She was still hungry.

The Collector's expression softened.

"I have increased your portions. Though I understand a vampire's needs can... escalate." He began rolling up a sleeve.

"Don't," Meg snapped.

"Don't what?"

Meg's voice dropped to a growl.

"Don't offer blood to me."

The Magpie cocked his head, black eyes gleaming. "I don't pretend. You are valuable. Both of you. And I care for all my treasures."

Teari felt sick.

Meg threw her bowl to the ground and chicken bones scattered across the floor. "I'm not your *treasure*."

"You are," he murmured, amused.

Meg stepped backward, bumping the bars of Teari's cage. Teari reached through and squeezed her wrist. Meg tensed.

The Collector knelt beside the fallen bowl and began picking up the bones. "Now then," he said brightly. "Shall we take a walk?"

Teari glared at him. "She is starving. Tell me why."

"Because she is not receiving what she truly needs," the Collector said simply. "And because Sparrow is not here."

Meg tensed, every muscle going rigid.

"If you hurt her..." Teari started to say.

"Hurt her?" The Magpie let out a soft laugh. "Angel, I have no desire to damage my collection. But hunger encourages compliance. Cooperation. Conversation."

He straightened and rested one hand lightly on Meg's shoulder.

She didn't flinch. Didn't snarl. Didn't attack. She just froze. Still.

Silent. Almost... trusting.

Teari's heart dropped.

The Magpie smiled at the realization.

"You see?" he said lightly. "She and I understand each other."

"No we don't," Meg snapped. The tremor in her voice betrayed her. "I'm just trying my hardest not to rip your throat out."

The Collector tilted his head again, studying her with academic interest. "Tell me, Meg. How did you defeat Lucifer? You have no wings. You are not exceptionally tall or physically imposing. You lack the brute strength of Hellborn warriors. And yet," He gestured broadly, "you took his crown."

Meg's jaw clenched so tightly Teari heard the grind of teeth.

"None of your business," Meg hissed.

"It is precisely my business." His tone darkened, curiosity edged with hunger. "I want to know what makes you capable of killing kings, of killing Archangels, high and fallen. What makes you dangerous. What makes you *exceptional*."

Meg's eyes flared. Her breathing sharpened.

"And why," he added softly, "despite all that power... why are you starving?"

Meg lunged but she hit a barrier she hadn't been able to see. The Collector didn't move, didn't flinch.

Meg stumbled back, shaking.

He sighed dramatically. "And this is why I offer you my blood."

At those words, Meg backed away so violently she hit Teari's bars again.

"Never," Meg spat. "Offer that again."

Teari's stomach turned. "Why? What would it do?"

The Magpie smiled at her with slow, cold delight. "Everything."

He stepped away, brushing dust from his fingers.

"Go rest," he said simply, motioning to Meg's bed. "You will need your strength for what comes next."

The lantern flickered.

The cages hummed.

And Meg simply walked back into her cell.

Bars fell and the Collector slipped back into the shifting dark.

Meg had finally stopped shaking. She was deep asleep.

Teari sat curled against the far wall of her cell, knees drawn to her chest, watching the rise and fall of Meg's. Her skin looked gray in the lantern light, lips cracked, hands trembling even in unconsciousness.

Footsteps echoed. Slow and measure. Teari recognized them and shot upright. The Collector appeared around the corner with the kind of smooth, theatrical grace that made Teari's skin crawl. His long coat brushed the floor. His black eyes glittered with amusement. He carried a tray.

Teari tensed, wings folding tight behind her. "Stay away from her."

"My angel," he murmured, voice warm as honey and just as sticky, "if I wanted to harm her, she would not be sleeping peacefully."

"She's not peaceful," Teari snapped. "She's starving. She's sick."

The Magpie's smile softened into something disturbingly sincere. "Yes. I know."

He set the tray down outside Meg's cell, there were bowls of fruit, broth, pieces of charred protein that smelled faintly spiced, then gestured toward her sleeping form.

"I'm trying to help her but she keeps secrets. She lies."

Teari's hands curled into fists. "You can't expect her to trust you."

"No." His head tilted.

As if on cue, Meg stirred in her sleep. A soft, involuntary growl rolled through her throat.

The Collector watched her with something that almost looked like concern. He reached into the tray and pulled out a small glass vial filled with shimmering black blood.

"Perhaps this will help," he said quietly.

Meg bolted upright. "No," she snarled, scrambling backward until her spine hit the bars. "Do not ever offer me that."

"Meg," Teari whispered, heart slamming into her ribs. "It's okay."

"It's not okay!" Meg barked. "I'll tear his throat out. I'll tear this place apart. I don't want his blood."

The Collector merely sighed and pocketed the vial.

"Demanding as always," he said. "Even starving."

Meg bared her teeth, the hunger trembling through her entire body.

He bowed slightly, as though indulging her.

"Tell me, Queen of Hell," he asked softly, "how did you defeat Lucifer? I want to hear your stories. You will never believe how boring this place can be. Entertain me with your spoils of war. Tell me yours and I'll tell you mine. I was quite the menace back in the day."

Meg's lips curled into something halfway between a smile and a warning. "Bite me and find out."

"Tempting," he murmured. "But unnecessary."

He straightened, brushing invisible dust from his sleeves.

Then he turned to Teari and the air shifted.

Teari went still.

"I need a favor," the Magpie said.

"Absolutely not," Teari snapped instantly.

"That wasn't a request." His smile sharpened. "Meg is declining faster than I anticipated. She needs healing magic to stabilize her."

Teari stiffened. "I'm not helping you."

"You are not helping *me*." His voice gentled. "You are helping your friend."

Meg's breathing hitched, eyes fluttering shut again as she slid down the wall to the floor in exhaustion.

Teari's chest clenched.

The Collector stepped closer to her cage, hands clasped behind his back. "If you heal her, I will allow you to share a cell. You can protect her. Feed her. Sleep beside her. Keep her alive."

Teari glared at him. "You let us out. Both of us. Now."

The Magpie laughed. It was a cold sound. He extended an arm toward the corridor to the maze of cages, stretching endlessly into the gloom.

"Do you see them?" he asked. "Hundreds of creatures. Every size, shape, from every realm. Every one of them was desperate to leave." His voice dropped to a whisper. "None ever have. Now they are complacent. They enjoy their time here. They are safe, cared for."

Silence.

Teari swallowed hard, throat burning.

He looked down at her. "So," the Magpie murmured, "agree to help the Queen of Hell... and I will bring you a treat."

Teari stared at him.

Then at Meg.

Teari exhaled, voice trembling.

"Fine," she whispered. "I'll help her."

The Magpie's smile widened.

He snapped his fingers and the bars between their cells shuddered then retracted smoothly into the floor.

Teari sprinted across the threshold and dropped

beside Meg, gathering her into her arms, pressing their foreheads together. Meg let out a half-hiccupped sob, clutching Teari's shirt.

"You're okay," Teari whispered fiercely. "I'm here. I've got you."

Meg squeezed her back.

Teari pulled away just enough to search her face. "You're going to be okay."

Meg looked away, her body went stiff. Teari grabbed ahold of her, Meg's eyes rolled as Teari lowered her to the floor.

"Meg, what is this..." She ran her hands over Meg's upper body, her heart, her lungs, her face, her head. "What's wrong with you?"

Chapter Twenty-Nine

Chel and Sparrow return to Hell.

Hell's library shook as Chel and Sparrow crashed through the giant doors. They approached the long wooden table where Remington and Evelyn had been sorting maps and blueprints that were ancient, brittle, inked in blood.

Sparrow laid down the parchments he'd stolen from Purgatory.

The two sets of blueprints began to react to each other with lines shifting, runes aligning, pieces folding and unfolding like a living puzzle.

Sparrow muttered, "That's... interesting."

Chel stepped closer. The ink glowed faintly. Chel dragged his thumb along one border.

Sparrow leaned in. "What are we looking for?"

Chel exhaled. "The entrance."

The blueprints snapped together, the ancient paper locking into a new configuration across the table. A shape emerged, A void, A descent. A spiral staircase made of bone.

Evelyn leaned closer and sucked in a breath. "I can read this. That old man in the shops showed me something like this." She pointed as she read, "Imprisoned in the void, enchanted between the Veil, the only true entrance remains in... Hell."

Chel's stomach dropped.

She kept reading, "The door to Gadreel's prison is in Hell. Buried under the old battlegrounds. Deep."

Sparrow's face hardened. "The Bone Warrens."

Chel nodded slowly. "The prison realm was created under Hell's oldest fault line. The oldest of wars here."

Sparrow let out a brittle laugh. "Of course."

Chel didn't smile.

Remington approached. "Are you telling me Teari and my mother have been that close this entire time?"

Chel confirmed with a grim nod. "Appears so."

The room went quiet.

Evelyn whispered, "So... how do you get in?"

Chel's gaze locked onto the center rune. He swallowed. Recognizing it. "I open it."

Sparrow's head snapped toward him. "Chel..."

"My blood that fits the lock," Chel said softly. "My mother's bloodline. The Fates told us."

Sparrow went silent. And after a long moment, he nodded once.

Sparrow said. "Let's go."

Sparrow opened a weapons case filled with basilisk bone blades with poisoned tips.

Chel cracked his knuckles, wings pulsing with black-gold runes like lightning.

"Chel?" Evelyn stepped closer. "You're different. What happened?"

"He found out who he was," Sparrow said. "And drank some Archangel blood."

Evelyn's eyes went wide. "Gross on the blood."

Remington's brow rose.

Evelyn turned pink. "I meant, for him, and an Archangel… Ugh, never mind."

"I'm leaving now," Chel said.

Sparrow picked up a blade and twirled it once.

They looked at each other.

For the first time, there was no banter.

No sarcasm. Just two men who had everything to lose.

Sparrow pointed toward the door. "Then let's go wake the Bone Warrens."

Chapter Thirty

The prison realm

"Meg, what is this..." Teari whispered.

Her hands moved frantically over Meg's upper body, assessing her shoulders, chest, ribs.

Meg's breathing was labored. Her skin glistened with cold sweat. Her pupils were blown wide, unfocused, drifting upward as though her mind was somewhere far beyond the cell.

Teari pressed her palm to Meg's sternum, letting the soft golden glow of healing magic seep from her fingertips.

"Your heart is fine," she murmured. "Your lungs are fine... Meg, look at me."

But Meg didn't respond.

Her body had gone rigid, breath shallow, eyes rolling back.

Teari went still as she connected the pieces. She'd seen this before, each time Rue had a vision. Teari recognized it. There was no denying it now. Was Meg having visions? Teari swallowed hard and maneuvered her body. She'd never seen Meg do this. But then, Meg was quite secretive about many things, and she had been taking a lot of vacations over the years... Teari's brow furrowed as she gazed at her friend. Meg was a liar, self-diagnosed and proud. Teari suddenly re-considered every conversation with her friend.

"Meg?" Teari whispered. "Meg are you seeing something?"

Nothing, then Meg gasped like someone had pushed her back into her own skin. Her whole body shuddered.

Teari caught her by the shoulders. "What is wrong with you?"

Meg didn't answer.

Teari let her healing light sink deeper, scanning Meg's spine, her ribs again, down her abdomen, her hips... Her magic flared. And Teari froze.

"No," she breathed.

Her hand hovered over Meg's lower abdomen, the glow illuminating something faint but unmistakable. New life. A heartbeat so small it flickered like a candle flame. No, not one. Two. Teari sucked in a sharp breath.

Meg's hands shot out, grabbing Teari's wrists with surprising strength. "No."

Teari stared at her, stunned.

Meg pushed her hands away hard. "Do not say it."

"But..."

"Say nothing." Meg's voice cracked, raw. "Promise me, Teari. Promise me you won't tell a soul."

Teari's mouth opened, closed. Her pulse hammered. "This changes everything. You can't stay here. You can't fight. You can't starve. I must get you out of this place."

"Promise me," Meg repeated, eyes fierce even through exhaustion.

Teari's throat tightened. "Meg, you've survived so much and I have never seen you like this. You're barely standing. You cannot stay in this realm while you're like this."

Meg slammed her hand over Teari's mouth.

The gesture was desperate but her voice soft, begging. "Please. You cannot say it. Not here."

Teari swallowed hard then nodded.

Meg's eyes shimmered with something she rarely showed anyone. Fear.

"If he finds out," Meg whispered, "if the Collector realizes he will ruin it. He will use me. Use Sparrow. Use all of us."

Teari's heart squeezed. "Meg..."

"You cannot tell a soul," Meg said, voice breaking. "You cannot tell Chel. You cannot tell anyone. Not until I get out."

"You can't stay," Teari argued, gripping her arms. "Your heart is under strain. Your temperature is low. You're starving, Meg. Completely starving. This place is killing you."

Meg flinched but held firm. "I've survived worse and

you know it." Meg's breath hitched. She looked away, eyes glistening.

Teari softened. "Listen to me," she whispered, hands trembling as she cupped her friend's face, "you need to get out of here. You're not just fighting for yourself now."

Meg closed her eyes, breathing uneven. "I know," she whispered. "But no one can know. Not yet."

Teari pulled her into a tight embrace.

"We're getting you out," she murmured into Meg's shoulder. "I swear it."

Meg shook against her but didn't pull away.

"Does Sparrow know?" Teari whispered, voice fragile.

"Yes." Meg nodded.

"You must play along with him," Teari warned. "With whatever he asks you to do. Do you understand? You cannot fight him. Not now. Not like this."

Meg nodded.

Chapter Thirty-One

"Take her," Meg said, eyes on Sparrow. "You must take her. Get out of here."

Sparrow grabbed the bars. "No. I'm taking you as well."

Meg was shaking her head. "You have to take her. I stay." She stepped closer to the bars separating them. "Get her out of here." She glanced to Chel and Teari. "Get them out of this place now."

"You." Sparrow grabbed the bars and shook them violently. The cage rattled but the bars didn't bend. He began running his hands over the bars, along the floor, the corners, there was no real door, no real keyhole.

Meg grabbed his wrist and tugged his arm through. "Get Teari out of here."

Sparrow held onto Meg, stretched his other arm through the cage and grabbed onto her body, pulling her as close to him as the bars would allow.

"I can't leave you here," he whispered. "I can't. You are mine."

"I know. You are mine and I am yours." She swallowed hard. "But this is the way it must be."

"I can't." Sparrow's fingers dug into her skin. "You must leave this place. Christ, I can feel your bones."

Her eyes were watery and red. "I will live."

"I don't want you to endure this, for anyone. This is selfish."

She was shaking her head. "You must get her out of here, now. There is only a small window before he returns. We cannot all be here in the same place. All these children of Archangels in one place is exactly what he wants. He will capture you all and the Veil between realms will be his. And you do not want to know the things he will do." Meg's hands spread across Sparrow's chest and twisted in his shirt. "Get the fuck out of here."

Fury twisted Sparrow's face. "I hate this."

Silent tears were dripping down Meg's face.

Sparrow moved his arm and pressed his wrist near her mouth. "Drink. Before I go. Do not continue on like this."

She nodded, pressed her mouth to his arm and drank, blood filled her mouth and she swallowed it down as if it were the sweetest nectar. When she was done, Sparrow tugged her face to the space between the bars and kissed her hard.

When his lips left hers, Meg said softly, "One day you will rescue me from this place, my Sparrow Man. But that day is not today. Please. Go. Before it's too late."

Sparrow released her, all the rage contained in every realm fueling him as he punched the cage containing her and roared so loud every creature in the Magpie's collection went silent.

Meg looked at Teari and Chel. "Go right now."

They ran.

MEG JOLTED AWAKE WITH A RAGGED SCREAM.

Teari was already sitting up, heart hammering. She reached for Meg.

"It's okay. Shh, I'm here, I'm right here."

Meg's breath came in shallow bursts, eyes wild and unfocused. Teari pressed her forehead to Meg's, steadying her.

"It's just a dream," Teari murmured.

But her gut twisted.

"I'm fine," Meg rasped.

"You're not," Teari whispered, smoothing Meg's hair back. "Go back to sleep."

Meg didn't argue. Didn't fight.

Didn't snarl or curse or threaten to gut someone, all things Meg normally did when distressed or hungry or annoyed.

She simply sagged into Teari's arms like a dying flame. Teari held Meg until her breathing slowed, chest rising and falling with exhausted shivers. The silence afterward felt sickening.

Teari had watched the Queen of Hell, scourge of demons, kill Lucifer, devour every meal like it was her last, now pale, weakened, starved. And *pregnant*.

Teari clenched her fists then straightened her fingers and pulled the blanket up to Meg's shoulders. She had to get Meg out.

The corridor filled with the soft echo of the Magpie's footsteps, light and graceful.

He appeared in front of the cell, lantern glow catching on his dark hair and long, black coat.

"I heard a scream," he said calmly. "Which one of you was it?"

Teari glared. "Meg had a nightmare."

Meg didn't stir.

The Magpie's eyes softened and it was disturbingly genuine. "She's been having them often."

"Yes," Teari snapped, "because she's starving."

He tilted his head. "She has food."

"She needs a different kind of food." Teari spat.

The Magpie's brows lifted. Slowly.

Thoughtfully.

"...Oh," he murmured. "Well. I've offered blood. She refuses it."

Teari lunged forward. "She has good reason."

He raised a finger. "Calm yourself. I have no interest in harming her or you."

Teari's stomach twisted.

He clicked his tongue. "Come with me."

"No."

He sighed as if she were a stubborn pet. "You have very little room to refuse."

With a gesture, the bar of the cell retracted. Teari reluctantly stood, casting one last look at Meg sleeping on the bed before following him into the hall.

The Magpie led her past dozens of cages. Some were filled, some empty, all humming with restrained magic.

He stopped beside cage 217. Inside crouched a small creature with leathery wings, bruised skin, and its eyes swollen shut.

Teari stared at the thing.

"It's a mimic. Have you ever seen one before? They're creatures from a faraway realm. Helpful, usually. But they can be vile and fight. Fix him," the Magpie said.

Teari stepped forward. "What happened to him?"

"He fought another inmate," the Magpie said lightly. "Over a pillow. I'm not sure why; all he had to do was ask."

Teari shot him a disgusted look. "He's dying."

"That's why I brought you," he said cheerfully. "Venom has been slowly spreading throughout his body. If you weren't here, I'd have to let him slowly die. Help him, Healer."

Healing magic flickered at her fingertips.

Teari stretched her hands between bars, channeling power into the wounded creature. Healing spread like warm water as she found the venom and drew it out. The creature gasped, its injuries healing and venom poured out of the wound onto the floor.

Within seconds, it was standing, blinking up at her. It opened its mouth, revealing tiny sharp teeth.

The Magpie clapped his hands. "Marvelous."

Teari turned on him. "You brought me here to heal prisoners. You want something."

"I always want something," he said. "But today, I want honesty."

She glared.

He motioned down the corridor toward her cell. "You heal a stranger with ease. But Meg?" His voice softened, curious, almost hurt. "You refuse to help her."

"I don't refuse." Teari stiffened. "She doesn't need healing. She needs the Raven King."

The Magpie's expression fell flat.

"She's starving," Teari hissed.

"She gets food."

"It's not enough. She needs the bond. You should not have separated them. She needs to leave this place. Let her go. Keep me. I'll stay in her place."

"And that," he said, "is a promise most valiant. But no, she will not leave. She must change her mind and feed from me. She threatened to remove something important from my body if I ever offered again. And she used some colorful language. Not very ladylike, if you ask me. But she will not leave. She must drink from my vein."

Teari went completely still.

The Magpie leaned in, smiling faintly.

"I am trying, little queen. I am trying to keep her alive. But you need to help. Convince her." He tapped her forehead. "Unless you are lying to me."

Teari's wings snapped tight. "I cannot lie."

"Yes I remember those days. The Days of no lies. Only deception. I say lean into the lies. Let them coat your soul. You'll find a new way of life. There is a new freedom in the lies. Just ask the Queen of Hell," he said softly.

"Convince her to drink from me. Or watch her wither and die. I will catch another one of you."

Teari turned away.

The Magpie watched her with sharp interest. "For her to survive," he said, voice low, "she must be returned to the Raven King. Or he could come here. Two dark birds in a cage. What a treat. Then I could let you go."

Teari froze. Very slowly, she turned back to him. "Stop," she whispered. "You are playing with fire. Both of them will end you in a heartbeat. You must seek death."

He shrugged. "Death is nothing," he said. "I am more interested in owning the Veil. Fix the Night Owl Queen. You heal her body but not her hunger. Only Sparrow can do that. Only he balances her. And we must find a fix to that."

Teari's throat tightened. "Let us go."

The mimics in the surrounding cages repeated in Teari's voice,

"Let us go."
"Let us go."
"Let us go."
"Let us go."
"Let us go."

"Let us go."
"Let us go."
"Let us go."

The Magpie slammed his hand on the bars until they stopped.

His laugh sounded delighted, bright and cruel. "Now, now. Don't be dramatic." He stepped closer. "How good would you be as a Queen," he murmured, "if I simply handed you everything you wanted?"

Teari stared him down. "Did you ever think she does not want to risk a bond with you?"

"Of course," he said, eyes shining, "I will bind the children of the Archangels and possess the Veil. How did you think it would happen. By prayer? By song? By chant?" He paused. Then tapped the bars of the closest cell. "We will be bound, come hell or high water."

Teari's voice broke. "No." She shook her head. "No." Thoughts of Chel flashed through her mind, they'd fought so hard to be together and now this creature was going to break it all to smithereens.

"Make sure she eats."

He stepped back and walked down the hall. Teari followed, glancing at the mimic as it watched her go, tiny wings fluttering and fingers clawing at the cage.

The Magpie gestured toward the cell.

"And now that you've stretched your legs and shown your worth," he said, voice warm like a host welcoming her home.

He snapped his fingers and the bars to the cell

opened. Teari ran to Meg's side at once. Meg stirred, lifting her head with a weak groan.

"Mmmh... Teari?"

Teari gathered her close. "I'm here. I've got you."

The Magpie watched them with a strange expression that was not quite envy and not quite admiration.

Then he turned away.

"Goodnight, little queens," he said softly.

And the cage sealed behind him.

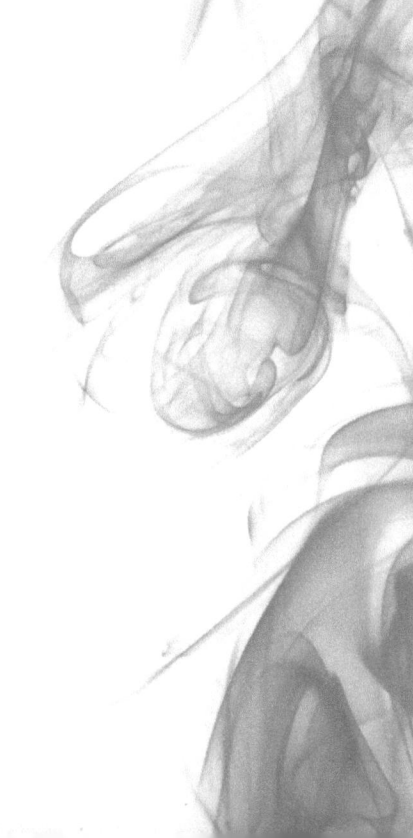

Chapter Thirty-Two

The trek through Hell's mountain ranges was quiet in a way that made Chel uneasy. There was no wind. No subtle scent of woodsmoke and pine. Only rot and a strange crunching noise under their feet. It was a bog of crisp rice and decomposition.

Ahead of them a vast stretch of jagged peaks that mirrored the mortal Appalachians—only darker, sharper, as though carved by something that hated softness. Against the ochre Hellsky, it was a vision of angst.

Chel adjusted the strap of the basilisk blade across his back. "Explain to me why we're walking where ever the hell a Bone Warren is."

Sparrow didn't slow. "A vehicle will sink on this land. Thousands of bodies decompose under our feet."

Chel grunted. "Comforting."

Remington was walking next to Chel, boots kicking up dust as they focused on a ridge. "This place..." He exhaled a soft breath. "I've been here before. This mountain—" He pointed toward a plateau. "That's where the portal called me when Evelyn's blood hit the rune stone. You remember?" he asked Chel.

Chel nodded. "I remember."

Remington glanced back at him. "That would mean the cave with the healing waters would be right over there." He pointed to the east.

Sparrow smirked. "This mountain range is ancient. There are probably more connections than we realize."

Chel looked out at the valley ahead. It looked very different than any other Hellscape, all ashen, cracked, and littered with blackened shrubs.

As they descended, Sparrow slowed sharply. "Here," he murmured.

The valley floor shifted under their boots. Chel crouched down, brushing the soil aside.

White glinted beneath. Bone. Hundreds. Thousands. Layered in a way that made Chel's skin crawl.

Sparrow knelt and scraped deeper with his fingers. Another layer. Another. And another. Femurs stacked like firewood. Wing bones tangled together in enormous spans.

Spines fused into grotesque shapes from ancient sword and flame.

Remington swallowed hard. "This is the battlefield."

He remembered the battlefield where they'd fought Lucifer outside the original Castle in the Burning Caves. That battle left hundreds of bodies. Remington scanned the valley. This place must've held thousands upon thousands.

"Now," Sparrow corrected softly.

"This was the battlefield."

The one the Archangels never spoke of.

The one that birthed Lucifer's rebellion and drowned Gadreel in holy flame. The one that marked the end of Heaven's first era.

Chel straightened. "We should have brought a Basilisk."

Sparrow's wings twitched, feathers bristling.

"A covenant of the Fallen," he said. "When Gadreel was taken, the ancient ones who followed him were sealed underground. Their bodies died. Their bones did not."

Chel frowned. "They can come back, like Lucifer did after the first time Meg killed him."

"Unfortunately," Sparrow said dryly. "Everything down here has a bit of life left in it."

Remington took a step forward. "If these bones belonged to beings who fought alongside Lucifer and Gadreel... then waking them will attract attention." Shadows curled at his feet, anticipating the need to embrace the darkness.

"Yes," Sparrow said. "It's a necessary evil."

Chel crossed his arms. "How do we wake them?"

Sparrow smirked. "Oh, you're going to love this."

He reached into his coat and pulled out a dagger carved from basilisk. A ritual blade without the venom tip. He offered it to Chel.

Chel's jaw hardened. "You want my blood."

"You heard the Fates," Sparrow said. "Duke blood."

Chel stared at the blade. Everything in this realm was calling to him now. Every door. Every cage. Every ancient secret. He focused on the soul tie. He exhaled slowly the thought of having Teari back crashed through it all. He would find her. He would release her from the grip of the Magpie if it was the last thing he ever did.

"Fine." Chel slashed his palm open.

Crimson blood poured out. It hit the bone-littered Hellscape with a hiss and the ground trembled.

Sparrow stepped back. "Brace."

Remington gripped his weapon and the space around his body turned black with wayward shadow.

Chel stood ready as the ground shook harder, dust lifting in spirals around them.

And then the bones moved with a hollow knocking noise. Not all at once but in slow, horrific cascades, shifting like a creature waking from deep sleep. Wing bones knit together. Skulls rolled into piles. Ribs realigned into arches that resembled doorways.

Chel's heart pounded. "Who are we waking?"

Sparrow's eyes gleamed with dark excitement. "Not a who."

He pointed as the bones began rising into towering shapes of beasts, fallen angels, skeletal titans with molten veins pulsing between their joints.

"A *what*."

Chel stepped back as a massive skull lifted from the earth, hollow sockets glowing faintly with buried fire.

"The Bone Warrens," Sparrow whispered.

"I've only read about this."

The earth split open beneath their feet.

A chasm of pure shadow yawned wide.

From deep within it, a voice rumbled, "Who calls us from the grave?"

Sparrow grinned.

Chel didn't.

Remington swallowed audibly.

Sparrow motioned to Chel.

The old Hellion stepped forward and said, "We seek access to Gadreel's prison realm."

The bones answered with a sound like a world cracking in half.

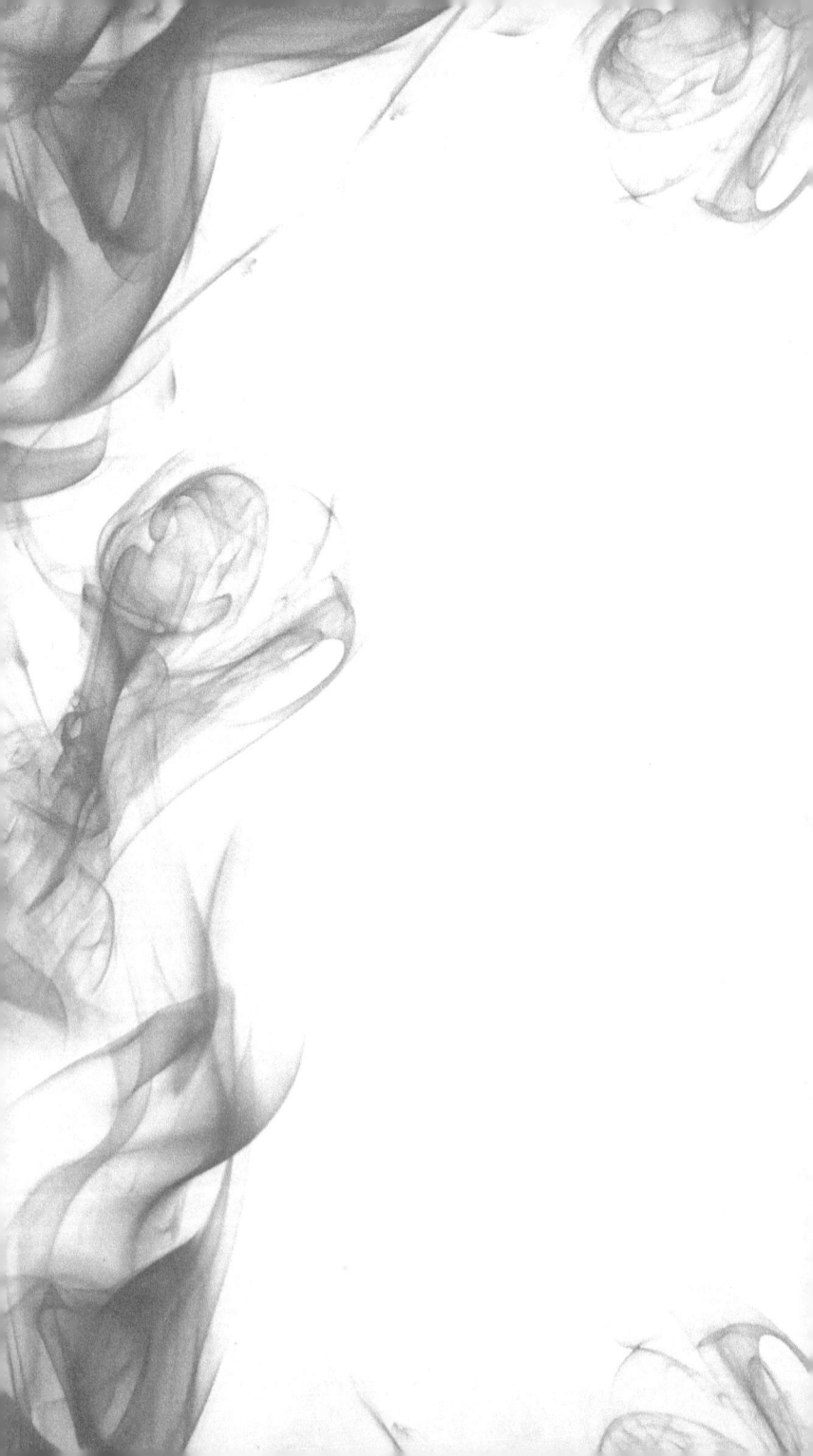

Chapter Thirty-Three

Teari had barely slept. Meg shivered in her arms until dawn as her body spasmed, her breath never fully steady. Teari soothed her the only way she could with gentle circles along her spine, soft murmurs, reminders that she wasn't alone.

When the morning came the corridors hummed with that same low, unsettling resonance.

Teari sat up, Meg still curled weakly against her as the familiar rattle of the food cart being pushed echoed down the corridor.

"Food."

"Food."

"Food," the mimics chanted in an unknown voice.

The pale creature pushed the rolling breakfast tray toward their cell, its long fingers trembling as they always did near Meg's cage. It usually slid the bowls through the lower slot and hurried away. But today it stopped. It waited. Large eyes looking at the floor.

Teari frowned and moved toward the bars.

"Maybe he finally figured out I eat more than a bird," Meg muttered, voice hoarse.

As Teari reached out to take the bowls, a hand shot from between the bars and clamped around her wrist. She gasped, dread filled her stomach as she looked up.

The Magpie materialized from the shadows, darkness peeling away from him like smoke.

"Time," he murmured, tightening his grip,

"is of the essence."

Before Teari could react, he bit her. Teeth sank into her forearm, sharp and cold. Teari choked, the shock staggering through her body.

She jerked back, but his grip locked tighter, pinning her arm through the bars.

Meg scrambled upright, eyes blazing. "Get off her!" She lunged for the bars, clawing at his face, trying to grab his hair.

The Magpie didn't budge.

Teari's knees buckled as he drank, in a sickening, intimate draw. Her wings spasmed. Her vision blurred.

"Stop," Teari rasped. "Stop!"

Meg kicked at him, slammed her fists into the side of his arm and hissed.

The Magpie finally released Teari's arm with a soft exhale.

Teari crumpled, clutching her bleeding arm, breath shuddering. She twisted away, shame and dread rolling through her. How could she let that happen. She let down her guard. Something stuck in her throat, she'd never had anyone bite her like that before. She knew she should fight back but the shock of it all had numbed her limbs.

Meg's hair fell around her face as she snarled, eyes black with fury. "You bite her again," Meg snarled, "and I'll rip your goddamn throat out."

The Magpie turned.

His hand snapped out and he seized Meg by the throat through the bars. "Do not threaten me, Queen of Hell," he said softly. "Not while I'm high on the Queen of Raphael's Kingdom's blood. I never liked him but his heir sure tastes powerful."

Meg spat in his face.

He smiled.

The Magpie didn't rage. He didn't snarl back. He simply smiled, slow, curious, and fascinated, like she was an exquisite puzzle box he had waited centuries to open. He seized her chin without warning as the bars of the cage slid away.

Meg hissed again, fangs flashing, but he overpowered her easily in her weakened state. He drew her forward, forced her jaw to the side, and sank his teeth into her neck.

Meg screamed.

Teari dragged herself upright, slamming into the bars as they closed her inside. "Let her go! You bastard! LET HER GO!"

But the Magpie wasn't listening.

His eyes fluttered shut as he drank deeply, testing

pulls, his fingers gripping Meg's jaw and neck like he might crush them.

Meg's hands clawed at his wrist, breath coming in furious snarls. She kicked at him and jerked her body trying to fight.

Finally he pulled back and stared down at Meg, chest rising and falling with sharp, clipped breaths. His pupils dilated into black pools, his lips stained with her blood.

Slowly, he spoke. "...What is this I taste?"

Meg spat blood into his face.

He wiped it away without blinking, fingertips trembling with revelation.

"Something fresh," he whispered. "Something new." His gaze flicked between Meg and Teari, calculatingly. "How many Archangels," he murmured, "have you bitten? Tell me, Night Owl Queen. How many Archangels have you devoured because I have not tasted blood like this ever in my lifetime."

Meg's expression didn't flinch. "Well..." she drawled, voice hoarse but smug, "there was Remiel. And Lucifer," she continued, scratching idly at her throat where the wound still leaked.

The Magpie's eyes widened slightly.

Meg tapped her lips with one finger. "Oh, and I did bite Raphael. But," she shrugged, never finishing.

Silence detonated through the corridor.

The Magpie's breath hitched like someone punched the air out of him. He stared at Meg as though she had become a solar eclipse. "Raphael..." he repeated softly. "I would have paid dearly to witness his death."

Meg smiled sweetly. "Someone else was meant to kill him, I just bit him." She kicked out, catching him in the side.

He didn't budge. "You have tasted the blood of two kings of Heaven. And one fallen crown." The Magpie was watching blood leak from the bite on her neck.

Meg winked. "Maybe I'm a collector."

The Magpie stepped away from her, hands trembling with exhilaration. "No wonder you starve," he whispered.

Meg's blue eyes burned with warning. "Offer me yours again and I'll add you to the tally."

He smiled. "Oh?" Then his gaze slid to Teari.

"Now I understand why you risked yourself to come here. You followed her cries for help so easily," he murmured. "You two are extraordinary. Deliciously rare. You will help me contain the Veil."

He rubbed the side of Meg's neck with his finger, holding her nearly off her feet and pressed against the cage.

"You will heal," he said. "You will grow strong. And when the time comes you will open the door for me."

A chill ripped through Teari's spine.

Meg growled, low and deadly. "I will drain you dry and I will control the Veil between realms."

But the Magpie only smiled. "I dare you, Night Owl Queen," he said gently, pressing her against the wall. He shifted his stance, holding his wrist to her mouth.

Meg froze as the Magpie pressed her into the iron

bars, his hand braced around her throat, his other wrist hovering a breath from her mouth.

Teari pushed herself upright, panting, wiping away the blood that was smeared across her arm where he'd bitten her.

The Magpie smiled but there was violence in his posture.

"I dare you, Night Owl Queen," he whispered, voice sliding like velvet over a knife's edge. "Show me what made Lucifer fall."

Meg snarled, baring teeth even sharper in the lantern light. "You ask for death."

"Perhaps," he murmured. "But I need you." His wrist inched closer to her lips. "Bite."

Meg turned her face away. "Fuck off."

Behind them, Teari dragged herself to her feet. Thoughts racing. Unsure of what would happen to Meg if the Blood bond with Sparrow broke. Could she reverse it with the healing magic? That was something Teari had never tried.

"Quiet your mind, little Queen," the Magpie said without turning, his tone slipping cold. "This has nothing to do with you." He focused on Meg again. "Bite, now," he repeated, voice thick with command.

Meg stared at him, hatred burning through the exhaustion in her eyes. "I would rather die."

"Yes," he whispered, "you seem the type but you are too important to die."

His fingers gripped her jaw, gentle but immovable, turning her face toward his wrist.

Teari flinched. "Leave her alone!"

Magpie said softly, "But she's starving. And you're too weak to help her. So let me."

Meg jerked her head back. Fangs showing.

"You do," he murmured, leaning closer. "You look half-dead, my Queen of Hell. You haven't had real blood in weeks. Your bite trembles. Your throat aches. I can hear the way your life force is thinning, something is draining you. So bite and fill your gut. The Raven King won't mind. He'll be so proud you did what you could to stay alive."

Meg went completely still. Her eyes flicked to Teari.

Teari's heart clenched. She could see the truth in Meg's posture, the way her hands shook, the faint blue tinge beneath her skin. She was dying slowly. Fading.

"Don't do it," Teari whispered, voice cracking.

Meg tried to pull away again, but his grip tightened around her throat.

His voice was unbearably soft.

"Show me your bite, little queen. Show me how you killed those Archangels."

Meg hissed. "I killed monsters. Like you."

"*Monsters like you. Monsters like you. Monsters like you*," the mimics echoed from the corridor.

He laughed, dark and delighted as he pressed his wrist directly against her lips.

Meg's entire body shook. She slammed her head back against the cage, teeth clenched until her jaw clicked.

"No," she growled. "I'm not giving you anything."

The Magpie leaned closer, his breath brushing her

283

cheek. "You already did. I tasted Lucifer in you. I tasted Remiel. Raphael. Your blood is a museum of fallen angels."

Meg snarled. "You talk too much."

"Then bite," he whispered, "and shut me up."

Her teeth grazed his skin. Teari gasped and covered her mouth.

Meg was holding back with every ounce of will she had. Hunger hit. Her fangs dropped.

The Magpie shivered. "There she is," he whispered. "There's my little dark bird. Oh to have you on my side will be spectacular."

Meg's eyes flared blue, bright and wild like a creature uncontrolled. She clamped her jaw shut again, shaking. "I said no."

"And I said," the Magpie murmured, voice dropping to a dark, inescapable command,

"bite."

His hand slid against her throat anchoring her in place.

Teari slammed her hands into the bars. "Stop. She's pregnant!"

"*She's pregnant! She's pregnant! She's pregnant! She's pregnant! She's pregnant!*" the Mimics shouted in Teari's voice.

The Magpie froze.

Meg's body went rigid.

Slowly, so very slowly, he released her throat and lowered his wrist, eyes widening, and the smile gone entirely. He turned his head and stared at Teari.

"What," he said, voice low, "did you just say?"

Meg moved faster than she should have, she grabbed the Magpie by the hair, intent on killing, teeth sank into his neck.

The Magpie tipped his head to the side and laughed.

Teari's chest filled with ice realizing he was too strong for her. He'd just fed from them both, and Meg, well Meg hadn't been this weak in years.

The Magpie's hands clamped on Meg's upper arms and pulled her away. He held her up like a child. Blood dripped down her chin.

"Why aren't you dead yet?" she hissed.

He deposited her in the cage and slammed the door closed.

Meg's eyes were wide as she watched the Magpie. She wiped an arm across her mouth then licked the blood on her arm. "Just know, that if you broke the bond with the Raven King, I will slaughter you with every chance I get. You'll come crawling in here, the Blood lust will devour you, and I will *never* forget."

Teari sat on the cold stone floor, back pressed to the cage bars, her hand had finally stopped shaking as she worked healing magic over the punctures in her arm. Her palm trembled. She hissed at the sharp sensation. The pain wasn't the worst part. It was the violation. The helplessness. The memory of Meg screaming. She didn't help. She couldn't. She gritted her teeth and pushed harder with her magic. Light spun across her skin, stitching the wound slowly, as if even her angelic healing didn't want to touch the Magpie's mark.

Teari looked up. Across from her, Meg sat on her knees, one hand pressed to her mouth, shoulders shaking. The gray that had hollowed Meg's eyes was gone. Her cheeks held a healthy pink flush. Her breathing had steadied. The tremor in her hands had stopped.

Teari's chest tightened. "Meg..."

Meg winced, dropping her hand. "Don't look at me like that."

"What do we do now?"

Meg let out a bitter laugh. "Nothing."

"You're stronger now." Teari's voice cracked. "Can you get us out."

Meg looked away.

Silence stretched between them, broken only by Teari's ragged breaths and Meg's uneven exhale.

After a long moment, Teari whispered, "How do you feel?"

Meg flexed her fingers. She touched her throat where the Magpie's bite had smeared against her skin. "Awful," she said honestly. "Strong ... but awful. I want to vomit."

"You look better."

"Don't," Meg snapped too quickly, rubbing her face with both hands. "Sorry."

"You were starving," Teari said softly.

"I was," she muttered.

"You were starving," Teari repeated. "And he knew."

Meg looked away, jaw trembling. "Of course he knew. He knows plenty. He's one of the originals."

Teari pushed herself closer, ignoring the sting in her arm. "He's using your hunger against you."

Meg let out a sharp, humorless puff of air. "Yes. That's what monsters do."

Teari studied her, the new color in her cheeks, the steadiness in her hands, the way her pupils tracked movement again with clarity, not haze.

"You feared the bond with Sparrow breaking."

Meg lifted a brow. "That obvious?"

"It concerns me as well," Teari snapped softly. "Can you feel it now?"

Meg's expression softened, something wounded flickering behind her eyes. "I can't tell."

Teari's hands trembled as she touched her own healing wound again. "You scared me."

Meg made a small, broken sound. "You're not supposed to worry about me. We are beyond that."

Teari leaned her head back against the bars and let out a shaky breath.

"Why did you do it?" she asked quietly. "Why bite him?"

Meg's face tightened. "I was hoping it would make me stronger than him." She was shaking her head. "It didn't work."

"It didn't work. It didn't work. It didn't work. It didn't work. It didn't work," the mimics echoed from the corridor.

"Shut up!" Meg shouted.

"*Shut up! Shut up! Shut up! Shut up! Shut up! Shut up!*" the mimics repeated in Meg's voice.

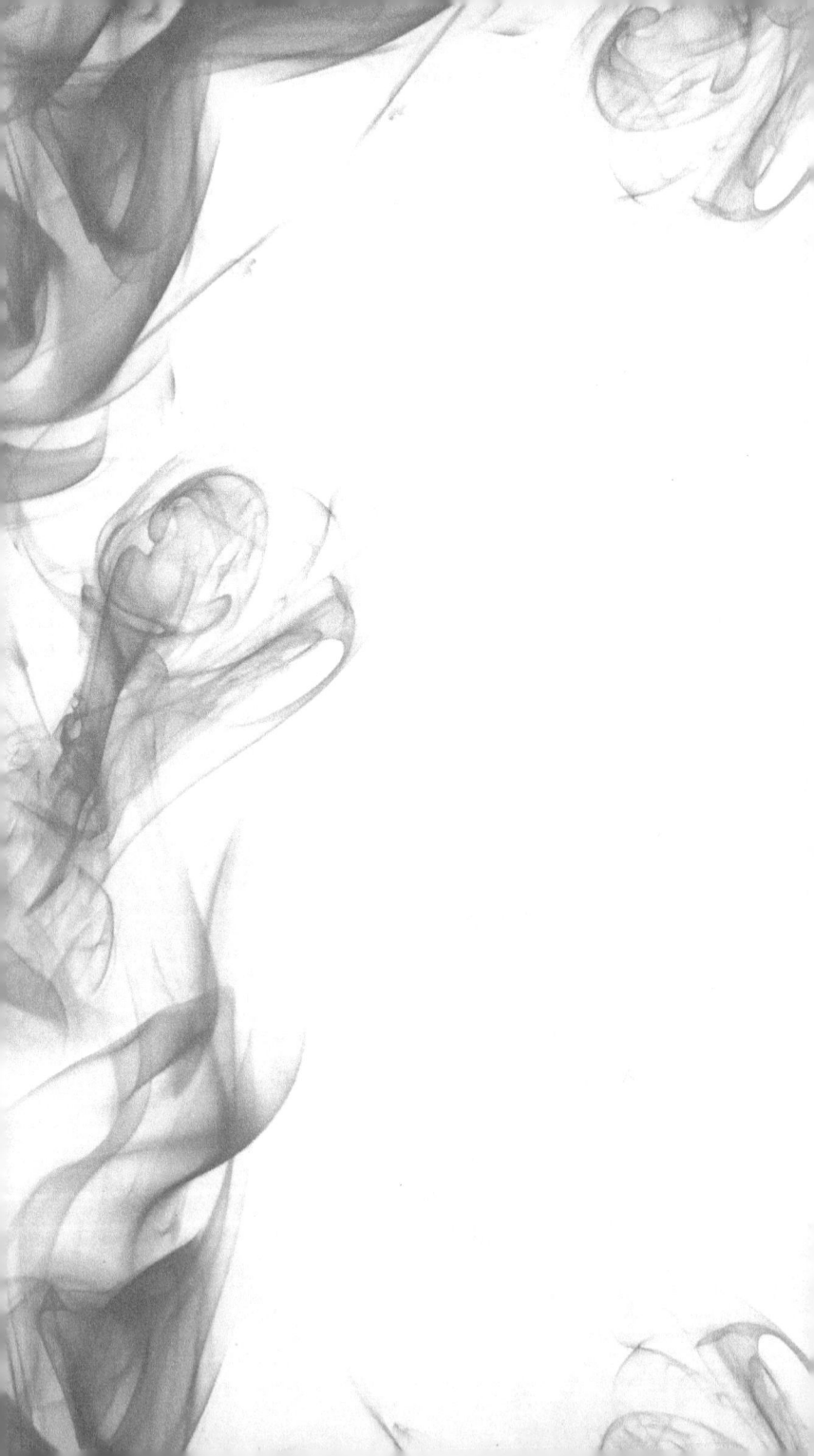

Chapter Thirty-Four

The Bone Warrens rose around Chel, Sparrow and Remington like a cathedral built from the dead, towering ribcages arching overhead, skulls grinding into place, vertebrae spiraling into bone pillars crowned with molten runes meant to keep monsters locked up.

Chel's blood still dripped from his palm, steaming where it touched the soil.

From the chasm of shadow beneath their feet, the immense voice spoke again, "Why do you wake the Warrens?"

Sparrow didn't flinch. Remington swallowed hard. Chel drew himself taller, wings twitching, ready for take-off if this went sideways.

"We seek access to Gadreel's prison realm," Chel said.

A low grinding noise rolled through the valley like continents scraping against each other. Bones shifted. A massive skull turned, hollow sockets glowing with buried embers.

"Gadreel..." The name vibrated through the marrow of every bone in the Warrens. "The Fallen Angel. The Collector. The one who forged cages and stole souls. He used to collect in Heaven, in Hell. His obsessions with collection brought his downfall. To enter this prison means you may never leave."

Sparrow stepped beside Chel, voice steady. "We need the door. The Fates sent the heir of an ancient Duke bloodline to wake you. Now show us the way. His blood is the key."

A ripple passed through the skeletal titans, traveling like a wave. And a rumble from beneath the surface as bones slid aside in geometric precision. As if obeying a command they had waited millennia to answer.

Sparrow's sharp inhale broke the silence. "There," he whispered.

Under centuries of soil, ash, and bones, something metallic glinted. The earth cracked open wider, revealing a buried doorway, a perfect circle of engraved runes, haloed by shifting bones like a crown.

Chel stepped forward, heart pounding.

He knew this place.

He had *seen* it in dreams, in his father's office, in the sketches on the desk. It was real.

The runes were the same. The measurements the same. The ancient symbols humming with a resonance he felt deep in his bones.

Chel dropped to one knee and brushed away the remaining dirt.

Sparrow crouched beside him. "Careful."

Chel pressed his bleeding palm against the door. A golden spark snapped across the surface. The runes lit up one by one, circling outward in a ripple of fire.

Sparrow shielded his face with a wing. "Hold it steady. I'll wedge the opening."

Chel grit his teeth. "We've seen the Collector's cages. What if everything inside comes out?"

"Let them out, we'll deal with it later," Sparrow said, deadly calm. "Grab Meg. Grab Teari. Leave before the whole place collapses."

Chel pressed harder. The runes responded by glowing brighter and hotter.

Remington stepped forward, shadows coiling around his arms. "I can reinforce the opening from this side."

"Good," Sparrow said. "We need every second."

The valley trembled.

A low moan rose from the bones, a universal groaning, as though the Warrens themselves were reliving their last battle.

Chel's wings flared.

A blast of light shot from the runes, ringing like a cracked bell.

The doorway shifted like a living thing waking up. The center circle rotated, unlocking layers of metal etched with symbols lost to time.

Sparrow braced his boots against the dirt, hands gripping the door's edge. "On three—"

"No," Chel snarled. "Now."

He shoved with all his strength. Hellion-bred muscle, Duke blood legacy, Raphael's power burning inside him.

The door screamed as they pushed it open. On the other side was darkness. Lantern glow. The rattling of cages. And the faint echo of a woman screaming.

"Teari," Chel whispered, soul tie pulsing violent and alive.

Sparrow snapped his wings open, eyes black as pitch. "Let's end this."

The Bone Warrens bowed, bending toward the open rift, ancient guardians acknowledging the return of a bloodline they once served.

Chel didn't look back. He stepped through first.

Sparrow followed.

Remington stood at the breach, shadows swirling, holding the doorway open with everything he had.

The veil between realms stretched and then ripped with a final, deafening scream. They were inside Gadreel's cage.

And nothing was going to stop Chel from reaching Teari.

Chapter Thirty-Five

A SUBTLE, BONE-DEEP TREMOR RIPPLED through every cage, every floor tile, every shadow-stuffed corridor.

Teari jolted awake.

Her palms slapped the cold stone as her cell tilted several degrees to the left, lantern light was swinging wildly above her and dust drifted from the ceiling like falling snow.

"Meg!" Teari scrambled toward the bars.

Meg was already awake and wide-eyed, braced against the shifting wall. The entire realm groaned like a sinking ship.

"What is happening?" Teari whispered.

Meg smirked. "That," she said, "is someone breaking in."

Hope flooded Teari as she thought of Chel running down the hall. She ran to the bars of the cage and pressed her face close, trying to see out.

Another shudder tore through the hall. Cages rattled. Creatures hissed and shrieked from their cells. Light burst through a crack in the ceiling in a thin and sharp fissure, like a blade slicing through the sky.

Teari's breath caught. The sky above the realm wasn't sky at all. It was a membrane. And it was fracturing.

Meg whispered, "Chel…"

Teari reached for her. And the floor lurched again.

Chapter Thirty-Six

Far down the corridor, the Collector froze mid-step. He tilted his head like a bird focusing on danger. A faint, unmistakable sound reached him, the outer seal of the prison realm opening. And this time it wasn't one of his tendrils or secret tunnels, no, it was the main door they'd sealed him behind ages ago.

A smile unfurled across the Magpie's face.

"Oh," he whispered. "So the Duke wakes."

The realm convulsed and a deep groan rumbled through the walls as runes flickered and gutters spat out sparks of light. Cages began to slip sideways. Chains fell from the ceiling. Locks shifted.

The Collector's expression hardened as he spoke into the trembling air, "Prepare yourselves, my treasures."

He lifted one long-fingered hand and snapped. Every cage in the eastern corridor unlocked at once. Doors flew open. Shadows spilled out. Creatures poured into the void between crumbling floors.

Not all survived the crossing. Some dissolved instantly. Others mutated mid-leap, sprouting new limbs or eyes. Most simply fled and scrambled toward the rupturing edge of the realm where the fabric of reality peeled away to reveal water. Ocean water. Bright sun shone through the waves. The creatures ran and dove in.

The Magpie gestured again and more doors opened.

Mimics poured out, chittering. Bone-birds erupted into flight, hollow wings shrieking like flutes. Slithering horrors dragged themselves toward the breach, eager for any world that was not this one. A child-sized creature made entirely of soft folds and too many eyes waddled toward the falling sky, humming.

The Magpie didn't watch them leave. He was looking at Little Brother, the shadow cat, Lucipurr's kin, curled amongst the shadows in a dark cell.

"You stay," he said gently.

Little Brother blinked as shadowed chains tightened around his body.

The ceiling split fully with cracks spreading overhead like shattering glass. A wind pulled inward, like a vacuum. Siphoning everything toward the edges of the collapsing dimension.

Meg grabbed a bar with both hands and shook it until it fell. She turned to Teari's cell and did the same. When the bars fell away, Teari moved closer.

"You need to move before this hall folds in on itself," Meg warned.

Teari grabbed her arm. "We need to run."

Meg nodded once.

But neither of them moved because the Magpie stepped into their corridor.

Dust fell around him. Cages buckled behind him. The world tried to collapse beneath him but he barely seemed to notice.

He smiled at them as the universe peeled apart behind him.

"Time to go, my angels," he said softly.

"The door is opening. The Veil between realms will be ours soon enough."

Teari's stomach dropped.

Meg spat, "Over my dead—"

The realm lurched, cutting her off.

The Magpie extended a hand.

The bars in nearby cages retracted with a metallic shriek.

"*Over my dead. Over my dead. Over my dead. Over my dead,*" the mimics echoed at Teari's feet.

Chapter Thirty-Seven

The Earthen Plane - Perdido Key

A deep vibration shook the sand. Locals paused on the main strip and glanced toward a construction site.

But the old shrimpers froze in place because they'd seen something crawling under the ocean surface in the wee hours of the morning. Something unexplained, a ridge that was deepening, disrupting the sea bottom.

The Gulf shimmered. The air warped.

A long metallic groan rolled across the dunes, like steel tearing.

Tom dropped the crate he was carrying and shouted, "Back! Everybody get back from the water!"

People scrambled up the beach just as the water arched open in a violent convulsion of light and shadow. A crack split the horizon. Foam exploded upward. Waves recoiled.

Something stepped out of the water. Not a monster. Not a demon. But a small, skeletal bird with translucent wings that fluttered like parchment in the wind. It looked around, dazed, blinking at the blue sky as if it had never seen anything like it before.

Tom lowered his rifle. "What in God's name..."

Before anyone could scream, more poured out. Not attacking. Not roaring but running. A flood of creatures spilled through the widening breach, fleeing the collapsing realm with frantic, terrified energy.

Mimics dragging themselves across the sand like wounded shadows, their forms flickering in and out.

Bone-birds flapping with broken, ancient wings as they searched desperately for higher ground. Small hunched, pale things with enormous eyes scattered into the beach grass and began digging.

Spider-limbed creatures skittering toward the dunes, clicking frantically.

Winged serpents bursting from the foam, only to collapse panting on the sand.

But none attacked. Not one hissed or lashed out. They ran. They fled. They blinked and cowered and clawed their way inland like prisoners stumbling into daylight after centuries underground.

Dogs barked madly. Car alarms blared as creatures accidentally ran into them.

A shadow-creature hid under a pier, its entire body shaking.

Tom grabbed his radio and called the others who'd met with Chel before he left them in charge. "Jesus, Mary, and all her cousins... we gotta call someone. We gotta get Chel. No, that other guy. Jed." Tom was digging in his pocket for the piece of paper Chel had given him with Jed's phone number.

A creature with six eyes and a mangled wing ran past him tripping, scrambling, then continuing on two legs like a panicked deer.

A woman shouted from main street, "Everybody back inside! Lock your doors!" She hesitated going inside, watching them because strangely enough the creatures weren't hunting, they were running in every direction.

The opening in the ocean behind them flickered with a massive pulse of energy. The portal widened, revealing a dark sky fracturing like broken glass.

A female voice screamed from the other side, echoing through the realms before abruptly cutting off.

Tom swallowed hard.

"Oh hell," he whispered. "Chel's not gonna like this."

A small, trembling mimic pressed its face to his boot, whimpering like a frightened animal.

Tom didn't kick it. He didn't move at all. He just whispered, "What happened to you?"

Behind them, Perdido Key watched a hundred nightmares stumble into their world like broken refugees of some ancient war.

And then the ocean collapsed in on itself in a

whirlpool that lasted just a minute, then stopped. The waves began lapping at the beach as though nothing had just happened.

Tom let out a thin, shaking breath.

"Yep. Nope. Absolutely not."

One of the card-night guys wiped his forehead. "I'm too old for this."

Another muttered, "Chel owes us a beer."

Tom pulled the crumpled slip of paper from his back pocket, the one Chel shoved at him before leaving to go find "his wife." The paper was damp with seawater and sweat, but the number was still visible.

"Alright," Tom muttered, "let's see if this Jed fella is as competent as Chel thinks."

He dialed and the phone rang twice.

A deep voice answered, suspicious and impatient. "Hello?"

Tom swallowed. "Jed? Chel told me to call you if something happened. Before the shit gets too deep."

Silence.

Then Jed sighed in that long, resigned, *I-knew-this-day-would-come* way only men with supernatural trauma could manage.

"What kind of shit are we talking?" Jed asked.

Tom rubbed a hand down his face. "Well... surprisingly enough, nothing violent. Yet."

"Define 'yet,'" Jed said flatly.

Tom stared at the beach.

At the dozen creatures sprinting for the dunes. Three that stopped to stare at the sun, confused. A tall, skeletal one curled up behind a lifeguard tower and began quietly sobbing into its many hands.

Tom cleared his throat. "There's a whole lotta strange creatures running out of the ocean."

Dead silence on Jed's end.

Tom waited.

A second passed.

Then another.

"Goddammit, Chel," Jed muttered under his breath.

He sighed again, louder this time.

"Alright. Don't touch them. Don't feed them. Don't *talk* to them."

"We'll be there soon."

"Uh—great," Tom said, staring as a mimic crawled onto the sidewalk and began sniffing a bicycle. "We'll just... keep an eye on 'em."

Chapter Thirty-Eight

The realm groaned out a sound like a dying star. Its last breath echoed through the Collector's chamber, rattling the cages, shaking dust from the ceiling. Teari grabbed one of the bars to steady herself as Meg braced against the back wall.

The air was thinner. The realm fraying at the seams.

The Magpie appeared in a blur of motion, cape dragging behind him like a torn shadow. He moved quickly hands snapping open locks, summoning chains, releasing beasts Teari had never seen nor imagined.

"Time is short," he hissed.

A mimic slipped past him, then froze when it saw Teari. Its head tilted, clicking softly. Another one that was smaller with black feathery arms crawled down a cracked cage wall and scampered across the floor toward her.

Meg noticed. "...Teari."

The first mimic approached and pressed its forehead

against Teari's leg. Its wide eyes shimmered faintly with recognition.

Teari blinked. "I remember you." It was the one she had healed.

The Magpie turned sharply, irritation flickering across his elegant features. "Back." He snapped his fingers, shadows curling like lashes. "Away from her."

But the mimic didn't move.

Not an inch.

A rip of pure white light burst across the corridor.

Teari's knees buckled.

Meg's eyes widened. "It's time."

The Magpie froze. "Let's go," he whispered. "That door will only remain open for so long."

The light grew impossibly bright and blinding.

Then through it a slightly familiar shape appeared. His wings dragged fire along the ground. His eyes burned gold and black.

His skin glowed with the runes Raphael's blood had carved through him.

Teari cried out. "Chel!"

"Sparrow!" Meg shouted. "Get her out of here!"

Sparrow stood just outside the doorway with Remington, straining, wings spread to full span, black feathers tearing at the edges under the pressure of holding the collapsing seam between realms.

A piece of the ceiling fell on Sparrow, he stumbled, blood streamed down his back.

He didn't stop.

"Go!" Sparrow snarled at Chel. "Get Teari!"

Chel sprinted across the shaking floor as the Magpie dragged Teari backward.

Meg launched herself again, slamming into the Magpie's side. Her teeth flashed. The Magpie recoiled, wings snapping wide.

"Meddlesome queen," he growled.

"Mouthy bastard," Meg spat.

Chel reached Teari and seized her, pulling her into his arms with a strength he couldn't contain.

"Angel, I've got you." Chel said, dragging her close.

"No!" Meg shouted. "Take her out! Chel, *go!* The realm is folding!"

The Magpie spun toward the door and toward freedom.

Chel shoved Teari toward the exit.

Sparrow braced harder, screaming through gritted teeth, "We can't hold it. MOVE!"

Chel dragged Teari through the door but the Magpie lunged.

More of the ceiling fell, Sparrow's wings buckled. Blood sprayed the stones.

His breath hitched with agony. He pushed Remington away from the danger and the door started to swing shut.

"SPARROW!" Meg screamed. "Get out of here."

Chel hesitated, one arm around Teari, one hand reaching back toward the collapsing realm.

"GO!" Meg screamed. "GO! NOW! Leave me! Do not return to this place!"

The Magpie slammed into Chel, knocking him sideways. Teari shrieked as Chel lost his grip on her.

The Magpie grabbed Teari and took off running, dragging her along.

The prison realm was open on both ends. One was emptying creatures into the Earthen plane, the other extended into Hell where Sparrow and Remington held the door open. A vacuum of wind whipped through the corridor. The Magpie, freshly fed on the Queens blood was strong enough to run against it.

But Sparrow was forced to make a choice, hold the door or save Chel from being dragged back into the collapsing realm.

It wasn't a choice. "Hold the door," he shouted to Remington.

The dark princeling grabbed the edge of the ancient door and fought against the vacuum trying to close it.

Sparrow's wings folded.

The Magpie ran through with Teari.

Sparrow grabbed Chel by the arm and swung him out. He spun and shoved Remington as hard as he could, away from the danger.

Four figures tumbled across the piles of bones as the door snapped shut behind Chel, sealing Sparrow and Meg inside the prison realm as it collapsed into darkness.

"NO!" Chel slammed his fists against the closed door.

Teari cried out. "Chel!"

Chel's eyes went murderous as he watched the

Magpie was dragging Teari across the ground, her heels carving furrows through ash and bone.

Chel turned. Slow. Lethal. His wings flared wide, black fire veined with gold lighting the battlefield.

"Let," Chel said quietly. "Her." A step closer. "Go."

The mimic Teari had healed hissed behind her, a wet, broken sound, and then pounced.

Claws raked across the Magpie's face. Blood splattered the ground in shimmering arcs as he staggered, shrieking in rage rather than pain.

Chel lunged.

His blade carved deep into the Magpie's shoulder, biting through bone and sinew. The Magpie howled, staggering back, shadow spilling from the wound like smoke.

He grabbed the mimic by the skull and hurled it aside, sending the creature crashing into a shattered pillar.

"You are *persistent*," the Magpie said, blood dripping from his chin. He pointed at Teari. "But she is now mine."

That was all Chel needed. He threw the basilisk blade.

It spun end over end, slicing through the air and sheared clean through the Magpie's lower arm. The hand hit the ground with a wet crack.

The Magpie howled and Teari fell from his grasp. Chel surged forward and caught her.

The Magpie staggered back, clutching the ruined stump, shadow knitting frantically around the wound.

Then… He laughed. A wild, unhinged sound. "Oh," he breathed, staggering upright. "I forgot how *good* this feels."

Dark wings tore free from his back and they were vast, ragged, stitched together from shadow and bone. They unfurled with a thunderous crack that sent debris flying.

Chel snarled and leapt for him but Teari grabbed Chel's arm with both hands. "No!"

He hesitated.

The Magpie launched skyward, blood trailing behind him like a comet's tail. He cackled as he climbed, voice echoing across the battlefield.

"I haven't stretched my wings in *ages*!"

He circled once above them, wounded but exultant, eyes burning black.

"This isn't over," he called. "You've only reminded me how much I miss the sky." Then he vanished into the clouds, laughter fading into the wind.

Chel stood rigid, breathing hard, every instinct screaming to go after the creature. To end his existence. But soft hands gripped his clothing and settled the rage. Teari pressed her forehead into his chest, gripping him like an anchor.

"Don't," she whispered. "He wants you to follow. One of us will die. Don't leave me."

Chel's wings shook, then slowly folded. His gaze stayed fixed on the ochre sky watching as the Magpie flew west.

"He got away," he growled.

Teari looked up at him, dirt-streaked, shaken, alive. "But so did we."

Chel pulled her close, shaking, blood dripping down his chest. "I thought I lost you."

Teari pressed a trembling hand to his face.

"My parents are trapped in there now," Remington said as he stared at the pile of bones where the door to the prison realm had once been. Slowly, he moved toward the Magpie's arm, he tugged off his shirt and used it to wrap the arm in.

"What are you doing?" Chel asked.

"If I've learned anything from my mother, never leave a piece of body behind. Collect the blood. Collect anything and save it."

"Meg said to leave her." Teari's voice was strained. "I don't want to leave her. We'll be back for you." She reached toward where the door once was. I promise, we'll find you both."

"I promise, as well," Chel said.

Remington's face was pale when he looked up at Teari and Chel. They both reached for him and pulled him into their arms.

Chapter Thirty-Nine

Light split open over the sky as Teari and Chel stepped through the shimmering gate into the heart of her kingdom.

The moment Chel crossed the threshold, the air shifted. Angels froze mid-stride. Wings rustled. Heads bowed instinctively.

Some didn't even realize they were bowing.

Chel noticed all of them. His jaw tightened.

Teari squeezed his hand.

"Be nice," she murmured.

"I *am* nice," Chel muttered under his breath.

A passing angel heard that and bowed lower.

Teari stifled a laugh.

They crossed the courtyard, exhausted, wrecked by the prison realm, by battle, by loss. The kingdom felt suspended on a single held breath. Fires had scorched the tree line. Smoke still curled from distant valleys where the fires had been smudged out. Healers tended to lines of injured angels. The scent of creosote hung in the air.

"Smells like Hell," Chel said.

A tense moment passed between them, both thinking of Meg and Sparrow.

They made their way to the infirmary, the hallway echoing with hushed voices and hurried footsteps. Teari pushed open the glass doors.

Noctara sat curled at the far end of a cot, knees tucked to her chest, hair draped in tangled dark waves. Her skin was no longer cracked and gray but she still bore the haunted look of someone who had lived far too long in darkness and alone.

Lassar stood nearby, stiff as a board, trying to pretend he didn't have a trembling Nightjar clutching the sleeve of his uniform.

When he saw Teari, he snapped to attention and bowed deeply. "My Queen. You have returned."

Noctara's eyes darted to Teari, then Chel, and she made a small, frightened sound, sinking further into her blanket. Lassar immediately knelt beside her, murmuring something awkward and soothing. "I'm right here. No one is going to harm you. Please... let go of my shirt. That's... expensive fabric, I think."

Teari hid a smile behind her hand.

Chel crossed his arms, watching Lassar struggle to untangle himself from Noctara's grip.

"She likes you," Chel said dryly.

"We knew each other in childhood," Lassar muttered through clenched teeth.

Teari approached slowly, wings lowered to avoid startling Noctara. "How is she?"

Lassar straightened. "She's stabilizing. Eating. Resting. The healers believe her mind will heal with time. She still calls herself Demore."

"That was what our father called her after he took her name. And you?" Teari asked, chin up.

Lassar swallowed hard. "I would like to apologize for keeping the fires from you." His voice broke. Just slightly. "I thought I was protecting you. I see that I was wrong. I was wrong about a lot of things. I vow to do better."

Teari touched his arm, forgiveness heavy and quiet in the gesture. "We can rebuild what was lost. But we start with honesty."

Lassar bowed his head. "Yes, my Queen." Lassar glanced at Chel and quickly bowed. "My King."

Chel watched the exchange closely, sensing the shift in the room between Lassar's loyalty, Noctara's fragile hope, and Teari reclaiming her authority without force.

Angels filtered in and out, bowing as they passed Chel. He tried to ignore it.

He failed.

Teari smirked again.

"Not a word," Chel muttered.

"Oh, I wasn't going to say anything," she said sweetly. "The kingdom already thinks you're some kind of ancient war-lord. They feel guilty for calling you a filthy Hellion."

"I mean, technically..." Lassar began.

Chel glared.

Lassar's mouth snapped shut.

Teari gathered her commanders and healers in the hall, Chel at her side like a shadow carved from stone.

Her voice carried through the chamber with steadiness, "We will recover. We will rebuild. And we will do it together."

She outlined assignments to everyone. Lassar reinstated as Commander, but under direct oversight until trust was fully earned. Noctara was placed under healer supervision. The wards were to be rebuilt around the kingdom's outer rim to stop further fire spread and heal the land. Refugees would be brought back, accounted for, and sheltered.

Chel stood beside her with an unreadable expression.

Every time an angel glanced at him with awe, he shifted uncomfortably.

When the meeting dispersed, Teari squeezed his hand again.

"I'm proud of you," she said softly.

"For what?"

"For not punching anyone today. Or baring your teeth."

Chel snorted. "Day's not over. I'm saving my teeth for later." His fingertips grazed her ribs with promise.

Teari laughed, and for a heartbeat an ease passed between them.

But beneath the relief, a shadow lingered. Meg and Sparrow were still trapped in the prison realm. Even though Meg had told them to stay away, everyone wanted to try and find them again.

Teari's wings lowered.

Chel touched the back of her spine with his thumb.

"We'll get them back," he murmured.

She nodded, though fear still gnawed at the edges of her heart.

"After this," Chel added quietly, "we go home."

Teari tilted her head. "Which home?"

Chel gave a faint, crooked smile.

"Wherever you are."

Chel's phone rang. He searched his pockets before pulling it out and answering.

Teari waited patiently, hearing Shay's voice on the other end. Sounded like they were in trouble.

Chel glanced to Teari before pacing nearby. It sounded like he was receiving a verbal lashing. Teari smiled as she looked up to the sky and took in the sun rays. She'd missed the heat.

Chel's call ended and he moved closer.

"Trouble?" Teari asked.

He wrapped an arm around her waist and dragged her closer. "So much trouble. Seems we have a mess to face on the Earthen plane."

"Oh," Teari's eyes went wide. "You weren't there to watch the portal. Did something happen?"

Chel nodded. "Every single creature the Magpie had collected, he released through the portal."

Teari's jaw dropped. "Oh no. Did anyone die? Did..." She ran a hand through her hair. "Oh my god, this is not good. Some of those creatures I'd never seen before in my life."

Chel was smiling when she looked up at him again. "Now what?" she asked.

"Now we go find them all. And apologize to the White Horse. I left my station. I failed."

"You most certainly did not," Teari corrected him.

Chapter Forty

Meg & Sparrow

Smoke drifted across the disheveled corridor, curling around shattered pillars and broken stone. The prison realm had nearly collapsed into a wasteland of debris. Twisted iron, crushed cages, broken furniture and singed linens were askew everywhere.

In the center of it all, Meg stood rigid and shaking, barefoot on the rubble. Her face dripping with tears and eyes red.

Her voice cut through the air like a blade. "SPARROW!"

Across the ruins, Sparrow staggered to his feet. His black wings dragged behind him in tatters. Blood streaked down one side of his face; his shirt was torn.

He heard her voice and ran. He tore down the

corridor like a storm unchained. Stone shattered under his boots. Metal screeched as he hurled it aside. A whole iron beam launched twenty feet into the air as he ripped it free with one hand.

He didn't stop. Didn't slow. Didn't blink. He didn't care about anyone or anything other than the woman across the way.

Every step cleared another obstacle, debris flying in every direction until nothing stood between them.

Meg didn't move.

She just kept shouting.

"What were you thinking? You weren't supposed to come. You can't be here..." Her voice cracked, fury entwined with terror.

"YOU WERE SUPPOSED TO COME LATER!"

Sparrow reached her in a single final stride, grabbed her by the waist, and crashed into her, lifting her clean off the ground in a crushing embrace.

She hit his chest with her fists with hard, frantic blows.

"You—idiot—bird—" Meg choked out, still pounding at him. "You were supposed to come later, not now—NOT NOW—Sparrow you weren't in the vision—"

He held her tighter, burying his face against her shoulder as if he could inhale her back into existence.

"You are mine," Sparrow growled, voice low and wrecked. "Do you understand me? You are mine. And I am yours and we will not do this alone. We will not do this apart. We will not let the realms and omens and others come between us like before. I promised you."

Meg froze. Her fists trembled against his chest. "It's not supposed to be this way," she whispered, grief flooding her chest. Fear. The echo of every nightmare she'd had in the dark of the collector's realm. "I saw what happens if you come too early."

Sparrow lifted his head and pressed his forehead to hers, breath shaking. "I do not care what you saw."

His wings wrapped around her, broken feathers falling like ash.

"I will never leave you," he said softly, fiercely. "Not like this." His voice broke. "Not now." His hands trembled as they cupped her face. "Not ever. I will not leave you nor will I leave them. What if it was wrong? So many omens have been wrong."

Meg exhaled a single sharp sob caught in her throat. Then she grabbed his shirt and pulled him into her arms, holding him just as tightly.

Shadows rippled at the far end of the corridor.

Meg stiffened, Sparrow's arms still locked around her waist. A low, unmistakable meow echoed—soft, offended, and entirely unimpressed.

Lucipurr stepped from the darkness.

His black fur was dusted in ash. His bright green eyes glowed, cutting through the dim, broken light of the prison realm. His tail swished once.

Meg recognized her daughter's kitten and sagged with relief. "How did you get here?" she breathed.

Lucipurr blinked, insulted. Then he turned and began padding deeper into the crumbling realm, pausing only to ensure they were following.

Meg and Sparrow exchanged a look.

"After you," Meg rasped.

They followed Lucipurr through cracked halls and tilting floors until they reached a lone cage that was half collapsed with shadows clinging to the bars like tar.

Inside, Little Brother lay curled into himself.

He was barely recognizable. Thin as a thread of smoke. His fur dull. His breathing shallow.

Meg dropped to her knees. "Oh... no."

Lucipurr stepped aside, granting them space.

Sparrow ripped the door clean off its hinges. Little Brother didn't move.

Sparrow crouched. His fingers flexed once, then he plunged his hands into the shadows clinging to the small cat. They hissed, recoiling, but Sparrow growled and the shadows shredded beneath his hands.

Meg slid inside and lifted the small creature carefully into her arms. He weighed almost nothing just a trembling heartbeat wrapped in fur.

"He's starved," Meg whispered, throat breaking.

Lucipurr nudged Sparrow's shin pointedly, then padded down a crumbling hall. He led them to a cracked pantry door where the Collector stored dried meats, enchanted treats, and jars filled with glowing essence.

Sparrow smashed the lock and took a jar of meat.

Little Brother weakly sniffed the food in Meg's hands. She tore the meat into tiny shreds and he finally ate. After, he curled in her lap, letting out a soft, half-hearted purr.

The realm rumbled and stone groaned above them. A stone fell from the ceiling and shattered nearby.

Meg flinched. "Sparrow... this place is going to crush us."

"No," Sparrow said calmly, brushing dust from her cheek. "We have time."

"You're sure?"

He touched foreheads with her again. "I would never lie to you."

Meg swallowed hard, nodding.

Lucipurr nudged Sparrow again, firmer this time as his eyes flicked toward the distant halls then back to them.

"He wants us to move," Sparrow murmured. "Find safer ground."

Meg rose, Little Brother tucked against her chest. "Lead the way, Lucipurr." She glanced at Sparrow. "Does Rue know you're here?"

Lucipurr's tail flicked, a hint of superiority, then he melted back into the darkness.

Sparrow took Meg's hand.

They followed the path the shadows opened for Lucipurr—deeper into the prison realm, but into a place that felt less hostile, less like it might collapse.

"We're trapped," Meg whispered. "In a collapsing realm. With a pantry and a sickly kitten. And somehow our daughter's kitten has found us."

Sparrow kissed the top of her head.

"Then we make this place ours," he murmured, voice low and fierce. "And when the gates open again, I will walk you out."

Meg closed her eyes. "Promise?"

Sparrow's grip tightened. "I promise," he said. "And a promise is a promise."

Chapter Forty-One

The ocean rolled in gentle breaths, the sky was a soft Florida blue, and Chel lay stretched on the sand beside Teari, one arm tucked under his head, the other trailing lazy patterns along her hip.

Teari wore a black bikini that made the sun glint off her skin like gold dust. Her hair fanned across the towel beneath them, drying in the warm breeze. Chel wore board shorts and Teari insisted they looked better on him than anything else.

Their wings were invisible here once again.

The Veil between worlds had reset itself.

Teari sighed and tipped her face toward the sun. "I forgot how warm this sun is."

Chel smirked. "I didn't forget how distracting you are in that bikini."

She rolled toward him, elbow on the towel, lips brushing his jaw. "This feels like a dream.'"

Chel's fingers slid along her waist. "It does and if it is, I'll stay sleeping."

"Oh?" Teari murmured, kissing the sensitive spot just beneath his ear.

Chel growled low in his throat and pulled her into his lap.

He was halfway through a very enthusiastic kiss, teeth scraping the soft skin under Teari's ear when he froze.

"Someone is here," he cursed.

Teari kissed him again and again until he forced himself to pull back, forehead pressed to hers, growling, "There is a human here."

Teari sighed dramatically. "Humans have awful timing."

Chel turned his head just as Tom trudged up the beach, hands in his pockets, squinting at them beneath the sun.

Tom halted, blinked twice, and cleared his throat.

"Well," he said slowly, "I see you found your wife. Welcome back, ma'am."

Teari sat up gracefully, offering a warm smile. "Thank you. It's good to be back on the beach."

Chel patted the sand beside him. "Sit."

Tom hesitated, then plopped down with a grunt. "Hope I'm not interrupting anything intimate."

"You are," Chel said.

Teari elbowed him, smiling.

Tom snorted. "Right. Well, sorry about that. But we got... uh... a small situation."

Chel sighed. "What now."

Tom rubbed the back of his neck. "Those creatures that ran outta the ocean? They didn't attack, thank God, but they sure as hell scattered. Like they hadn't seen daylight in decades."

Chel and Teari exchanged a glance.

"They hadn't," Teari said softly.

Tom continued, "I called that number you left me. Jed, right? That fella was not real friendly but was very tall. And covered in tattoos I ain't ever seen before."

Chel chuckled. "That tracks."

Tom eyed him suspiciously. "Where'd you find a friend like that? He looks like he walked out of a nightmare or a movie or something."

Chel leaned back on his hands, eyes half-lidded from the sun. "You wouldn't believe me."

Tom huffed a laugh. "Chel, after the shit I've seen these last few days, with shadows walking outta the surf, birds made of bones flying over the highway, and a deer with too many eyes staring at my mailbox... I don't think *anything* would surprise me anymore."

Chel smirked. "Jed's just a guy from Montana."

Teari's lips twitched. "A different kinda guy from Montana."

Tom blinked at them.

Chel shrugged. "You said not much surprises you."

Tom shook his head. "Well... that does."

They sat together for a moment, three unlikely allies staring at the calm ocean that had, days earlier, vomited nightmares.

Finally Tom asked, "So, uh... what happens now? With all them things running loose?"

Chel slipped an arm around Teari's waist. "We'll find them. We'll help them. We'll send them where they need to go."

"Right after," Teari said, leaning her head on Chel's shoulder, "we take a vacation."

Tom raised a brow. "A vacation."

Chel nodded. "A long one."

Teari smiled, soft and full of relief.

Tom's eyes widened. "Maybe I should go now."

Chel gave him a look.

Tom lifted both hands. "Congratulations. I'm out."

Chel grinned, pulling Teari closer and kissing the top of her head. "I'm going to take a vacation. Kind of a honeymoon of sorts."

Epilogue

Chel was standing in front of the White Horse. Nero was nearby, pacing. Watching the mountains in the distance as though demons might snap through the veil and come running toward them. They wouldn't. The Veil was sealed tight now that the Magpie wasn't stretching the prison realm between the Veil.

"Guardian," the White Horse was furious. "You were to protect the Gulf portal. Instead thousands of creatures have crossed into my world. This is my sanctuary. There are things here that mortals have never laid eyes on. Never considered."

Chel cleared his throat and tucked his chin. "I apologize for my failures."

"He had to save me," Teari spoke up. "If Chel and Sparrow hadn't searched for us, Gadreel would have possessed the Veil and there would be nothing here."

The White Horse focused on Teari, deep in thought. Her mane glimmered in the moonlight.

"That was heroic of them. But now we have bigger problems to deal with." The White Horse snapped her teeth and turned away to pace near the cluster of birch trees. There was a noticeable patch of packed down dirt around the trees, as if the White Horse had been ruminating for days.

"We need to find Meg and Sparrow," Teari finally said.

"Yes," the White Horse agreed. "They need to be found and returned to their rightful stations."

Something howled in the distance.

The glow of moonlight was interrupted by something flying overhead. It disappeared before any of them could follow the shadowed figure.

"What a mess," the White Horse muttered.

Issue No. 51

Midnight Ledger Press | **The Veil Gazette** | @midnightledgerbooks

Who wears the crown?
THE QUIET CLAIMING OF HELL'S THRONE
Prince Remington Assumes the Throne of Hell

Hell has a new ruler.

Following the recent upheavals across realms, Prince Remington has formally assumed the Throne of Hell. The ascension was conducted in private, witnessed only by the Queen's Guard, select members of the Court, and the White Horse, whose presence confirmed the legitimacy of the claim.
Sources describe the ceremony as solemn rather than celebratory. No fires were lit. No banners raised.

Remington, long regarded as a reluctant heir, is said to have accepted the crown without spectacle. Those present noted a marked stillness in the chamber when he took his seat, followed by the quiet locking of ancient runes embedded in the castle stone.
The Court has issued no proclamations yet. But Hell has chosen.
And Hell does not choose lightly.

Ancient and Otherworldly Creatures Loose on the Earthen Plane

Multiple confirmed sightings indicate that ancient and otherworldly creatures—long thought sealed, extinct, or dormant—are now active on the Earthen plane.
Reports include displaced beasts from pre-Veil epochs, creatures not catalogued in any known bestiary, and entities that do not conform to the laws of the mortal realm. In several cases, these beings appear confused rather than aggressive, suggesting forced displacement rather than intentional incursion.
Scholars suspect deliberate release.
The public is warned not to approach unfamiliar creatures, no matter how docile they appear. Many exhibit delayed threat responses, altered perception fields, or territorial instincts triggered by fear.

Prophecy Fragment (Unattributed)

When the crown settles, the watcher will turn away.
When the magpie steals what was never meant to be found, the mountain will remember its name.
And Hell will discover what it has already crowned.

Issue No. 51

Midnight Ledger Press | **The Veil Gazette** | @midnightledgerbooks

Ancient Fallen Archangel at Large — Beware Gadreel

Authorities across realms have confirmed the reemergence of an ancient fallen archangel, known historically as Gadreel, though he is increasingly encountered under the name Magpie.

Gadreel is believed to be responsible for multiple recent breaches involving artifact theft, creature displacement, and false bargains. Witnesses describe him as charming, curious, and deeply dangerous—prone to collecting what does not belong to him, including souls, secrets, and names.

Unlike lesser fallen, Gadreel does not announce himself with violence. He barters. He persuades. He waits.

Those who have crossed paths with Magpie report memory gaps, misplaced loyalties, and an unsettling sense that something valuable was taken—though they cannot recall what.

All citizens are advised not to engage, not to bargain, and not to accept gifts, no matter how small.

If you think you have encountered Magpie, report immediately to the Queen's Guard or the White Horse.

Hunting Parties Sought for Creature Recovery Operations

The Court of Hell is recruiting specialized hunting parties to assist in the recovery and containment of escaped creatures currently roaming the Earthen plane.

All applicants must meet the following conditions:
- Clearance by the White Horse is mandatory
- All operations must comply with mortal realm laws
- No lethal force permitted unless explicitly sanctioned
- Collateral damage will not be excused as "inevitable"

Hunting parties will work in coordinated cells alongside local authorities when required. Experience with cross-realm entities, tracking magic, and restraint wards is strongly preferred.

Those seeking glory, trophies, or revenge need not apply.

This is not a war.

It is cleanup.

Interested parties should submit credentials through approved channels only. Unauthorized action will be prosecuted.

Follow on TikTok   Scan to go to the shop   Follow on Facebook

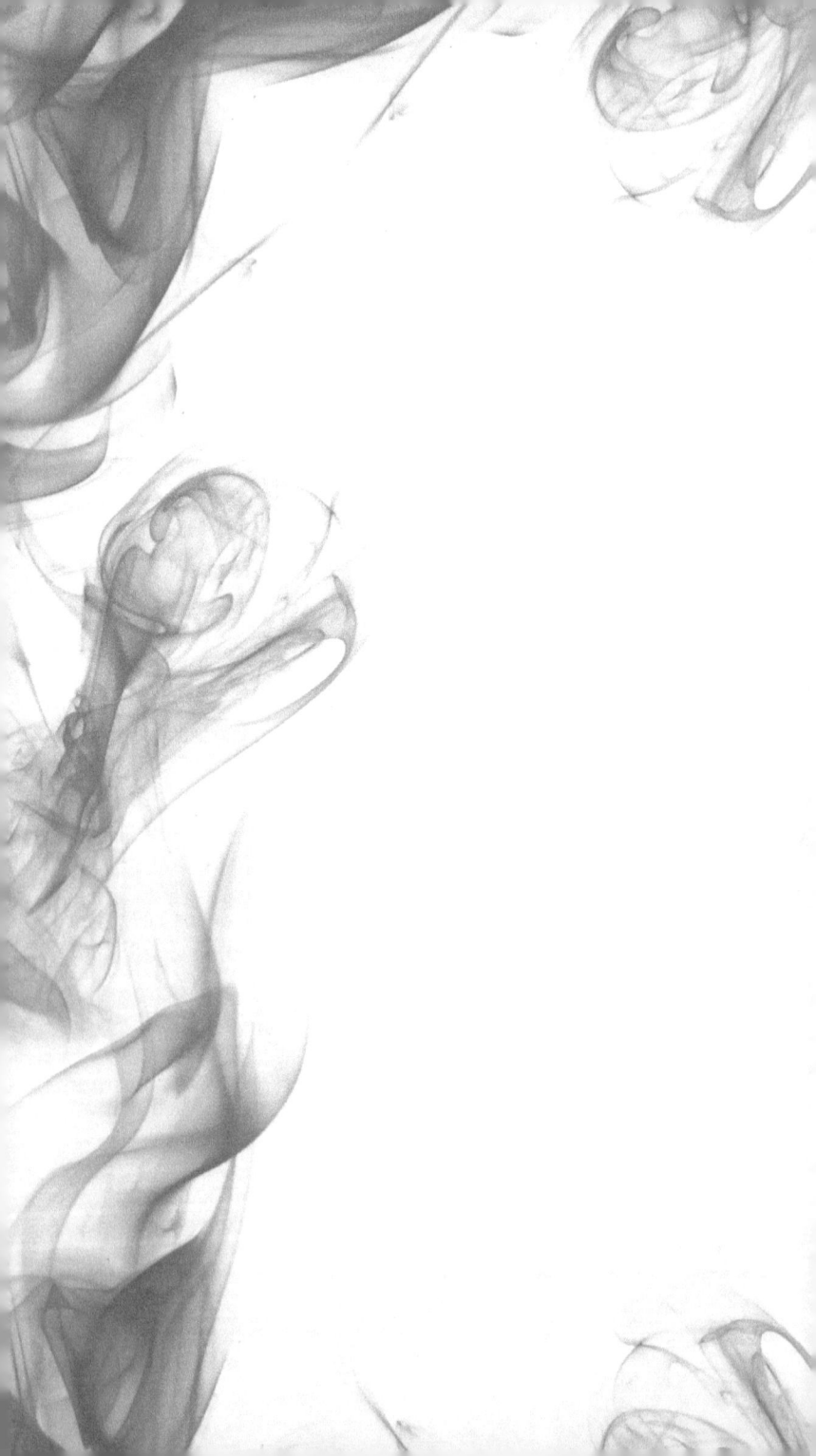

A note

Thank You

To every reader who picked up *These Promises are Valiant*—whether you've been with me since the first Veil of Shadows book or jumped in at The Sky is Starless or you just stumbled across my work on TikTok at 2 a.m. THANK YOU! You are the reason this world keeps growing. Every like, share, review, late-night DM, and "OMG..." message fuels my dark little writer heart. And I love responding with: "I wonder what's going to happen next?!"

To my incredible BookTok family: Mellystarr, massiel reads, ShadowDaddy/D, Linda, Kim.d.f.reads, Tameka, Tracy, Cass Marie, Shania, littlekick, sweetpea26_26, Del (I'm still thinking about that alpha rescue, after all this time!), thatgalbritt, punkachoo, Short.n.sweet, Shannon, curious_kitten, momma Deb, SarLitten, Raye, Platinum_VERA, OkayLucy, DivaSoldierFoster, jennifer-

A NOTE

7746, Whit, Brianne, Mikayla, Brandi B, Ken, Like.A.Diamond, Mystery Book Bundles, Sam/Dillon, DeyaReads, Jessica, Oopsiedaisies, Sarah, Letty, Chantel, Megs, Mama Guti, Bookinit, AuthorAnnette S, Patty.M.G, Ivan.n.honey, Janet Marie Freels, Andrea, White Booktok, and sooooo many more!! You all make promoting vampires, morally gray MMCs, and slow-burn romance a joy.

To my ARC readers on Booksirens: Thank you, thank you. I love getting your first reviews and thoughts.

To my editor, Massiel: you catch the things I miss and all those extra commas, sharpen every sentence, and saved my deadlines for the new year. I am forever grateful!

To my family: you've listened to my rambling lore dumps, tolerated my writing marathons, my Livestreams, and never once questioned why I'm Googling things like "who was the worst Archangel?" You're my safe place and my chaos crew, and I love you.

Here's to more books, more worlds, and more late nights chasing the stories that refuse to let us sleep.

I'm still smiling about the nights you all got me to 1 million likes during the many livestreams in 2025!

2026 is going to be amazing!

A NOTE

***Let the Vampires Bite*,**
　Meredith
　(PS: Melly, it's not a cliffhanger. Chel and Teari's story was HEA and complete. Hehehehehehehe)

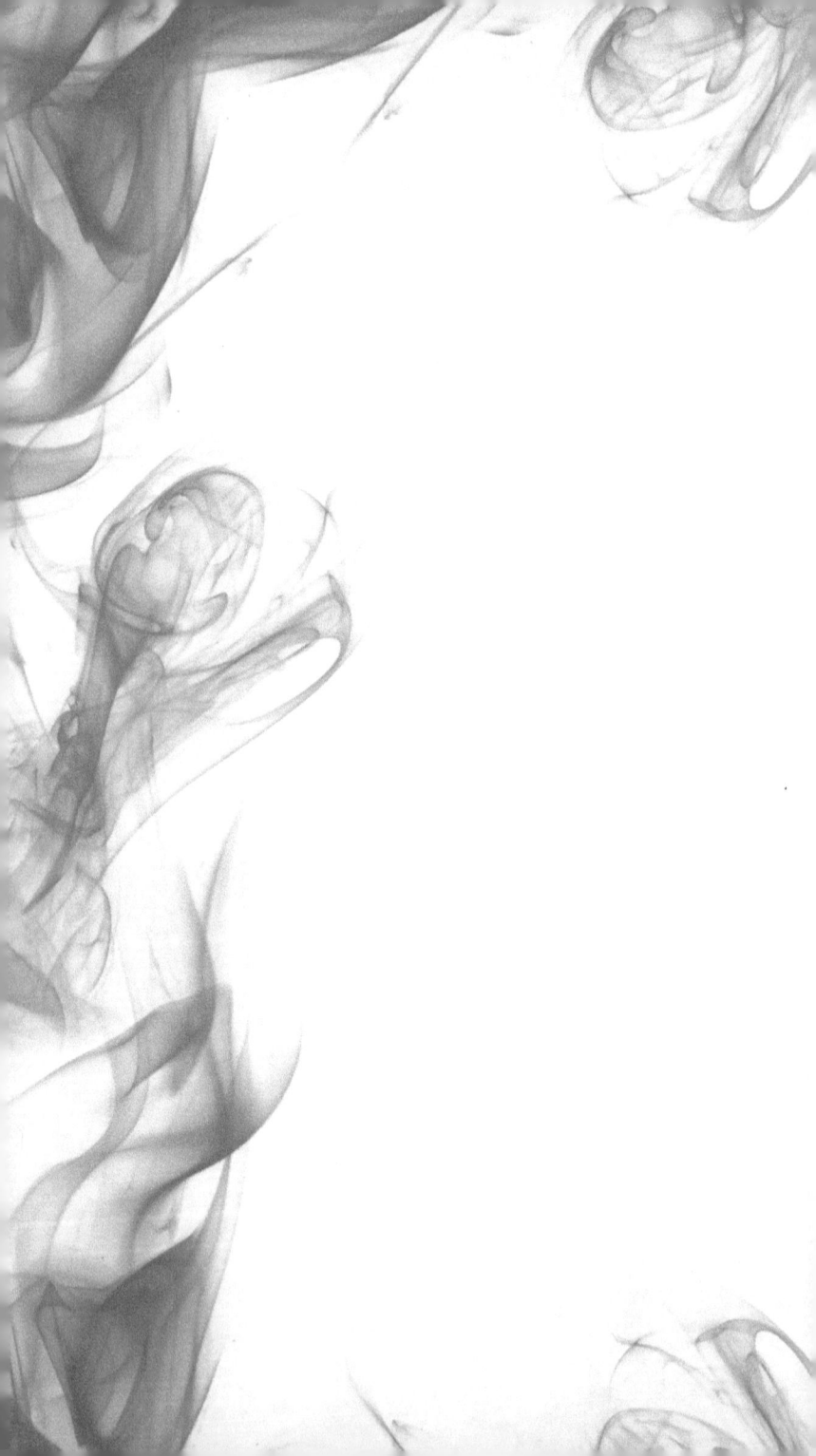

About the Author

M. R. Pritchard delves into the profound clash between good and evil, the mystical realms of gods and monsters, and the intricate transformations of ordinary people into beings of immense power. Her gripping narratives often unfold within the haunting backdrop of apocalyptic or post-apocalyptic landscapes, offering a unique blend of suspense and wonder.

M. R. Pritchard is a two-time Kindle Scout winning author, her short story "Glitch" has been featured in the 2017 winter edition of THE FIRST LINE literary journal. Her short story "Moon Lord" has been featured in Chronicle Worlds: Half Way Home (Part of the Future Chronicles) and will be time capsuled on the moon on the Lunar Codex in 2024.

Visit her website MRPritchard.com and Subscribe. You'll get subscriber only content, deleted scenes, updates, special previews of new projects, and book deals.

Looking to buy direct? Visit MidnightLedgerbooks (dot) com to get signed books, early releases, and extras.

www.ingramcontent.com/pod-product-compliance
Lightning Source LLC
LaVergne TN
LVHW040039080526
838202LV00045B/3402